youthjuice

youthjuice

e.k. sathue

ЯENE
GADE

RENEGADE BOOKS

First published in the United States in 2024 by Hell's Hundred, an imprint of Soho Press
First published in Great Britain in 2024 by Renegade Books

1 3 5 7 9 10 8 6 4 2

Copyright © Erin Mayer 2024

Hebe Illustration: duncan1890/iStock

Interior design by Janine Agro

The moral right of the author has been asserted.

A CIP catalogue record for this book
is available from the British Library.

Hardback ISBN 978-1-408-74922-7
Trade Paperback ISBN 978-1-408-74923-4

Printed and bound in Great Britain by Clays Ltd, Elcograf S.p.A

Papers used by Renegade Books are from well-managed forests
and other responsible sources.

Renegade Books
Carmelite House
50 Victoria Embankment
London EC4Y 0DZ

www.dialoguebooks.co.uk

Dialogue, part of Little Brown, Book Group Limited,
an Hachette UK company.

To Benjamin, Mom, and Steve.

"The secret of remaining young is never to have an emotion that is unbecoming."

—Oscar Wilde, *The Picture of Dorian Gray*

HEBE.

HEBE

Hebe (hee-bee): The Greek goddess of youth, daughter of Zeus and Hera.

At HEBE, we believe beauty is your birthright. You were born perfect, but life drained you of your vibrance. We return your inheritance. From the boardroom to the bar bathroom, HEBE's products tap into your natural vitality, making you glow from within. After all, the world belongs to those who bathe in abundance.

In 2013, Tree Whitestone founded her blog, *The Dew*, with the understanding that peering into someone's bathroom lets you see their soul. She carried that philosophy forward into our curated line of luxurious (and accessible) skincare and makeup. You are what you put on your face, and our products are made from the purest ingredients. No toxins, no parabens, no artificial fragrance. Just the good stuff. Because we think you should look your best—always. Remember: Beauty is possible.

May

1

We bathed in their blood to stay young. Slick, fatty liquid kept us alight in our wild beauty. Their blood was the fountain of youth, burbling through our very own veins. Platelets are the secret to radiance. The key to a brighter complexion. Blood, with the fortifying run of an egg yolk's slow drip, is the opposite of tech. It's messy, never sterile.

To care for one's skin is a learned art. Tree famously wore sunscreen every day from age five onward. First applied by her mother before Tree picked up the mantle of self-care when she turned twelve. She was the master and I her apprentice. The world is one assault on the face after another. The bloodbath was all we could do to survive.

AN EMAIL. GHOSTLY at the top of my empty inbox. It's from Marigold Vreeland, Assistant to the Founder and CEO. *Tree will see you* in the subject line. The body is blank.

Tree Whitestone's office is at the end of a long hall. I shake the wrinkles from my first-day skirt. Japanese designer with a complex system of pleats. Borrowed from Dom. I bury my gloved hands into the pockets, posture lifted, and head for the frosted glass door. Stationed out front at a kidney-shaped obsidian desk is Marigold, her hair a center-parted bob swishing on either side of her freckled face like the panels in a car wash. She works her flat lips into a mirthless grimace. No teeth.

"Hi, I'm—"

"The new Creative," she finishes. "Welcome. I'm Marigold, Tree's assistant. You'll work with me to schedule appointments with the founder and CEO."

She extends an arm. I shove my right hand, sheathed in flimsy lace frayed at the seams, into hers and we shake. Marigold pumps with a propeller's force. "You may go in."

A Lucite desk, the transparent mirror of Marigold's, is the centerpiece of the room. Through it I see Tree's cigarette trousers tapered to crossed ankles, the impressive bend of her knees, which are pressed together, calves set neatly to the side like a ballet dancer in repose. Her eyes are closed, the wall behind her splashed with old campaign imagery. Light spills through the tall windows. A quiet bell chimes.

I take a tentative step and clear my throat.

Tree's eyelids unfurl like electronic window shades. She stares and stares and then—she smiles. She says, "Soph." As if she has been waiting decades to hold my name in her mouth. "Please. Sit down."

Tree gestures to a pink velvet settee and moves over to a beverage dispenser on a rattan table in the corner. I sit on the couch, taking in the room: the collaged photos of dew-soaked women behind the desk, the faux-bohemian accents, the product prototypes with naked, malformed packaging spread on a teak and gold tray. I must be one of the first in the world to see them.

Beside the desk is a library cart with two rows of books, the spines battered. Some are old. Binding peeling away from the pages. I can't read the titles from this distance.

Tree's narrow torso blocks my view as she hands me a glass of lemon water and rests on the opposite domed cushion. "Soph," she says again. No one has ever felt the need to shorten *Sophia* before. "Welcome."

I balance the glass on my knee. The gloves affect my grip so that I'm often on the verge of dropping something. Richard, my boyfriend, calls me *butterfingers*. Inside my left pocket, my index nail worries a dent in the thumb's knuckle. The urge to bite is strong. I rub the uneven ridge through the glove's lace weave.

"I'm so happy to be here," I say. "This is my dream job."

"You're already a vital member of our team," Tree replies. "You've been given a computer? And the products? Everything you need?"

"Yes, thank you."

Tree waves. "No need to thank me, I have moisturizer coming out of my ears. And everywhere else." She winks.

I blush and force an echoey laugh. She is, indeed, incredibly moisturized. Her forehead flashes, a boom light. Her shoulders glimmer in her sleeveless top. I feel it coming off of her in waves, a hissing mist. Tree laughs heartily, from the gut. She laughs and laughs. Slaps a knee.

I sit there, smile frozen, an ache burning my cheeks, clutching the glass.

Her white-blond hair, parted down the middle, grazes her shoulders as she shakes her head. "Loosen up. Beauty is fun. That's one of HEBE's guiding principles."

Hebe. The Greek goddess of youth. Serving ambrosia to the gods and goddesses of Mount Olympus.

I laugh, softening into it, and settle farther into the couch's embrace. I'm suddenly tired; I could nap. I touch the water glass to my inner wrist, hoping for a jolt, but it's lukewarm.

"Let's talk business for a sec. Your first major project will be next Wednesday; Gem will fill you in on the details, but we have a shoot for a new launch. And please, come out for drinks with us tonight! My treat."

Gem is Gemma. HEBE's Lead Storyteller, my boss. *She hates the word boss*, Tree said in our final interview. *I do too. It's so masculine. Call me your True North.* She plucked the final word from the air with a finger curl.

"I would love to, but—"

She cuts me off. "Ah, time for my next appointment. Take your time settling in. The real work starts soon!"

I'm nodding, hard. Picturing my head rolling off my neck. I see it plunging onto the creamy rug, dripping the wrong pink for the color scheme. There's a light knock and we both turn toward Marigold's spooky face pressed to the door, summoning me.

It isn't until I'm back at my desk that I realize I'm still holding the glass of water, tight enough that I'm surprised it doesn't break.

DRINKS ARE IN the bar of a hotel around the corner from the office. I've walked down this street countless times and never noticed the entrance, an industrial door framed by a coat of ivy. Tree, Gem, and I tunnel through the archway of greenery. SoHo recedes, the leafy walls narrow, rustling and mobile, until they spit us into a dark room. A smell like new leather, like flowers on fire. Santal 33 by Le Labo. I'm wearing it too. We're all wearing it—Tree and Gemma and the plush and slim-shouldered women milling about the candlelit bar, pencil rubbings coming to life as I adjust to the dark.

The maître d', reedy in a black dress, straightens at our approach. "Ms. Whitestone! How are you this evening? May we seat you at the usual table?"

"If it's available," Tree says. Magnanimous, but also like she might unhinge her jaw, snake-like, and swallow the maître d's head whole if the table is, in fact, not available.

Tree's usual table is in the back corner of a smaller, quieter dining room. The table doesn't seem large enough to fit the three of us, but we manage to fold our limbs underneath. It's not comfortable. If I move slightly to either side my knee will graze one companion or the other. I aim to stay completely still, legs pointed forward, back straight, breath held. Already there is a twinge, a muscle jumping near my tailbone.

"Have you been here before?" Tree asks. "It's my favorite place near the office."

I shake my head. "First time."

The server drops three menus. The beverages are named after yoga poses. Downward Dog. Warrior One. Upon closer inspection, I realize they don't contain alcohol. I haven't had a drink since I was a junior in high school, and it's such a relief not to be saddled with water at a bar that I order at random. The Namaste. Moments later the server returns with our drinks and a bowl of rosemary-dusted almonds. In my glass, a lavender sprig floats serene on a foam cloud.

Tree shakes her drink. She raises the glass. Gemma and I lift ours in return. "Beauty is possible," Tree says.

We clink, swallow. The Namaste is slightly gritty; my throat resists as the drink eases down. In the candlelight, Tree's lips are slicked wet patent leather. The second sip of The Namaste is not nearly as shocking as the first. I start to enjoy myself.

"So," Tree says.

"What brings you to us?" Gemma says.

The conversational volley feels like another interview. Maybe I dreamt signing the offer letter, the placid pink office, a stretch of marble with a sticky note denoting a nebulous square as belonging to me, the bags of makeup weighing down my overstuffed purse. "Well, as you know, I majored in fashion merchandising at LIM—"

Tree looks at Gemma, back at me. "Tell us what's in your heart."

The women, my coworkers, stand out in the swampy dining room. Hair and skin and cheeks and teeth. The moment I knew I wanted to work for them took place on the corner of Prince and Crosby. I waited to cross so I could meet Richard at the outdoor café across the street. I spotted him at our favorite table in a blue shirt, reading a book with the cover rolled back, and smiled at the sight of his natural state, how he was when he thought he was alone. The weather was warm but not yet hot, and SoHo bubbled with the Friday afternoon rush. My happiness, as it always was when it came, was restless. I checked my phone as a sleek car with tinted windows passed, imagining someone famous inside, maybe Brad Pitt, maybe Margot Robbie, maybe Viola Davis. These were the celebrities that came to mind.

Then, a bright splash on the horizon. A billboard. The image: serene pool blue transposed over the HEBE logo on a white background. Beneath: *Coming Soon.* Such a calm, blank space suspended above the downtown throb was arresting.

"The company branding stuck with me," I say to Tree and Gemma. "It's like a visual meditation. That's what we need, isn't it? To be soothed. To find a moment of peace among all the . . ." I toss my hand toward my phone, screen up on the table. "Noise. I want to give that to people."

"Aesthetics are *so* important. That's why I founded a beauty brand in the first place. When you look good, you *are* good. You know?"

And Tree must be the absolute best, because she is breathtaking. Her white hair and geometric eyeliner, the ceramic tone of her skin, the backless dress. Was she wearing that before? I don't recall. She drains her cartoonish drink, pulls a compact and a tube from the bowels of her Staud handbag, and applies the tiniest rub of HEBE balm to her bare lips. I study her mannerisms, try to memorize the delicacy with which she handles the tube, tosses it into her bag, and snaps the closure shut, after which she calls, "Waiter!" and waves an arm. "Another round, please."

Three fresh drinks appear. But my first languishes near the bottom of the glass. Foam streaks the sides.

"Drink up, Soph!" Gemma says. My cheeks turn warm. *Sophia* is a recent grad with a secondhand Louis Vuitton Neverfull in her closet, an obvious blow-out, and dry skin on her knuckles. *Soph* is a spotless professional. Her clothes and hair and teeth exude money.

There is no harm in drinking another Namaste. Nothing in the drink will turn me sour-mouthed and vicious. Only calories, which the other women don't seem worried about. I take the largest sip I can manage, swallowing hard and chasing with water. Lavender floods my sinuses. I blink and a tear drips down my cheek.

Tree grabs my wrist with one hand. The other cups my chin. She wrenches my face so that I'm staring right at her.

"Oh, honey," she says. "Don't cry." She releases me, presses an index finger to the single tear, absorbing the liquid into her skin, lifting the damp finger to her lips. Her pink rabbit's tongue darts out and licks. "Mmm, salty!" she says, and giggles.

I should be disturbed. My new boss just touched my face. Just licked my tears right from the palm of her hand. But my new boss is Tree Whitestone. And she's smiling like a maniac, like she's been waiting for me all her life. And the funny thing is, I feel like she has. I feel like I might have something that she needs.

As if in answer, she says, "We're so happy to have you."

THE DEAD BOLT on the apartment door is kicked out and nestled against the frame. What time is it? Some minutes ago, Tree put me in an Uber XL. The driver offered a mini Fiji, an organic breath mint I sucked on merrily as we threaded through lower Manhattan. Not drunk but shadowed by the memory of drunkenness, I am loose and spilling over my edges.

I push the door open. It slams against the wall. "Fuck! Dominique!" I twist the dead bolt. It retreats and the door slots into place. I lock it behind me. On my bedroom floor, legs splayed in a lazy straddle, hair a dark beehive held in place with a scrunchie, Dom, my roommate and best friend, does her makeup. She's taken the full-length mirror off the wall and placed it against the bed in a characteristic display of dominance that I resent.

"Full name. I must be in trouble." Dom keeps eye contact with her reflection.

"What are you doing in here?" My eyeliners are scattered on the rug. She's wearing a black lace thong and a striped tube top, as if she got distracted in the midst of dressing.

"Going through your makeup."

I throw my bag on the floor, sit down next to it, and shed my gloves. "Like you don't have enough of your own?"

Dom's blog, *MAKEUPSEX*, is popular enough to keep her as rich in eyeliner as she is in everything else. She started publishing her writing online during her one semester at the School of Visual Arts. All the great artists kept diaries, but hers needed a hook that would keep others interested; she chose to tell the story of her life through makeup, which she used as a window to parties, dates with semi-famous people of all genders, and her various drug addictions. A post on the best liquid lipsticks to wear while giving a blowjob went viral, and she dropped out of school to devote herself to the project full-time.

Now she makes a modest income from ad revenue and sponsorships, and she would make more, if she bothered to update the site regularly. Her lifestyle of expensive pills, Prada and Margiela clothes, and nightly dinners at a rotation of Michelin-starred restaurants is bankrolled by a substantial trust fund. Our Lower East Side abode came as part of her inheritance when her maternal grandmother died.

Dom and I lock eyes in the mirror. She crawls toward me on her hands and knees. Closes her eyes and tells me to guess. One wing is sharp, with a dried-down glossy finish. The other, smudged like a remnant from Ash Wednesday.

I point to one eye and then the other. "Stila Stay All Day, Urban Decay 24/7 Glide-On."

"YES!" Dom rests on her heels, flinging her arms. Collapses

onto her hands and knees, elbows straight, and kisses me on the forehead.

I examine her up close. Rheumy eyes and a constant low-level sniffle put her at about a four-and-a-half, maybe a five, on the sobriety scale. Dom is never completely clean. She can't handle *raw-dogging reality*, as she puts it. She needs a constant hazy scrim between her and what she refers to as *all that shit*. In other words, life.

It's not too bad tonight; she's holding herself upright. And her eyeliner is perfect.

"Where were *you*?" A suspicious twist to the mouth, as though biting lemon pulp.

"Work. Remember? First day."

"Work! Yes! With *Tree Whitestone*. How was it?" When Dom is like this, fully awake, she fires one question after another.

"Good? They didn't give me much to do. But we have a big shoot in a few days. I'll learn more then. And we went out for drinks after."

Dom crinkles her brow. "Drinks?"

"Non-alcoholic. Tree told me pretty much everyone at HEBE is sober. And vegan."

"Sounds like sooo much fun." She flips onto her back, head in my lap. "I'm working too. I'm going to dance till dawn, make out with someone sweaty, sleep on non-silk pillowcases and see how my wings hold up in the morning. Wanna come?"

"Sorry, babes, I have to wake up early. Work, remember? That's how the plebes get by."

I shake Dom off and climb into bed. Lavender Namastes thrum in my system, lulling me, baby-like, toward sleep. A flicker of guilt when I think about my nighttime skincare routine, but the pillow is calling and I sink.

"Earning an honest living, I respect it." Dom stands, picks with pinched toes at the rumpled fabric of her skirt on the floor where I left it, then picks it up and hikes it over her curved hips, tugging at the zipper.

"Thanks for letting me wear that today," I say, drifting.

"Anything for you, sweetheart." She blows me a kiss and leaves.

2008

After school with Mona. Knee propped on the sink while she applied eye makeup in the bathroom, the ball of the other foot dug into the linoleum, skirt hiked around her upper thighs. She wanted to be sexy for the boys who passed while we sat on benches in the town square, far enough away from school so as to be outside faculty jurisdiction and halfway between our two houses. Those boys wore their dads' leather jackets and their older brothers' cologne, a cheap musk that couldn't hide the smell of stale cigarettes and skunky weed, the scarier ones sucking on chewing tobacco, working it with their teeth. These were the boys on whom we harbored crushes; the ones we would let touch us at parties. We felt we had the power to change these boys, to make them men. Mona, with her saucy cat eyes and her foisted-up tits, and me with a white T-shirt tied high and a schoolgirl skirt circling.

She'd hold out the brush tip of her eyeliner pen. "Let me do your eyes?"

I never let her. It frightened me, the power of ink. The harsh lines Mona carved with a Q-tip traced her pale skin, making her older in the wrong way, like the waitress with a smoker's cough at the twenty-four-hour diner where we choked down black coffee to feel cooler, more adult, than we really were. The tugging required to wash it off on nights when she didn't fall into bed with makeup on, waking in the morning with racoon smudges under her eyes, the liner clinging, as much a part of her face as her nose or freckles.

I could see, already, how this would age her. How these habits would be sexy and endearing until, one day, they were not. Even though Mona was more beautiful and free-spirited, everything we were taught men and boys wanted, I felt superior. When I closed my eyes, I saw a woman, many decades older, wearing my face. The skin a bit slackened on the bone, yet smooth. Plumped. I never smiled in these visions, but it was there anyway, the suggestion of a grin.

I didn't touch makeup besides my grandma Lucy's lipsticks and a cake-scented gloss swiped from the drugstore, until the Homecoming dance when Mona told me I'd be practically naked in the photos, helped me apply a cast of foundation, a sweep of smoky shadow, body glitter on my cheeks and shoulders. She was right; I liked myself in the bedroom mirror, and later, when the photos were uploaded, I was a woman on the arm of my date, who wore a busted leather jacket over his white shirt and tie. Feminine and sweet. Pliable, like a doll.

But, for now: Mona in the bathroom. Mona, radiant amid the grout grime. Her girlish movements, flick of the wrist, tilt of the chin, a self-possession born and not made. She remains there, trapped in the amber of my memory. An innocent fly, beating her wings. I visit her often, whenever I close my eyes.

2

Pigeon calls pull me from princess-sleep. Feet to the floorboards, I stretch my neck muscles while looking at the calendar on the wall across from the bed. If I flipped forward two months to July, my thirtieth birthday would be circled in red pen. Thirty on the 31st.

I perform a few yoga poses on the mat I keep sprawled on the floor. I read once in a magazine that to encourage exercise in the morning, you should have everything you need ready to go as soon as you wake up. My spine moves nimbly through cat and cow, curling into downward dog. In child's pose I turn onto one cheek and inspect my face in the mirror. No breakouts. Plump lids. Smooth planes. But a flash of decay lurks. Mirrors are portals to the future; my wrinkled face overlays my young one.

I bury my forehead onto the mat and breathe.

The routine goes as follows: cold shower, a scream as I step under the spray, counting to ten before I slowly introduce warm water until the temperature is tolerable. I address keratosis pilaris on my arms and thighs with a lemon and walnut powder exfoliating bar, use two pumps of HEBE neroli body oil to cleanse. Heady floral steam fills the shower's narrow column. Next, I wash my hair with charcoal exfoliating shampoo followed by a deep conditioning mask that stays on while I shave my underarms, legs, and bikini line with men's shaving cream from the drugstore and a pastel razor from a company that sends replacement razorheads in the mail every three months. Then I stand under the water for an extra minute, blast the hot water for a second, let my raw cuticles sting.

I towel off and mist oil onto my damp skin, comb knots out of my hair. I wish I could afford a silk pillowcase like Dom's to make sleep frictionless and clean. Sometimes she lets me borrow one she isn't using. I dust the mid-lengths and ends with texturizing spray, wrap my hair in a second towel exclusively for this purpose, demarcated by a urinal hue from scalp residue. By this time the body oil has absorbed, and I coat my limbs with colloidal oatmeal moisturizer and slip on my robe. The shower opens my pores, leaving me generally pliant and unfurled. I can appreciate my unfocused reflection within the haze of the just-wiped mirror.

This morning, the HEBE skincare range forms a curvaceous army on the sink's rim.

I skip cleanser—over-washing increases oil production and thus breakouts—and apply three pumps of rosewater toning mist directly onto clean skin. Serum (a vitamin C and ferulic acid blend followed by hyaluronic acid) comes next. I fan my hands to hasten the dry-down, then distribute a pump of eye cream between both ring fingers. Pressing semi-circles around the orbital bone, I massage until the white cast disappears. It's sealed with a generous dollop of sunscreen that leaves a flypaper tackiness.

When I'm alone, like I am this morning, Richard at his own apartment and Dom surely passed out elsewhere, if she ever made it to sleep, I prepare my coffee pour-over style. Feeding the boiling water into the cone, watching the level sink—akin to meditation.

I bite the nails on my unoccupied hand and scroll Dom's late-night messages while the coffee brews:

I heart
Sixteenth and
Remember when?????/
Sparkly tootoo
Or wait TUTOO
TUTU GODDMANNIT

Between the sentence fragments is a text from Richard, asking about my first day. He apologizes for not calling when he got home late from client drinks at Russian Samovar. Richard works in advertising and paints on the weekends. He is thirty-two and graying at the temples.

I add a scoop of chaga mushroom powder to the coffee and take it to my bedroom. There, I do my makeup sitting on the floor in front of the mirror where Dom left it: oil primer for a clean-girl glow. Concealer on the bruised cavities under my eyes. Fleshy powder to cut the shine of my T-zone. I don't need blush—I have a natural flush—but I open a new tube of HEBE's cream highlighter from my work bag, apply it to my cheek- and brow bones. Lip balm dapped in the center of my mouth to cheat thin lips to fullness.

I once came across a tagged candid of myself online, lips bare, mouth open, an alarming, ringless hole under my nose, a portal for spirits to fly through.

All that effort adds up to not much. I am myself made holy.

My reflection is a dewy dumpling. A baby angel glows at me in the mirror. Worthy of love and saving.

A true answered prayer.

MARIGOLD DROPS A turmeric latte in front of Tree, leaves the conference room, and stands guard with her back to the glass. Gemma has the upcoming launch, the subject of Wednesday's shoot, in an acrylic box under the desk. She clutches the lid so that I cannot make out more than a few splotches of pink, terra-cotta, white, and purple. My own hands, latticed in my lap, hidden in the white lace gloves I wear every day, mirror her tense grip.

Gemma places the box on the table to a rattling chorus, the sound of heavy marbles rolling inside. She pops the lid and I tip closer, peering at the contents. Pill-shaped vials, each capped with a different color. A shudder inside me, the sensation like a baby kicking.

I knit my hands tighter across my stomach. I coo, indeed the way I would whilst bending over a newborn, and compliment the packaging, lifting one chunky pill from the box. The colorful half comes off to reveal a tiny nozzle. "What are they?"

"Love Flush," says Gemma.

"Multi-use stains," Tree says. "Eyes, lips, and cheeks."

The customer is low-maintenance. She does her face in the back of a taxi, at her desk before happy hour without a mirror. Always without a mirror, unless she is at home, taking her time. Applying her makeup over a glass of wine before a date. That's the only time she deigns to look at her own perfect face. She is young forever by accident, a confluence of genetics, luck, and SPF. And the right products. Our products.

Terra-cotta liquid spurts from the nozzle. On the side, the

shade name and fluid ounces are printed where milligrams would be on an actual pill. Warm bronze drips down, bleeds into my glove like runny flesh. A bitch to wash out, but for now I don't mind.

"Collagen. That's the secret," Tree says.

"It will come in eight universally flattering shades," Gem adds.

The door creaks. Marigold wheels an easel on which rests a collaged canvas filled with inspirational images. Impressionist paintings I recall from long-ago art history classes: Monet, Degas, Cassatt. Blurred ballet dancers, flowering fields, women in high-necked blouses with bonnets tied at the plumps of their chins. Dusky-cheeked girls brimming with hydration.

"They're very pigmented," Gemma says. "You have to be careful."

"Gemma will take the lead on tomorrow's shoot, but don't be afraid to jump in with your ideas. We don't have room for wallflowers at HEBE," Tree says.

Gemma shows me headshots of the models for the shoot. One girl has an acne scar in the shape of Marilyn Monroe's birthmark. A spray of light brown freckles shower another girl's nose. All of their necks are cocked at broken angles. Wide-awake corpses, freshly killed.

The girls are something more than beautiful. Accessible, but further elevated by this quality. Like I could look like them, with the right moisturizer. I do look like them, a little bit. We all do.

And they all look like Tree.

RICHARD IS AT a two-top facing the door when I arrive at the restaurant, a bottle of my favorite mineral water on the table by the bread basket. He waves when he sees me. I kiss him on the cheek and hang my bag off the chair.

"Have you been waiting long?" I ask.

I hadn't wanted to go out the night I met Richard, but Dom had tickets to a Chairlift show in Williamsburg and was in a wild mood, flying on molly, wearing a ruffled pink onesie over a turquoise bra, eyes aflame and limbs liquid. I didn't want to leave her alone, but she charged into the crowd the second we entered the venue and I quickly lost sight of her. Richard found me at the bar, sipping seltzer with lime. He had on a mesh long-sleeved shirt under a cardigan. "I lost a bet," he said when I inquired, and charmed me with a cheeseball wink. "Your friends ditch you? Mine too. Let's get out of here?"

Before we went home together we ordered giant slices through a window at the pizza place next door, ate them standing on the corner. I suspect this is the Sophia Bannion he has in his mind, the one with vivid grease dripping off her chin and a sense of abandon in the press of her jaw. Not long after we met, I went vegan.

"I dreamt about this meal," Richard says when the food comes.

I force myself to chew each bite of whole wheat pasta with lemon and oil twenty-five times. Richard asks about my first week, jerking his chin supportively every third sentence or so, like he's timed his response.

If, as a child, I had drawn a diagram of my dream man, Richard would be the blueprint. Foppish sandy brown hair. Body defined by muscle yet cushioned enough to lie on. A caring gaze, artistic aspirations, family money. Under a tailored jacket, he's wearing a $200 T-shirt with a bear on a skateboard. He chews his lasagna like each bite is the last he will ever eat and fully lowers his utensils onto the plate. He never takes his eyes off me.

It can be suffocating, this focused attention.

The waiter clears our plates. I turn down a box for leftovers, deny Richard's attempts to cajole me into sharing tiramisu, and order an oat milk cappuccino. Richard's eyes and mouth tighten, but he doesn't argue.

Instead he updates me on the progress of the Harry Styles triptych he's finishing for his application to an emerging artists' grant. This year's theme is "The New Masculinity."

The waiter brings two spoons for the tiramisu anyway.

I KEEP MY face neutral, light, girlfriendly, in the cab home. Richard doesn't understand that I'm on a wellness journey. If I didn't know better, I might accuse him of ordering the tiramisu to rile me. But he's incapable of deception. He probably just wanted dessert, and thought maybe, this time, I might want some too.

Besides, I can't stand Richard's face when we fight. The flesh becomes doughy and his cheeks droop toward his jowls. His eyes do this melting chocolate chip thing. His sweetness further enrages me, a hot flare in my chest, and I want to slap him, claw at the pillow of his mouth until it bruises and swells. Violent urges that occasionally grip like iron fists on my spine.

Richard squeezes my knee. "Everything okay, babe?"

Hands curled into fists, nails biting palms, I say, "Fine. Just tired."

A dark figure is slumped on the sidewalk in front of the building. It's Dom, attempting to light a cigarette with a battered Bic. Her finger skids uselessly over the spark wheel. Her hooded lids drift to the open cab door as I climb out, and she yells, "Baby!"

Behind me, Richard slams his door. I feel him tense when he spots Dom. He disapproves of her, though he's too kind to admit it.

"What's going on, babes? Did you forget your keys again?" Hiking up my skirt, I squat and gesture for the lighter. Cigarette dangling from her lips, Dom leans toward the flame, waits for the end to catch. Leans back and takes a long pull. She removes the cigarette from her mouth and tries to put the moist end into mine, but I move away just in time. "Thought you were trying to quit," I say.

She rolls her eyes. "Okay, Mom."

"Hello, Dominique." Richard stands close to the curb, hands in his pockets.

"Richie! Help me." Dom spiders her arms. Her palms are clammy. She's wearing a lace bra as a top. Ribs convulse as she breathes.

Dom rests on my shoulder in the elevator. In the apartment, she flees to the kitchen. By the time I reach her, she's valiantly attempting to jam a corkscrew into a bottle of wine. She gives up, puts the bottle down, sits on a stool, and starts rolling a joint. Her fingers move with incredible precision.

Richard pops his head in from the hallway. "I'm turning in. Sophia?" An invitation to leave Dom with her bottle and continue our night in private. She will pass out on the couch in five minutes, tops. But there's that nagging voice that says catastrophe could strike. And then there's the part of me who just wants to be a girl in that way you can only be with other girls.

"I'm gonna stay up for a bit."

Richard leaves without protest, but his disappointment

echoes with the sound of his shoes. I hear him slam the bed-room door. I grab the discarded corkscrew and open the wine. Like a pro, even after all these years. Dom licks the seam of her joint and produces the lighter from inside her chain mail purse. I'm poised to assist, but she draws flame on the first try. Inhales like she's dying.

I take a swig of lukewarm lemon water from the S'well on the counter. Water bottles are scattered all over the apartment. Sometimes I open one and take a sip before I see it's stuffed with moldering fruit, reeking of sweet rot.

An extended silence, scored by the wine as it slaps the cords of Dom's throat, the dry scratch of breath as she smokes, descends. I strip off my gloves and set them on the kitchen island's marble, shed snake skins. My hands crunch as I stretch them.

Dom places the joint carefully on the edge of a heavy silver ashtray, her focus sharpening. She gets up; her footsteps creak the floorboards, I hear a door open—the linen closet—and she returns with a glass vial of cuticle oil. She spreads a paper towel and reaches for my hands. She begins to rub the oil on them in steady circular strokes, working finger by finger. It smells of almonds and vanilla. The scent intensifies with friction. She hums an old Italian hymn that her grandmother taught her.

This is our ritual. At the end of a long night, I take off my gloves, let Dom see the scars while she massages my hands back to some semblance of normalcy. Not even Richard is allowed to touch them with such intimacy.

I could cry, not from the pain, which only makes me drowsy, but from the exquisite pleasure of being known. Almond mixed with vanilla. I rest my chin on my breastbone and start to nod off. When I open my eyes, I'm at the table alone and the room is cold.

3

The interns are dew fresh. The interns are blond, brunette, redheaded. They have waves, bobs, ringlets. Glossy lips and eyelids. Dresses with side cutouts and patterns of flowers, of fruit, of space. They are turning their faces to the sun. They are scaling back, into the shadows, afraid of damage. The interns are wearing hats.

The interns have French saloon art and velvet fainting couches in their one-bedrooms. The interns live next to the Brooklyn Bridge, in the East and West Villages, on the Upper East Side. The interns wear matching lingerie and vintage door knocker earrings, tiny cardigans with nothing underneath, unbuttoned to the pastry swell of their small breasts. How do their nipples not chafe?

The interns carry our lavender satin drawstring pouches with phone, keys, and matte lip stain inside. Matchbooks from Balthazar or Jimmy at the James. Receipts from Dimes. No wallet. Not even ID. If they are killed, if their bodies are found, they will be Jane Doe.

They don't care, they are dancing in backless dresses. They

don't care, they have nail art. They don't care, they have a new rib cage tattoo, do you wanna see?

The interns didn't read that, but they posted the books so you know they would read them if they had the time. There is never enough time. The interns love the artist, want to be the muse. They say, draw me. They say, paint me. They say, sing me.

The interns have symmetrical faces.

The interns carry our lip balm, a status symbol, candy-colored tubes jutting from pockets and rolled shirt sleeves like packs of cigarettes. The interns wink and say, *Got a light?* Smoking isn't cool anymore, moisturizing is. Health is the new smoking. The interns understand this, and they keep their vices locked tight. They drink green juice and eat kale salad for lunch. They reach for ephemeral ethical consumption with reusable grocery bags and recycled bamboo sundresses that disintegrate in the wash.

And our products. Gilding their cheekbones, kissing their lips, telling them they are perfect and holy and worthy. They are beautiful, luminous, and we make them more so.

The interns, they want and want and want. We give them what we can.

MANY RUMORS: TREE is a natural brunette. She's a natural blonde. Her father is a politician. Her mother, a descendant of Mary Shelley. Tree dropped out of Wesleyan or she graduated Phi Beta Kappa. Tree sleeps for fifteen hours a night. Tree never sleeps. No one can say how old she is, exactly. She sprung from the womb fully formed, ageless.

Someone finds, in the annals of the internet, or a friend of a friend of a friend's basement, a yearbook photo. Sixteen- or seventeen-year-old Tree, a black turtleneck gripped around her neck, draped with a circular diamond on a delicate platinum chain. Her white-blond flashbulb hair parted threateningly down the center, follicles marching in a succinct line that exposes her skull. Diamond studs twinkle on her earlobes. Wide-set eyes settle under the broad canopy of her eyebrows. Her smile is tight and compact. Why doesn't she let her teeth show? I know they are perfect. White and square, the kind in toothpaste commercials. Teeth that dentists dream about. Maybe she paid for them later.

But I don't think so; I think she was born that way. An ideal smile with both rows visible, and noninvasive gums.

DUSK. THE GIRLS from work gather on the roof, sucking anti-inflammatory turmeric root from vape pens. Tree reclines on a lounge chair, leather slides kicked off and legs hidden inside her pleated midi. The party orbits her. She's freshly bronzed from a week at Amangiri. Not truly tan, though, not burnt.

Gemma appears at her elbow, perches like an exotic bird on the footrest, and feeds Tree a wedge of cashew gouda off an ivory plate. It feels like something I shouldn't witness, and I look down at the street, leaning on the partition that encloses the deck.

Soft material brushes my arm and I rotate into the turmeric cloud encompassing the roof. A navy headband. One silver hoop earring. Brown eyes.

"You're the new girl," says a petite brunette, her face broad and plain as the bottom of a new shoe.

"Sophia."

"Emily."

"Nice dress," I say, and I mean it. It's black with skinny jeweled straps, rocket ships and shooting stars printed on the fabric. Something I would wear.

"Thanks. Vintage." It's not vintage; I saw it on a mannequin in a shop a few blocks from the office. Considered trying it on. But I couldn't afford it, so I didn't bother.

Her lie lands as a blatant challenge. I let it settle, the weight of her fib and my sympathy for her need to seem cooler than she is. Taste, real taste, is curated, not designed.

We nurse mocktails. Nothing I think to say sounds interesting, even to me, so I say nothing for a minute, two. Then, because the silence is oppressive: "Nice night."

Emily snorts. "Yeah. A dream."

"So, what do you do?"

"I'm Senior Editor of *The Dew*. I took over the blog when Tree switched gears to launch the product line." Emily pauses, sips amber liquid from a plastic coupe. "I was the first intern," she adds. The phrase has the stilted, rehearsed cadence of something she's repeated so often that it's been stripped of its original meaning.

HEBE's origin story is well-publicized. Tree started taking grainy DSLR photos of her glamorous friends' bathrooms when she was nineteen, quoted them at length about their beauty routines, and published the results on her website. She saw the appeal in voyeuristic glances at the innermost quarters of the borderline famous. *Borderline* being key; these women could not be garishly notable. A pop star or a legendary actor would defeat the point, which was the attainability illusion. The women she profiled—sought-after DJs, infamous party girls, fashion bloggers, magazine editors, and the occasional novelist—were, in a way, less reachable than the household

names, origin stories shadowed, wealth and connections con-
cealed.

The site's most-viewed article was a profile of a reclu-
sive best-selling author. I had memorized the salient details
ahead of my HEBE interview. My favorite part is the author's
response to Tree's question about how she maintains her signature chin-length bob: *I trust my hair to stay out of my way
and, mostly, my hair listens.* The profundity of beauty that has
the decency to leave you alone.

"Should I cut my hair?" I say it out loud, though I didn't
mean to.

Emily laughs. She twists her un-split ends around her fist
and lets them go. "I take it you've read the Dianna Smart
interview on our site?"

We giggle like children.

"Sometimes when I edit interviews I'm thinking, damn, I
should be on the other side," she says.

"Photographed in your pool-sized bathtub?"

"Asked about my ideas *and* my favorite retinol serum."
Emily peers at the bubbles in her champagne. She puts her
coupe on a nearby table. Her lashes are dark, her lips sheeny,
as if she dipped her face in lobster butter. So healthy; Dom's
diametric opposite. And Mona's too, if I let myself go there.

Emily's eyes are brown marbles threaded with gold. She
lowers them and lifts the sleek black vape to her tawny lips.
Her too. Smog presses in, sweat gluing hair to my neck in
clumps. I dab my moist forehead with the back of a wrist. The
gloves are sausage-casing tight.

"Nice gloves," Emily says, and offers a pull on the vape.
"Turmeric root. It's supposed to cure cancer or whatever. I just
like the taste."

I decline reflexively, then worry I fractured a bonding opportunity. Emily's breath emits delicate spice. She asks how I enjoy working at HEBE, and I tell her it's the most fulfilling job I've had in my life, which may or may not be true but feels true at the moment.

Emily slyly purses her lips. Takes another turmeric drag. Our chatter embodies the camaraderie of two people who are not yet friends but could be. I leave the party before it gets awkward, a slippery Irish goodbye off the deck, through the office, and onto the street.

MARIGOLD IS SITTING on my desk the next morning. She looks rough. Red lipstick gathers in the cracks of her mouth and dark circles clump under her eyes, a washed-out layer of concealer poorly blended on top. Not ours. Something fuller coverage.

Her imperfection in the flame of office light is jarring. She stands. We square off behind my chair. She's much taller; my nose would graze her collarbone if we were to hug.

"Tree requests your presence," Marigold says.

Interns circle the open-plan like flies, distinguished by a shared demeanor. Taut yet expansive. They carry coffee trays and product samples, cutting a weave from the various enclosed offices of the C-suite.

"This way."

Half the lights are off in Tree's office, casting an apocalyptic glow. There's a second door at the back that I didn't notice before. Like a portal to another dimension. Marigold leads me through, into a pristine room that resembles a high school science lab. Cabinets on three walls, wide tables in the center bordered by tall stools. A full-scale anatomy model with no legs is nestled on a counter, the worms of her intestines bared.

Tree doesn't hear us come in; she's touching the plastic heart. I swear that it pulses as she takes her hand away. A smile swallows her face. Her hair sloshes. I see it now: Tree and Marigold have the same haircut. The same sheeting effect as they turn their heads.

Intensity gathers around Tree, an electric current. Suddenly, I don't want Marigold to leave me alone with her. But Marigold has already vanished, taking my escape hatch. Clicking the door shut. "Hi. Uh, Marigold said you wanted me?"

My mind plays tricks: Tree in a petal-hued lab coat. A steady, viscous drip, the sound like saline gulping through an IV tube. Tree's hand reaching, reaching, covered in red fluid. Her skin makes contact and brings me back to myself. It's just a sleeve brushing my cheek, then a thumb tracing a warm pulse down my neck. I smell her gardenia perfume. Huh. She really is wearing a lab coat. But her hands are clean and she's dabbing at my upper lip.

She licks a fingertip and wipes at me again. "You've got something . . ." Tree squints, her brow folding like the crease of a paper airplane. Botox must not be her secret. It doesn't allow the face to move that freely. "There. Looked like a chocolate smudge."

Tree's neck is so close, a pale runway. I jerk my head away. "What did you need?" I ask, with more force than intended. Tree perches on a stool. She pulls out her phone and starts scrolling. Maybe I can leave.

"Let me tell you a story." Tree touches the next stool. I take the seat, a reluctant RSVP. Salmon entrée, please. Only there is no wedding food, no boiled prom vegetables. Just Tree and her ghoulish skinned-alive mannequin in a fantasy science classroom from bubblegum hell.

We are breathing the very same air, our lungs pulsing in time.

The story goes: there is a girl who lives on the edge of a forest. In what town? "Doesn't matter," Tree says. "Any forest. Any town." She lives among the trees. What trees? "Doesn't matter. Douglas firs. Redwoods. Maples." Pick a tree, stick with it. That's the tree surrounding our heroine. She lives with her mother, who is covered in tattoos. The tattoos are all silhouettes of women. Mouths and hands, gesturing. Holding. A lipstick bullet trapped like a cigar between teeth. Curls of line work piled on an outlined face. The mother never talks about her life before the girl and the forest, but she keeps a collection of matchbooks in the top drawer of her armoire, from places dotting the coast of California.

"They live in California?"

No. They share a mismatched wardrobe. Nothing fits right. Zippers snag at the waist and the sweaters are large enough to fit both women at once. The girl doesn't know where the garments come from. Every few weeks, her mother leaves the girl with three cans of refried beans and disappears for a day or two, returning with a bulging garbage bag. They go through the bag together, pulling green taffeta and maroon silk from the plastic, laying the spoils smooth on the bed in makeshift outfits.

When they finish, the bedroom is the aftermath of a department store massacre. The girl doesn't ask where the clothes come from. She puts on a new silk slip with the straps that slip down her shoulder and tries to be grateful. The clothes are pretty, after all, and she was taught that pretty is a virtue one cannot afford to deny.

But she has suspicions. Whenever her mother brings a new batch of clothes home, her face is a little younger, too. Collagen-plump cheeks, fewer lines in her forehead. A bruised and bloodied lower lip. The girl asked her mother about it once. "One day you'll understand," the mother said, and handed her daughter a ruffled '80s party dress. "Here, put this on."

On a cool summer night, her mother comes home with blood on her shoes. Blood on the garbage bag. She tries to hide it, but the girl sees, and pretends she doesn't see.

Says, "Oh, what a lovely blouse!"

She doesn't forget though, and the following week the girl follows her mother to the forest border. It's the first time she's been beyond the tree line in as long as she can remember, maybe ever. Maybe she was born among the trees.

She trails the dirt road until it intersects with a highway and watches a black car pull up and swallow her mother. The girl waits until the door closes and the car peels off before she sticks out her thumb. Hitches a ride with a stale man in a stale Volkswagen bus, trailing the sleek car carrying her mother into a city. Maybe it isn't much of a city at all, not what you and I would call a city, just a flat, sheenless cluster of buildings. But it is as much of a city as the girl has ever seen. To her, it's a metropolis.

The girl starts to get out on a corner and the man puts his big hand on her slim thigh, the oldest story in the world, and she opens the door and throws herself onto the sidewalk. Knees and palms scraped, bleeding, she looks up as her mother vanishes into the crowd.

Here, Tree pauses. "I want to show you something," she says.

"What happened to the girl?"

"That's where the story ends."

Tree gets up, opens a cabinet over an epoxy resin sink. I'm thinking about the girl, the trouble the mother got into in exchange for all those thrift-store rejects and the swollen lip. The mob, probably. As my grandma Lucy would say, it's always the mob.

Tree returns with a white jar the size of a clementine. She unscrews the lid, sets it down on the counter. I notice a red dot in the center, pulsing in the hospital fluorescence. Inside the jar is a cream as white and smooth as fresh snow. It smells like crushed flowers, acidic and sweet. My gloved hands tingle with the urge to destroy.

Tree says, "Will you take this home and try it for a few weeks?"

"Me?" I ask, like an idiot.

Tree assures me that yes, she wants me. She tells me not to do anything besides wash my face. No retinol, no serum. Sunscreen is okay. And to record my results in a notebook, which she also provides. The cover is lavender leather, the HEBE logo stamped in the center.

"You're doing an important service for the company," Tree says, as I clutch the jar, with all its promise of a new face, a new life.

With that, I appear to be dismissed. Tree calls to me one last time as I move to the door. Her hand is on her long throat, psychedelic magenta swirls on her nails the only spots of color on her blotted disposition.

"There's nothing as sacred as a young face," Tree says, with closed eyes, like she's forgotten I'm there.

DOOMED DREAMS AND unease stalk me through the night. The cream is on the bedside table. Last thing I remember before passing out is putting it down, the white jar's cataracted eye staring into my bedroom's neverdark.

The morning holds a Saturday's traditional restless energy. A feeling like I'm late for a plan I don't remember making. I stare at my phone, pick at the tender dead skin haloing my thumbnail until blood bubbles to the surface.

Richard rolls over, his breath deepens. I tuck my bloodied thumb into the palm of my hand and hold my breath, watch the rise and fall of his chest. I imagine reaching over, snuggling into his side. Inhaling his musky night-sweat. I shift and his arm drapes a diagonal across my body, pinning me to the mattress like a butterfly mounted inside a frame.

I stare at the ceiling and count my breath. One on the inhale, two on the exhale. And so on and so on, until I reach nine, then I start over. I'm wide awake. I kiss Richard on the wrist and gently scoot out from under his arm. Satisfied that he's remained asleep, I put the coffee on and move through the apartment while it brews, examining my face in the mirrors.

In the bathroom, I try to identify the distinct sensation of my features—closing one eye and then the other, opening my mouth—but each gesture is more like touching a numbed tooth than the last. In the apartment entranceway, fragmented across three circular mirrors grouped above the table with its perennial stack of abandoned junk mail, I'm a child. In the toaster's reflection, I am not getting any younger. Closer to thirty than not.

The coffee beeps. I fill an old mug, NYU logo on the side and a chip around the rim that my tongue slips into with each sip. The mushroom powder gives it an earthy flavor that I hated at first but have taken to strongly; I miss it when I drink coffee without it.

Richard appears in the kitchen doorway, damp hair and a towel around his waist.

"Hey there," I say. "I didn't hear you get up."

"Figured I'd hop in the shower, be all fresh-faced when I see you so you don't leave me."

He kisses my forehead, takes down a mug from the cabinet, and fills it with coffee from the carafe. Shirtless in the sun-dappled kitchen, he appears like an apparition from a catalog.

I joke that Richard stays with me because of the apartment I share with Dom, which is beautiful and airy, splashed with yellow light in the summertime. She allows me to live there for a nominal fee, which, as I understand it, mostly covers utilities.

Which is to say, I would date me for the apartment, too.

Richard kisses me on the mouth this time, my coffee mingling with his toothpaste, and goes to get dressed. The next sip burns my tongue. All day I taste blood.

2008

Clark's Deli was on the main road, a quaint stretch past the train station where the traffic thinned, opening onto squat awnings announcing shops and bars. Inside was a linoleum floor, cheerful rows of gum and candy bars set into the counter, providing a garish contrast with the condoms and cigarettes and scratch-offs tucked out of reach behind the cashier.

Here, on this spot, on a rainy afternoon, Mona's feet set on a salmon-pink tile and mine on an off-white, our friendship splintered beyond repair.

I can't remember why we went to Clark's that day. We usually avoided the place, which was where the popular kids from school bought Arnold Palmers that the employees mixed themselves and poured into massive Styrofoam cups. They'd come to class five minutes late, those white cups flashing spotlight beams on the corners of their desks, squeaking with every sip. Nothing explicitly stopped Mona and me from purchasing Arnold Palmers before first period like our classmates, the same way nothing stopped us from leaving campus at lunch or shopping for polos and jeans at Abercrombie & Fitch in the mall. At the same time, these activities were aligned with a certain social class, counter to our stance of chosen loneliness, that it would look nothing less than desperate for us to adopt them for ourselves.

On this particular Sunday in early March, the sky had turned from cloudless blue to blank stone white in a matter of moments. Mona eyed the scene over her cigarette from our bench in the square, farthest from the church entrance so we could catch God coming.

She gave the air, suddenly chilly, a hard sniff.

"We should take cover," she said, and pulled me off the bench. She walked to Clark's with such purpose that, looking back, I wonder what she'd known. Her impassive face betrayed nothing as she stopped under the burgundy awning, aimed her eyes at me, lifted one shoulder in a characteristic shrug, and said, "I want an Arnold Palmer."

I was the one who opened the door and stepped inside.

Clark's appeared empty at first glance. The racks were too tall and cluttered, rendering the eye utterly confused, unable to make out where Pepperidge Farms ended and Lay's began. I blinked until the chaos settled, and I could make out the gleaming dome that housed prepared foods and salad ingredients, the menu suspended above and, between them, a tall boy with sharp cheekbones watching us. His dark eyes glittered like a raccoon's.

Mona had charged ahead by the time I broke eye contact with the boy. I hadn't seen him before, which wasn't unusual. Small towns outside of New York City were not so small, really. People passed through like ghosts, leaving nothing behind on their way to somewhere else.

I couldn't see Mona anymore, but used the crinkling as she rifled through junk food as a sonic map to locate her. In the back corner next to the refrigerators, she had a family-sized bag of Snyder's honey mustard pretzels in one hand and an Oreo liberated from its container in the other. "There you are," she said, and handed me the pretzels.

"Mona, what the fuck?" I whispered, gesturing at the Oreo. She bit into the cookie, sending a spray of black crumbs onto her chest.

"You want one?" Mona reached for the nearest bag. I pulled her hand away. "Ow! What's your problem?"

Mona shrugged and ate another pretzel. Then she left me in the aisle and moved back toward the entrance. I followed. The boy watched as we came around the bend, leaned back, arms crossed, a bemused dimple pressed into one cheek as though someone had poked him gently but firmly with the eraser end of a pencil.

I waited for him to call us out for stealing. Instead, he turned away in tacit permission. When I looked at Mona, she was chewing.

The craving came over me then. How long had it been since I'd last had iced tea or lemonade? Neither drink impressed my keenly developing taste buds. Sugar-sweet that hurt your teeth, or a bitterness that pruned your tongue. The one time I made lemonade as a child, I'd forgotten to add sugar. Sold it like that too, at a folding table on our postage-stamp lawn— mirthless lemon water for thirty cents a cup. I hadn't tasted it, and didn't understand why my customers' faces shrank after their first sip, why they shuffled away so quickly with barely a *thank you*. When my mother discovered me outside—I'd made the batch early in the morning while she was asleep, hoping to delight her with my earnings later in the day—she whisked the plastic cup I was handing to our neighbor Mrs. Greenwood out of my grip, took a sip, and spit the lemonade onto the lawn, spraying my bare ankle and moistening a patch of grass. She made me return Mrs. Greenwood's change, then watched from our stoop as I went door-to-door down the block, offering refunds.

I couldn't remember which of our neighbors patronized the stand, so I ended up digging into my allowance and paying every household on our street thirty cents.

I approached the counter. He was wiping down the grill station, pointedly not looking at me. I made a fist and rapped on the glass displaying hard discs of bagel stale from the morning, various cream cheeses, prepared salads.

He spun, a mangled rag dangling from one hand, the other perched on his hip.

"Can I help you?" he said, and his voice held a trace of amused irritation.

"Two Arnold Palmers," I said.

With exaggerated movements he pulled two cups from a dispenser and filled them to the top with ice. Mona shuffled up next to me, still chewing. She wiped her mouth with the back of her hand. Her upper lip bulged as she ran her tongue over her teeth.

The boy carried the cups to the register, slamming them onto the counter. The Styrofoam buckled under his fingertips. He rang us up, announcing the price in a hollow voice deeper than the one he'd used before. His tone fluctuated with the looping cadence of a lazy hand draped over piano keys.

Since I had ordered the drinks without asking Mona, and since she was poorer than I was and perpetually spending her meager allowance on mysterious pills and weed, I scraped around in my bag, took far too long to count out exact change.

I dumped the money on the counter, crumpled bills first.

Slowly, the boy lifted each coin and dropped them, one by one, into the register. The sound of coins jumping against the drawer's metal walls frayed my nerves. He didn't seem to be counting, an edge of antagonism punctuating his gestures, amusement playing at his face, as if it were all—us, Clark's Deli, this town, the whole world—a big joke.

And why did I feel such a pull toward him, when his smirking confidence should have infuriated me? The boys at school were similarly churlish, but you could tell they did it for attention and that it wasn't rooted in any real sense of superiority. They were as insecure as any girl; they just displayed it with the false masculine veneers that television and their angry fathers had taught them to adopt as protection.

This boy's attitude, on the other hand, had nothing to do with us. We could be abducted by aliens in the middle of Clark's and he'd hardly notice.

Mona took the cups, handed one to me. I felt the boy's eyes meander over the underdeveloped curves tucked into my light-wash skinny jeans, and that simple, human glance, that urge to look, is what burrowed into my skin, parasitic, and changed the course of our collective history.

My hand shook. Fingers turned smooth and rudderless. They rubbed, useless, against the Styrofoam as it slipped toward the floor. The cup tumbled, and then my legs, from the shins down, and the linoleum became sticky with liquid sugar. All I could think about was my mother's furrowed mouth spraying drops of lemonade on the grass.

To say that I wanted to die at that moment sounds dramatic. But I was sixteen, and everything was drama. The wind hurt my skin. Tears could be summoned in an instant, by an especially orange sunset, or the opening notes of a favorite song. Embarrassment in front of a cute boy (I had, between order and payment, decided that he was very cute) was more than enough to render me momentarily suicidal.

Mona was no help; she laughed, and her laughter was the most irritating bell. Fury took hold of me; I wanted to shake her. I had worshiped Mona since childhood, and never once before now had I wished for her to suffer.

Around us, Clark's turned flat and gray. The boy had returned to cleaning the grill, and I waited for him to notice the disaster. Time extended, traveling down a long and painful funnel, as he finally sensed us staring and whirled around. He came closer, squeezing the rag, glanced first at my empty hand, then at the cup on the floor, then at the vague brown liquid circling my feet. The lid had popped, remaining tangentially attached to the cup by the straw anchored through the lid's hole. Melted ice trailed onto the tile. I fought the urge to nudge the cup with the toe of my shoe and send it spiraling. To make a bad situation worse.

"Was that you?" the boy asked, rhetorically. His words snapped something within me, and I stooped to righten the cup, halfheartedly pushing some of the spilled ice back inside, which only left my palm slick and wet and freezing. I wiped it on my jeans, smearing a handprint.

The boy disappeared through a doorway at the far end and emerged wheeling a bucket and mop. He was giddy as he came around the counter, as if my klutziness were the single most exciting thing to happen to him all day.

I relaxed and smiled up at him. He was so tall. "Sorry," I said, and giggled girlishly.

Mona hadn't spoken in a while. She wanted to leave, but I needed to see how far I could take this. Flirting did not come naturally to me; I hadn't had much practice. I had no idea where to begin. The boy had no name tag. This felt deliberate, as though he had materialized with no history, no future. Only this very moment.

Mona and I stood still as he sloshed the mop around us for a minute, replaced it inside the bucket, and returned to his post. There, he prepared a fresh Arnold Palmer, and delivered it with a shallow bow, one arm tucked behind his back, as though asking if he could have this dance.

I took the cup. *Yes.*

The little bell on the door fluttered as Mona and I stepped outside. The sun had returned, and my mood was buoyant. My irritation faded. I felt like skipping.

"He was cute," Mona said, and sucked at her straw. The tip was crumpled and veined where the plastic cracked under her teeth. Mona mangled straws like they had killed her family.

He was cute. I heard it as confirmation. Acceptance of my burgeoning crush. Those days I did nothing without Mona's permission. I didn't know what I liked until Mona told me I liked it. We'd be in the car, a song would come on, she'd hum along absently, and from then on I would not be able to get enough of that song. We'd go to the mall and I would think I wanted some shirt or sweater until she shook her head or wrinkled her nose or told me it was *what a hooker nun would wear.* I'd protest as I slid the garment back onto the rack. But I put it back every time anyway. Nights in the park that ended behind the bushes with some boy started with Mona looking at him, looking at me, and giving a succinct nod. Mona's agreement that the boy from Clark's, whose name, I would later learn, was Chase, was cute—I took it as a sign.

I raised the cup to my lips, taking a drawn-out sip. Sugar hit my tongue, traveled to my brain, making me blissfully dizzy. I was filled with light and sunshine and all the beautiful things. Mona hit me on the arm and took off running down the block. I tossed the cup, still partly full, into a garbage can and chased after her.

When I think back on it now, I see the two little girls we still were running toward a future we could not possibly imagine. This is the one perfect instant I return to in the dark hours when I miss her the most, made all the more precious by its status as the one immediately preceding our downfall.

But ah—wait. Look, she's getting away.

4

I'm searching for women on the internet. Girls, really. They are so young, their flesh like unbaked clay. A mosaic populates the browser. I save profiles to show Tree and Gemma at our casting meeting. Some girls have tagged our brand so that I can find them easily. I prefer the ones who present the challenge of discovery.

At around one, Emily messages to ask if I want lunch. She's talking to the office manager, Starla, at the front desk when I get there. Near the pillowy couch for visitors is an ice sculpture of a goblet, the symbol for the Greek goddess Hebe, on a marble plinth. I heard it cost $50,000 to hire Aria, an up-and-comer on the Chelsea gallery scene, to install it at four A.M. ahead of Tree's photoshoot with the women-centered business magazine *Femisphere*.

Emily and I walk to a salad place three blocks from the office. The line snakes to the door. We slowly make our way through the queue. Emily requests feta for her Mediterranean bowl, cuts her eyes at me. "Don't tell on me. HEBE women don't do dairy."

At the table, I empty a packet of nutritional yeast and mix it into the lettuce. Emily asks how I like working for Tree. I say that I love it because it seems like I should. Truthfully I've been unsettled by what I've seen so far, yet I couldn't be anywhere else.

Then I add, "There are a lot of interns."

"It's weird, right? Tree is obsessed with mentorship, but I'm not sure how much mentoring she expects us to do when these girls cycle through the office every three weeks. I don't even bother learning their names. And Tree handpicks all the interns—have you ever heard of a CEO who does that?"

"No. I mean, that does sound weird."

Emily stabs her salad. "Where were you before?" She means, as people in New York always do when they ask this question, did you work somewhere I should care about?

I picture the espresso machine at the coffee shop I worked at before HEBE. Sleek chrome lines, the hiss of the steam wand. "I, um. I did photo research at this indie zine."

"Oh, which? I bet I've heard of it. I'm obsessed with zines; I collect them."

I chew a sliver of bell pepper until it is near liquid, biding my time to think up a plausible lie. "Actually, it's online? My friend runs a blog called *MAKEUPSEX*."

"Wait, you worked for *Dominique*? She's an icon. Don't tell Tree, but she's honestly my inspiration for *The Dew*. We can't get as edgy, of course—the investors wouldn't like it. But her work is so refreshingly honest. She understands that being a woman is, like, totally vulgar."

Emily blots her chin with a napkin. Resting her elbow on the table, she moves her hand from her face and crumples the paper in a fist spiked with small gold rings. She is pitched forward, listening intently. A squill of arugula slips down my throat and I cough, sip my water.

"I was sort of an editorial assistant? Just doing a bit of everything."

"And you guys are friends?"

"Ah, yeah. Best friends, really. And roommates."

"That's funny, isn't she a trust-fund baby? I'm surprised she needs a roommate."

"She doesn't like to be alone."

Emily slides her fork around the inner curves of the bowl, scraping bits of cheese and spinach and dressing. She sucks on the tines and refreshes an application on her phone by running her finger vertically over the screen. "So many emails," she mutters.

"Actually, I wasn't telling the truth," I say. "About working for Dom." Emily levels her eyes at me, narrows them. She puts her phone on the table. "I worked at a coffee shop before this. As a barista. I was there for almost eight years."

"How did you get this job, then?"

I slip my gloved thumb into my mouth, bite down, and then lay my hand firmly next to the salad bowl and splay my fingers, pressing the palm flat on the table.

"I embellished my resumé. Dom agreed to be my reference; she was like, *I'll tell them anything you want.* But they didn't seem to care much about that, honestly. Tree mostly wanted to know about my birth chart."

Emily twists the thread of gold on her left middle finger. "She has an Excel spreadsheet she uses to track the entire astrological makeup of the office. I've heard she consults her psychic on hiring decisions, but that might be hearsay."

I laugh. "Sounds plausible. I guess she liked that I'm a . . ."

I trail off and open Co-Star on my phone. "Leo sun, Aries moon, Libra rising."

Clearing the trash, we slip into the diffuse pink afternoon. The city closes in and I feel like I'm being observed by blinking eyes in the windows, hidden by smogged glass.

THE DAY WINDS down. I text Dom and Richard alternately about evening plans. Dom invites me to a brand dinner for a curly hair care line owned by a D-list soap opera actress at the Public Hotel, and Richard wants me to join him and his coworkers at Rose Bar. As I'm mulling the options, neither overtly appealing, the work chat pings with a company-wide invitation to Tree's favorite bar, the one she and Gemma took me to on my first day.

I open a private Slack message to Emily and ask if she's going. Three dots appear next to her photo and shimmer there for several seconds before the response comes through.

> **not srue I have a choice lol**
> ***sure** The ellipses appear again and then: **you?**
> **if you're going . . .**
> **everyone is going, I promise.**
> **even the interns**
> **especially the interns.**
> **ha**

I slip my laptop into my backpack, next to the lavender notebook from Tree. The backpack is fake leather from Forever 21. Plastic flakes onto the floor as I close the zipper. Emily approaches while I'm securing the buckle. She's wearing a real leather jacket. The material armors her shoulders. Zippers rattle as she moves. She smells like patchouli. Her floral maxi dress flutters in an undetectable breeze that I, at first, think must be the stir of heaven, but realize once it reaches me too is the flicker of cool air from a vent.

"Ready?"

Interns have gathered on the Ligne Roset Togo sofas in the lobby. Aria's ice sculpture melts onto its stone plinth. A puddle grows on the floor.

"My acupuncturist says I carry all my tension in the arch of my left foot," says a ginger intern. She slides her foot out of a platform slide and points at her puckered insole. "If anyone touches me there, I start bawling like a baby."

I don't look too closely at the interns as we pass. One girl on the edge of the couch stands out to me anyway. She has wide bug eyes and an insectile fold to her slim arms. She stares dead at me, not blinking. A chill patterns down my arms.

I expect us to be seated near Tree's usual table, but the maître d' brings Emily and me through the dining room and into a lush garden crowded with so much greenery that it no longer feels like we are in the city. Tree, Gemma, Marigold, and Starla are on either side of a glass-topped iron table with a long tray of sushi between them.

I settle across from Gemma, who gestures with a seaweed maki before putting it into her mouth. I scan for chopsticks but there are none. The other women are eating with their hands. I'm wearing my favorite Cornelia James gloves, a trellis pattern stitched into the tissue-thin Irish lace, flowers at the cuffs. A birthday gift from Dom that seems a little cruel in retrospect. Like she doesn't expect me to get control of my habit. But they are, by far, the loveliest things I own.

"Hey, are there chopsticks?" I say.

Everyone keeps chattering. I repeat the question, louder.

Starla hears this time and tries to get the waiter's attention. "We ordered more stuff," she says. "It should be out soon."

"I didn't know they had such a big menu," Emily says.

"This is the soft launch. Vegan, earth-inspired foods with nods to various cuisines," Tree says. Brown rice ringed with tar-like strips of seaweed. Jewel-toned pearls that resemble fish at first glance but, upon closer inspection, could be vegetables.

My mouth waters. I sit on my hands.

Eventually the waiter returns with more plates, utensils. Typically, I'd starve before eating sushi with a fork. In Japan, it's considered very rude. Mona told me that during her anime phase in the eighth grade and I never forgot it. We used to day-dream about going to Japan together. But everyone is eating. What else am I supposed to do? I can't remove my gloves, not here. Not in front of these women. I can't let them see my scars. And if I eat with my hands, I'll stain the lace.

I feel Marigold watching as I spear a maki through its bleeding red center. Beets that could almost not quite pass for salmon.

The interns file in, clustering around a second table. The bug-eyed girl is last, and all the chairs are taken. She glances at the door like she's considering an exit. My hand is in the air and I'm waving her over. I'm saying, "Come sit with us! Plenty of room over here."

She has a lion's mane of honey-tinged hair that catches the fading light, reflecting a brilliant rosy glow. Her smile is grateful. Uncertain and kind.

"Welcome to the grown-ups' table," Gemma says, stirring her iced matcha with a straw. She retracts the straw, flips it over, and sticks the soggy end into her mouth.

Straws, I want to say, *give you wrinkles.* Then I remember the prototype cream, unopened on the nightstand at home. I wonder if Gemma has used it.

Emily leans on an elbow, chin in palm. "Which one are you?"

The intern takes her saucer pupils to the side, like Emily couldn't possibly be talking to her. Finding no one else, she says, "Which one?"

"What's your name, she means," I say.

"I'm Jamie."

"Nice to meet you, Jamie," Starla says. An avocado-stuffed lettuce cup garnished with chili crisp travels her plate like a soft green boat. "When did you join us?"

"Monday was my first day."

"Welcome to the team," Starla says.

Seasonal food emerges from the kitchen in a decadent parade: fermented rutabaga slaw, soft tofu layered beneath roasted cauliflower and sunchokes, yogurt-stuffed dates dotted with pistachios, mint, and sea salt, fennel martinis and mugs of fluffy golden oat milk that we clink in the center, cheering, *"BEAUTY IS POSSIBLE!"*

Jamie watches us, curious, a caged tiger observing humans at the zoo, until I fill her plate with some of each dish. She takes a tentative bite, and then swallows ferociously. She seems like she hasn't eaten in days.

Fairy lights sway in the trees. Evening approaches in its lazy, summertime way. A backwaiter lights a row of tapers in tall candleholders, though it is not yet dark. The ambient lighting gives the garden a heady dread, shadows sectioning the dusk like puzzle pieces.

Unmoored, I grip the edge of the table. Jamie puts a soft, sweet hand on my shoulder.

"Nice gloves," she says. "Where did you get them?"

I say they belonged to my maternal grandmother. With a guilty pang I think of Grandma Lucy in her one-bedroom above Steinway Street and her artful flea market wardrobe.

"Family heirlooms make the best vintage," Jamie says gravely.

Tree, Gemma, Marigold, and Starla have moved on to a recent *New York Times* exposé. Harassment allegations against the CEO of a trendy artisanal jam company. "Her first mistake," Tree starts, jabbing a finger in the air, "her first mistake was putting it in writing. Don't put anything in writing." Lips stained beet red.

"Did you learn that from Daddy the Lawyer?" Emily says.

"Please. My father is *not* a lawyer," Tree says.

Emily looks at me and shrugs like *I tried*. We go on like this for a while, debating the ethics of threatening to bash an employee's head in and bottle the juices for a limited-edition flavor. Most of us agree the obvious hyperbole makes it a non-issue. Satire, we agree, is a lost art among the younger generation.

"Put it this way—would they have suspended her if she were a man? I don't think so," Gemma says.

Tree fixes her gaze on Jamie, who twists in her seat. "You have to understand. We'll only reach true equality when women can act barbaric and receive respect for it."

Jamie says, *totally*, like she's comprehended the lesson, but I think she just wants Tree to stop swallowing her with her empty-pool eyes. She pretends to rifle for something in her canvas McNally Jackson tote, and comes up with a mint HEBE lip balm, the tube well-worshiped.

The sky flames into brilliance, golden clouds on a pink

surface, then fades and darkens. I have to admit, Tree is run-down in the gathering dusk. Eyes withdrawn into sockets. A crinkle when she smiles. Slight collapse around the cheeks, and two lines curving around the mouth that deepen when she speaks. In this light, she appears almost human.

With a flash of horror I touch my own face, relaxing when I feel, through the weave of my glove, that the cheek is velvet and down, vibrant with all that is still good in this world.

The air is fresher than I'm used to, crisp and overly oxygen-ated. It stings the lungs, makes me feel young and very much alive. I haven't been drunk in a long time, close to fifteen years, but the remnants of wild nights stir like leaves kicked up in a strong wind. I close my eyes to relish the memory and Mona is there, dancing over the closed lids as if she never left me. I open them fast. The garden tips and whirls.

Someone at another table breaks out a guitar. Or, no. It's a speaker. From which tinny pop music unspools. The singer is on a bed waiting, waiting for you.

The garden blurs, music playing louder. The interns mul-tiply. Mating bugs in the summer night. Eyes wide like children in a Margaret Keane painting. We had one over the mantle growing up. An original that Grandma Lucy inher-ited from her mother. A child with short blond hair peered through a gap in a brick wall, one small hand resting on the stones. I loved that painting, and often tried to emulate its orphaned expression in the bathroom mirror, capitulating when my mother eventually banged on the door. Proving my point, really.

Interns couple up. Their movements start casual and fal-tering, gradually tightening into ritualistic waves of their wrists and hips as if meant to summon a primordial god.

I want to sneer at them from such a place of growth and superiority—look at me, no longer the age when grinding on your coworkers seems not only smart, not only acceptable, but expected—yet find that they remind me too much of myself and of Mona sitting on each other's laps in the town square, snuggling for the benefit of boys watching from a distance, planning their approach. With no men in the garden, Tree is who they perform for.

Hands clasping a fresh beet juice, Jamie studies the dancing interns as if gazing at a plant. Stiff in her chair, her mouth set in a line.

"Not much of a dancer? It's okay, I'm not either," I say.

"I have two left feet." She giggles shyly and rubs the sole of her left sneaker against the iron base of the table. Crisp white ankle socks, a pale crescent scar smiling on one knee, flush with want. She reminds me of younger me, and that makes me hate her and love her all the same.

Turmeric smoke mushrooms above the garden; Emily offers her vape and this time I pull on it, eager to be one of them. The sweet fragrance fills my lungs and I wonder how healthy this can possibly be. But it feels good. Anything that feels this good has to be right. Right?

A light, airy sensation spreads from my chest up through my throat, into the nasal cavity, reaching back into my brain and the space behind my eyes. The garden belongs to us, the women of HEBE. Tree Whitestone has a way of cleaving the world, carving a pocket of space in which she and her associates can purely exist, sans judgment or interference. It's intoxicating.

I tip my head back and exhale. Through the parted trees, the city recedes, and the stars multiply.

SOMETIME LATER, TALKING to Emily and Jamie. Sucking turmeric root like vodka through a straw. High on wellness. I managed to put Mona out of my mind, but phantoms never stay away for long. She skirts the garden's shadowed edges. Tosses taunting waves. Hooks her spindly arm around a tree trunk and dangles like a fishing line in the dark. Foolishly, I believed that she'd been finally banished to the far recesses, the palm-smeared outline of a charcoal sketch in my memory. I hadn't seen her clearly since I visited my parents at Christmas. Being home dredged her up, no doubt. That's natural. Home is where she lives for me. In the home of the past.

I can't pinpoint what brings her skimming to the mind's surface tonight. Could it be the garden which, in its proximity to SoHo traffic, resembles a scraggly, pubic cluster of vegetation alongside the highway where we'd go to smoke in high school? With headlights spiking through the branches, it hardly counted as a forest. Or maybe it's these girls, limbs and hair all jellyfish and seaweed in the aquatic moonlight, fat lips parted and wet with laughter.

Mona flickers in my periphery like the phosphorescent glow of a television in a dark room. I sharpen my focus on my coworkers, but Emily and Jamie are deep inside a conversation that I don't follow. Behind me, the other interns sing an off-key rendition of "Sweet Caroline." One of them is named Caroline, I think, and she puts her pink face in her hands and laughs.

My hands tingle as though crawling with maggots. I brush them together. I weave my fingers and push the clasped hands between my legs, sitting on them. Temporary relief, and then the itching intensifies and spreads, pushing to the brink of pain, bone-deep discomfort burrowing. My breath comes shallow and fast.

Emily's mouth moves without sound. Concern etched into her brows. She and Jamie blink like twins in the garden's fairy light.

"Are you okay?" Emily repeats.

"Be right back." I start toward the restaurant. Trees block the path. Reedy, sinister figures like an army of unremorseful men accused of sexual assault. I glance back. Far enough to see my coworkers as a stranger might. Hair long and witchy in the murk, clothes hanging, stony faces carved by the kinetic light. A ritual I've stumbled upon, a human sacrifice.

Pulled by Mona's essence, I lunge deeper into the garden, bypassing the restaurant's door and ending up in a plant-tangled alley.

I can't see her, but she's there, reaching for me with her insistent, childlike hands. She pulls at me like she always has, guiding the abdication of my body. Under Mona's influence, I am never in control.

The alley stretches and pulses. Whispers of the party bleed through the foliage, but very little light. An explosion of stars sharpens as my eyes adjust to the true dark. I'm in some kind of dream where night comes for New York like it's anywhere else and if Mona were here, really here, she would make sense of the stars for me by pointing out the constellations, bringing order to the sky. I search for the Big Dipper, the only constellation I can identify on my own, but the stars are slippery, rearranging just as they begin to coalesce. Headlights flash, blotting my vision, and when the lights settle, the stars are gone, and the sky is a milky haze.

The need to disrupt myself, to tear apart the equilibrium between skin and fluid, flares in the heat of my chest. An itch that is more an unbearable burning, like the crawl of fire ants. Flashes of Mona the last time I saw her, the whites of her eyes rolling like marbles, a painterly trickle of blood escaping from the corner of her mouth, a nightmarish ski slope bright and unreal as candy, stamp onto the sky.

If I had a knife, I would work the tip lovingly under the second knuckle of my left pinkie with deep consideration. Apply pressure until I hit bone. The culmination of all these years picking at myself until I bleed. The blissful plunge that comes from giving in.

I picture myself emerging from the band of trees. Listing to the side, the final girl of the apocalypse. Temporary relief followed by pain that takes over, becomes your driving engine.

When would it stop? Once I'd cut off a hand? An arm? And what would the girls from work say?

But there is no knife, and my hand is in my mouth. I have ripped the gloves straight down the center seam, easy as paper, and my teeth are doing what evolution designed them to do.

Anyone who bites knows the shameful satisfaction after a moment's hesitation, however brief, in which you think: *hey, maybe I can stop.* Underneath there is a stronger current that says: *once more for the road.* Before you've made a decision, you've already lost. The losing is its own victory. Proof that you are as weak and disgusting and self-sabotaging as you always suspected yourself to be. And why fight it? That's nature. The circle of life, or whatever. The circle of life is just failure.

The city and the garden within it come closer and closer, and then it's only me, it's me with the fingers I'm gnawing on, three at a time, filling the way food never is, and still never enough. My tongue travels over my pebbled nails, muscling like a pumping snake until it finds a hangnail and latches.

A tiny kernel juts from the skin, growing as I maneuver my tongue into the space where it lifts from my finger, a plane taking flight. With my teeth I pull at the flap of skin until it is no longer part of me. Fluid takes longer to surface. Perhaps it's a confusion of the cells, which sense danger, and relax when they see that I'm the agent of my own destruction.

The blood hits my tongue in a hot wave.

Who can say how long I huddle there, a pitiful vampiric ectype slurping under a tented sky, lofted by trees I cannot name. This is the first thing that comes to mind as I look backward and up, allowing the warm blood to dribble down my hand: pathetic, that the world is made of so much, flora and fauna, entire systems that function without human input, yet I walk around like Earth is a palace built just for me.

Humans believe we are special, preordained to a great destiny, but how are we different from worms writhing in the dirt, singularly eating and shitting? I'm one of the chosen ones, and yet I can't control my basest instinct to cannibalize myself. What right do I have, believing I'm any better than a leech or a fat-bellied mosquito that preys on flesh?

If anything, I'm worse. Because I should know better.

A siren tears the night in half. Brings me back and back until I am standing in the alley's oil-slicked light, tasting blood. Torn lace dangles from my right pinky. Rivers of blood race within the creases of my palms. Numb throbs down my forearm.

I've stripped a hangnail from thumb to wrist. Crimson beads collect in the divot of shiny, wormy skin. My cheeks are hot and damp. Pain gathers at the base of my neck, amorphous yet threatening to settle. When the sting lands, the flesh of my injured hand seared and prickling, I vomit against the side of the restaurant.

Rustling. Someone calls, "Sophia?" It could be Emily or Jamie, Starla. Definitely not Tree. They can't see me through the oddly dense brush of potted plants—they *are* potted plants, not trees—guarding the backyard from the view of the alley and the street beyond. I stay very still, holding my breath. The person is silent, hovering. Finally, I hear footsteps. I gather my hand in the cradle of my shirt hem, and begin to walk home.

I'M MAKING GREEN tea when Jamie takes a soy yogurt from the fridge.

"Hey," she says, closing the door.

My bad hand is tucked gingerly in the pocket of my corduroy culottes, fingers capped with Band-Aids and gauze. When I got home from the party, I assessed the damage. Nail beds purple and swollen, the nails split. A crater on the thumb where I'd pulled off the hangnail shining at me like a black eye. I ached all over like a long-lost hangover. My hand felt huge and puffy. I swabbed the cuts with hydrogen peroxide. Then, something glinted. I looked toward the cluster of jars and tubes on the nightstand.

Tree's cream, the domed lid gleaming like a hard extraterrestrial eye.

The bruised fingers twitched as I held the jar, twisted the smooth lid, wincing in terrific pain as the cold cream (and how was it so cold, so close to June in New York?) spread over my wounds like a kiss of frozen butter.

Now Jamie comes closer. A tiny rose gold ring is embedded in the cartilage between her nostrils. "You're alive! Where did you go last night? We were really worried." Fresh confidence in her demeanor sets me on edge. What had I missed?

"My boyfriend got locked out of our apartment." Theatrical eye roll. Look at me, blaming Richard. Richard, who called six times because he was worried I'd been kidnapped. But the question was there, without him saying: *Are you having one of your episodes again?*

"You live with your boyfriend?" Jamie's awe highlights the gap in our ages.

"He actually has his own place, but he likes mine better. And it's an easier commute to his office." The electric kettle whistles. I pour hot water into a mug and Jamie reaches for the drawer at my hip to retrieve a spoon. A tattoo marches up her forearm, typewritten letters nestled in the divot where muscle meets bone. It's too small to read from where I stand. "Nice tattoo," I say.

"They remind me of the body's impermanence." Jamie wiggles her spoon at me. "See you around."

On the way to my desk, I pass a long table of interns working on laptops. Only one chair is empty, the one next to Jamie's. I pause, ticking my eyes over each bowed head. Who is missing? The white blonde. Sweet Caroline. Her face, when I try to conjure it, escapes me. All I see is a lightning bolt of silver. Not natural, there's no way. Hers is blond from a bottle. Blond that crisps and curls waywardly, takes on a green pallor if she swims in chlorine.

No one acts perturbed by the absence, and I try to put it out of my mind. She's probably sick. People get sick all the time. Only in other jobs I've had, the sick people always come to work.

I can't stop thinking about Caroline's head. The strip of bare skin between space buns, like someone cracked a glow stick and let the vibrant liquid drip, burns yellow in my mind.

THE APARTMENT IS empty when I get home. Richard is working late at his rented studio, and I haven't heard from Dom in three days. I'll start to worry if it reaches five. Tonight, I'm glad to be alone in the temperature-controlled vacuum, where I don't have to think. When I'm home alone it's easy to pretend this place is mine.

I take a shot of honey-laced apple cider vinegar, draw the blinds in my bedroom, and sit on the bed with a first aid kit open on the quilt and a trash can on the floor by my feet. Take the left glove off first. The flesh is pitted with scars but lacking the bare shock of a fresh wound. Striated nails and mealy pockets of skin. I remove the second glove, the one that covers the new damage. Flecks of lace stick to the exposed adhesive along the edges of the bandages fattening my fingers, a layer of sickly gray fuzz. I spread my hands on an old issue of *Vogue*; a powder-dusted Kirsten Dunst dressed as Marie Antoinette pokes through the middle and forefingers. Starting at the thumb, I work the bandage until it lifts free and I am able to peel it like a citrus rind, then set it aside. Next, I move the gauze, speckled with blood, and lift my hand to inspect the damage. Only there is none. The skin is porcelain and creamy straight to the line of the nail.

I rip off the other bandages in a dazed fury, littering the bed with them until my hand is naked and gleaming in the splash of silver light from the bedside lamp. It is spotless. Even the old scars have faded to near invisibility. I want to cry or scream or tell someone, but there's no one here except for me and the bandages scattered like cicada shells, so I fall backward on my bed and smile like mad at the ceiling.

2008

Mona began to disappear. She'd blow off our plans with a text, *sorry, fell asleep, still luv me???* at 1 A.M. Or she'd show up on my stoop hours late, dazed, as though she'd been tossed into the back of a dark van and driven in circles, dumped at my front door.

I forgave her every time, of course, because what else could I do? What is a girl without her best friend?

Still, Mona's unreliability dawned a new era of unaccounted for time. She was not my only friend, per se, but hers was the only company I deliberately sought out. Her absence imbued me with romantic loneliness. While she was busy with whatever, I took my iPod on walks, shoving my dad's crusty old Sony headphones over my ears. Music full of longing that left me with a strong desire to act. I'd take off running on uncluttered streets, the drama of the moment and the firm drumbeats wailing within me. I hoped I could expel the desire through the soles of my feet pounding the pavement.

I thought often of the boy from Clark's on these brief jogs, which invariably ended with me doubled over on a street corner, heaving.

It took several weeks for me to end up there. Bored without Mona, and fluttery with lust for the boy behind the counter, I returned. My old reticence was back, and my heart pounded as I approached the vermillion awning. I felt sweaty and stupid, embarrassed before I'd done anything. I almost turned back.

The door opened. Three girls spilled onto the sidewalk, radioactive snacks dangling from their fresh pink talons. The Ashleys: Ashley Roberts, Ashley McDonald, Ashley Macdonough. Spray tans varying degrees of fresh, varsity cheerleading skirts cupping their thighs like knives. Three angry crows on a telephone wire.

Ashley R. slowed when she saw me. "Well, if it isn't Slut Two out for a little walk," she sneered. "Where's Slut One?"

Before I could respond, Ashley Mac sipped her drink, swished the liquid around between her cheeks and pursed her lips, aiming a sour-sweet spit cannon at my heels. Arnold Palmer.

I didn't flinch. The Ashleys opened their glossy beaks and laughed.

Ashley R. looked me in the eye and said, "Tell your whore best friend to keep her hands to herself. She has to pay for Oxy just like everybody else."

I had no idea what she meant, but I'd rather die than let her know that. "Tell her yourself," I said, pushing past the Ashleys and into Clark's.

He faced the door. Hands behind his back, that same wry smile pulling at the symmetry of his face. He'd probably seen the whole thing. "Hello there," he said.

"Hi." The boldness that had kicked up in my stomach as

a response to the Ashleys faded. I felt shy, and very young. Transparent, as if he could peer through to my rotten, desirous core. A house at night with the curtains open and all the lights on inside.

He was already reaching for the stack of Styrofoam cups. "Arnold Palmer?"

I scanned the menu boards. "Um, actually? Can I just have a coffee? Milk, no sugar?"

The boy clicked his tongue, impressed. "Well, well, well. Sophisticated taste." Mocking me, but jovially. We were developing a rapport. He poured the coffee, licorice black, into a small cup and brought it over to the register along with a dented milk carton. "Tell me when."

The bizarre intimacy of his words, the way they aligned us, made my breath catch in my throat. I watched as a stream of milk intersected the coffee's placid surface, spreading outward until the coffee was light and creamy in color.

"When." It came as a graveled whisper.

I paid, and he handed me the cup wrapped in several flimsy deli napkins that fluttered to the floor like petals as they changed hands. The boy stifled a laugh as I bent to gather them. This was perhaps the first genuine expression he'd made in the course of our brief acquaintance, and it warmed my chest.

The coffee was too light, but I drank it anyway.

Reluctant to leave without a tangible accomplishment, I paced the aisles. Pausing before a selection of Kettle Cooked Lay's, I touched several bags, pretended to deliberate over the flavors. Flamin' Hot vs. Maui Onion vs. Mesquite BBQ. All sounded disgusting weighed against the bitter coffee lining my mouth. Footsteps creaked, rubber on linoleum, and my heartbeat filled my ears, my breath shallowing, a limp wave breaking shore at low tide.

He was next to me. Long shadow. Solid feet encased in sneakers stained by simple syrup. He smelled like sugar and, beneath that, tangy cologne. All the time I knew him I wanted to ask what cologne it was, but I never did, holding on to the question as if its very existence would guarantee the opportunity to ask would come. And then it was too late, and I would never know.

"Take a walk with me?" he said. I followed him to the end of the aisle, where he surprised me by taking not a left toward the front door, but a right farther into the depths of the store. At the very back was another door that blended into the wall.

He twisted the lock and opened it in a practiced motion, and then we were in an alley next to a boulder of trash. He held the door open while he kicked a wooden triangle into the crack. When he let go, the door fell against the wood, leaving several inches of the Clark's interior visible. Then he leaned against the brick, fishing in the pocket of his splattered apron.

I switched my weight from foot to foot, reluctant to face him directly. Instead, I checked my phone for messages from Mona, or my parents. Nothing. I continued to press buttons anyway, furrowing my brow in concentration. The phone, a Samsung that flipped open and closed, had been a sixteenth birthday gift from Grandma Lucy the summer before. I was the second-to-last girl in my class to get a cell phone. Mona had been the last.

In the periphery, the boy took a lighter to the narrow end of a joint. I pressed a few more buttons, snapped my cell phone shut with a crack that echoed down the narrow corridor.

The boy pulled, exhaled, and said, "Chase." I looked up

and down the alley, at the ground, eyes going anywhere and nowhere. "And you are?"

"Oh, um. Sophia."

"Nice to meet you, Um Sophia." Chase offered the joint.

I stared at it, his long fingers wrapped around the tapered cylinder, the part where his lips had kissed pointed toward me.

The moment was suddenly far too real; I had gone from the familiar scenario with the Ashleys to this alley from another dimension. Shadows crisscrossed the ground and everything—the buildings, the trash bags, the overstuffed dumpster, even the small tendril of smoke quaking from the joint's tip—stretched out of proportion. The wave that brought me here had receded, but I felt it rising within me once again as I rode it to its logical conclusion.

I stared Chase in the eye as I pressed my lips over the spot where his had been.

I'd only smoked a couple of times on Mona's urging. My body was weak and unprepared; my head lifted gently off my neck, settling down at a skewed angle. The shadows stirred like tree cover. Chase's wolfish smile spread wider. My head hurt, my mouth tasted like tar.

I moved down and down until I found solid ground. The sun shifted from behind a cloud, illuminating the alley, chasing the shadows. Chase laughed. Pebbles embedded into my thighs and I tried to brush them away, but they multiplied. I was covered in grit.

Chase leaned over, he was so close, he was going to kiss me, his nose was close enough to nibble. He removed the joint from my lips, straightened up, and took a hit.

"Have you ever had weed before?" he said.

"I . . ." I shook my head. "I'm not good at it."

Then we both were laughing and I truly believed that we might never stop. Nothing in history had ever been this funny before. My organs rattled and the laughter turned to a cough and I doubled over, the pebbles scouring my palms as I pressed down, eyes watering. Chase flopped down next to me, his back against the straining plastic dumpster, his chest shaking its contents.

I sat up as though struck by lightning. The dumpster loomed large and ominous above us. Scared and intrigued, I wanted to be closer, inside the beating filthy darkness.

"Do you think there's a body in there?"

Chase twisted around, following the line of my pointing finger.

"It's just," I continued, "on TV, whenever there's a dumpster, there's usually a body. Dead. A dead body, I mean."

"Oh no, I got what you meant. You wouldn't go in there if you had a choice." Chase scratched the side of his head. His hair was much shorter on the sides than on top, nearly buzzed. The skin on his temples looked boyish and new. He habitually pushed the bangs off his forehead. I flexed my fingers, imagining running them through that thickness down the center of his scalp, gripping the follicles. Chase tensed, and I worried he had read my mind. My thoughts were so obvious, they drew lines on my face. I pictured words running over the pulsing pink ridges of my brain.

He raised an eyebrow, jerked a thumb over his shoulder. "Shall we have a look?"

"Look?" I parroted, tongue moony with THC.

Chase stood and held out his hand. Our palms brushed together like damp feathers, and I almost cried out in happiness when he did not let go, but instead brought me closer, weaving his fingers between mine and pulling me to stand beside him at the lip of the dumpster.

It is wrong to hope for disaster. I know this now as I knew it then, peering over the edge, staring into the dark maw with Chase's arm brushing my shoulder and his hot breath in my ear. But a small part of me, as I plunged my free arm into the depth between two trash bags, wished to find catastrophe waiting there.

One hand roamed over the varying textures, moving from wrinkled plastic to puddled gunk, while the other clung to Chase, the heat between us turning slick. I didn't wince. I felt renewed. No matter what happened next, this afternoon had already changed me. I pushed my hand deeper, and deeper still. I brushed something hard and rough, with a little give. When I tried to gain purchase and lift it, I found that it had the weight and heft of a child's limb.

"I got something," I yelled to Chase, though he was close enough to hear me if I whispered. Together, we leaned forward. I tugged. The object was thicker in the center, with several long, dwindling appendages branching like fingers and a rough surface.

My heartbeat pulsed in my ears: *this is it; this is it.*

The excitement and fear roiling in my chest, the panic behind my eyes, was similar to the confused conflagration of terror and desire I had experienced during a bomb threat that placed our school under a lockdown last winter. Cowering in a second-floor science classroom as we waited for either an explosion or an all-clear, wondering if I would die breathing blunted eraser fumes, I should not have wanted what was coming. And yet, when the moment passed without incident, the principal on the loudspeaker releasing us from suspense,

I felt disappointment. I didn't want anyone to get hurt, but I didn't want things to stay the same, either.

Horror enabled your life to change. Tragedy thrust you from *before* to *after*. I would emerge from the rubble as the person I was meant to be.

I pulled. The stuck limb—I'd decided it was a hand—refused to be unglued. Chase positioned himself behind me, hands on my waist. Our combined force pulled the limb free too easily; I fell backward, stumbled into Chase, and sent us to the pavement. I landed on his chest, in his lap, legs thatched over his hip. I looked down. I was holding a gnarled brown palm marbled by ridges. Four fat, misshapen fingers grew from the center.

Ginger root.

I held it up at Chase. He took it from me, studied it. Then he smiled, tossed the ginger root deeper into the alley, wrapped his arms around my waist, and pulled me into him. This time he did kiss me. It was fast, our tongues briefly mingling, and then it was over, and Chase had shifted his weight so that I was no longer sitting directly on top of him, but off to the side, our legs still crossed. He looked at me strangely, recognition scrambling his features, and then he stood, and my legs fell to the ground.

"Better get back in there before I get fired," he said.

The back door to Clark's thudded shut and I was alone, still seated next to the dumpster. Stupefied, as if I'd gone to sleep in my bed and woken up here. I closed my eyes and inhaled the sweet trash taint clinging to my body, pressing the moment into memory like a dried flower between the pages of a book.

Then I gathered myself, checking to make sure I still had my phone and my flimsy fold-over sunflower wallet with two five-dollar bills tucked inside. Chase hadn't made me pay for the coffee, which I had left on the counter. It seemed too late to go inside and get it now, though I wanted it. I smoothed my hair and straightened my clothes. At the last second, I bent down and retrieved the ginger root. Held it firmly and ran a finger over the coarse surface, wondering how, only minutes ago, I could have believed it was someone's hand.

JUNE

5

A new batch of interns takes over New York in the summer, with their citrus nails and Chloë Sevigny magazine tear-outs on their walls. They say, "Isn't Chloë Sevigny dead?" because at twenty-two, forty-nine might as well be dead.

These interns, they are Santa Monica at sunset. They are a crop top hugging a pair of exposed ribs like shards of china. They are a blurred camera flash in a Vaseline-smeared mirror. They roll fat joints and wear gossamer dresses. Fire escape grates dig grooves into their thighs. These interns collect matchbooks from downtown bars you've never heard of and carry lighters with cheeky sayings even though they mostly vape.

These interns. I watch them from the exercise ball that serves as a desk chair. I watch them from the terrace, sucking my turmeric root from the vape Emily gave me. It really does resemble a jewel, something polished down to its blackened core, a computer hard drive or a rock from another planet. Earthy smoke fills my lungs, and I feel my neck elongating, stretching, and then settling back. Like that time I smoked weed with Chase, I think, and put it out of mind.

Later, at home after work. I'm on the fire escape. Still vaping. A subtle charge ferments the air and courses through my nostrils as I lean back against the dirty window and inhale. Two teenagers stop directly below the apartment with their arms linked. They look at the ground, kicking sooty ovals of gum with their sandals, then at me on my deck. They wave. The taller one wears a Nirvana T-shirt and the shorter has her hair in pigtails. I wave back. They make me sick with remembrance.

A man stumbles from the bar across the street. Drunk too early in the day not to be dangerous. I see him before the girls do. He whistles, eyeing their firm bare legs with a vile hunger. It's a hunger I share, though the root differs.

"Hey, baby!" the man says.

Then, I swear to God, the man licks his lips. Spittle shines on them, a heavy coat of gloss. The girls look at the man, look at each other, laugh. I want to tell them: *I've been you.* I want to tell them: *You don't have to laugh.* The more skittish the girls are, the more they concentrate on the gum calcified to become one with the sidewalk, the quicker the man advances.

The girls shrink and pull at their skirts, which are too short to really go anywhere. The shorter girl tugs her ponytail elastic until it snaps and falls off, leaving an indent. Her friend says something loud about boyfriends who are totally waiting for them at Ray's Pizza, omigod they'll be so worried, we are *so* late. I see right through it, but the man is stupid. He backs off, gets very interested in checking his ugly, fat gold watch. He shuffles off in shame, back toward the hellmouth entrance of the bar.

Seizing their opportunity for escape, the girls run down Ninth, holding hands, laughing louder, their voices a hymn in the distance as they weave between taxis and are swallowed by the late afternoon rush.

My next puff tastes like blood. I can picture it easily, too easily. The girls' fluted necks in my mouth, the gristle snapping under my teeth. Blood spurting down my throat, thick as a cheesy roux. Screams like music. Dancing in the fluids like a pagan goddess. Rejuvenated by the flood of life-giving plasma. The vision startles me and I shake my head, suck on the vape pen. The spice hits my throat, calming me, and the image scatters. My cells constrict. I feel high, and I don't think it's the turmeric root, or not only the turmeric root. Instinctively, I touch the cuticles on one hand with my thumb. The skin is too smooth, I could pet it for hours. Sometimes I do. Stroking my hands like the soft underbellies of kittens, like cold milk, like the leather cover of the HEBE notebook that rests on the nightstand. Lulling me to sleep as Richard's snores fade and I sink further into the bliss of myself.

DOM'S FAVORITE RESTAURANT of the moment is so self-consciously hip that it's annoying. Orbed light fixtures dangle like UFOs. Girls in spangled dresses squeeze against their dates, men noosed into expensive ties, as they fight to claim space at the bar. The waitstaff is young enough to intern at HEBE, with beaky bone structure and wire-hanger shoulders. Fist-small portions of grains, veggies, and fish arranged at the center of each vast white plate. Even with the new job I can't quite afford to eat here. Dom insisted on paying for all our shared meals when I made $8 an hour as a barista, but my current salary—$65,000 a year with benefits—makes me feel compelled to contribute.

Glassy-eyed, Dom brandishes a cigarette from her jacket and puts it in her mouth. She seems to have forgotten that she can't smoke inside. I take the cigarette from between her lips and rest it on the table.

It's then that she notices. Her mouth falls open. She pushes up the cuff of my sleeve. "Your hands . . ."

I pull my arm away as the waiter brings our drinks. The virgin martini is sour. The sensation of swallowing like inhaling chlorinated water: a stinging tingle.

Dom swirls her wine. "You stopped biting," she says.

"I'm doing a new meditation therapy." Meditation as a cure appeals to me. I've tried it several times. In college, I sat on my dorm floor using a rolled blanket for a cushion and closed my eyes for twenty minutes twice a day. All that silence did was make me want to saw my hands off at the wrists so I wouldn't have to feel them anymore.

Dom narrows her eyes. The food swoops in before she can reply. Next to the gleaming oils gathered in the curves of the pasta on Dom's plate, my salad is crude and saturnine. Like a child's drawing of food. Usually, the nourishment is enough. But it's hard to eat this way around Dom, whose notched collarbones do not betray her taste for carbs and dairy. She eats with such joy and relish, swirling her tongue behind her lips and between her teeth. Each bite lasts forever. I watch her butter-glossed mouth envelop a forkful of dripping fettuccine alfredo and spear a piece of lettuce with my own fork. Chickpeas and vegan cheese roll off, leaving behind the leaf shined with red wine vinegar and olive oil.

While I chew, I tamp down my irritation. I don't like being annoyed with Dom. I can't help it, though. I hate the way she treats herself, how that carelessness spills over. Dom colors outside the lines, taking up more than her share of space. Her unwieldy crayon erases everyone else in her path.

"If you get tired of meditating, I can always give you some Xannys. Makes you feel like you're floating; you won't remember you even have hands. I keep telling my psychiatrist that I don't need them, but she's convinced anxiety is my problem," Dom says. She rolls her eyes. Then, "Y-U-M. I could eat pasta for every meal."

TREE IS READING in one of the Ovaries, a pair of egg-shaped conference rooms separated by a slim hallway. I rap softly and step in without waiting. "Do you have a minute?"

"For you? I have an hour. My office?" She closes the volume on the table and tucks it under her arm. The way the light plays in the room renders her skull-like, cheeks sucked in and eyes bulging.

Tree's office is charmingly disheveled. Shades are drawn over the windows, and a sage green weighted blanket is draped on the velvet couch, a stack of books next to it. The top one's title reads *The Blood Countess* in gothic font. Balanced precariously on top of the book is a mug with a vial-shaped tea infuser sunk beneath a half-inch of murky green water.

"Excuse the mess," Tree says. "What can I do for you?"

I'm wearing gloves again, in case. Now I brandish one like a plaintive white flag, stripping it from my hand and wiggling my fingers at eye level.

"My hands used to be covered in scars." My voice shakes. I might cry. "I bit my nails so often they never completely healed, and they would break all the time. The skin was cracked and ugly. I've tried absolutely everything to quit—meditation, yoga, hypnotherapy, ketamine treatments, prescription steroid creams, clear nail polish. Nothing worked. It was like the harder I tried, the worse it got. I used some of that cream you gave me, and look—they're totally healed."

Tree draws close, grips my wrist in both hands, and pulls it up to her face. I feel her breath on the knuckles. She squeezes my fingers, hard, and I gasp. "Beautiful."

"What's in this stuff? It's seriously magic, I've never used anything like it. And it's not just the physical aspect; I haven't even wanted to bite my nails in days."

Tree lets me go. I push my hand into my dress pocket out of sheer habit. I feel naked with it exposed. Tree studies me for a moment, eyes bright, mouth set in a line. Then she smiles. "Great! I love to hear that. Keep using it, and write your observations down in that notebook I gave you. We'll chat more soon."

SCULPTED THIGHS IN high-performance navy spandex push into downward-facing dog. The thighs belong to Gemma. A matching sports bra with a zipper down the center neatly cups her breasts like two reaching hands. Through the gap in her thighs the pebbled muscles of her core move as she glides into chaturanga.

Saturday morning hot yoga hosted by a rival beauty brand at Om, a studio near my apartment. When we got the invite, girls from HEBE joked that it was a trap, they'd be waiting for us with spiked baseball bats, chains, and nightsticks. The class settles into child's pose and I glimpse Emily's sporty ponytail peacocking over her shoulder. Bangs stuck to her forehead. The walls pulse and the succulents in the corners of the room seem to grow in rapid time lapse.

Colors splash my vision, and I think I'm hallucinating when a dark-haired girl crashes into the room. Hair a spun-silk beehive held in place with a red silk scarf. Betty Boop tattooed on a sinewy bicep. She got it done last month at a studio on West Broadway.

I know because I was there.

The instructor's tree pose remains steady as she glares at Dom, who selects a mat from a pyramid of equipment that wavers as she walks away. Did I tell her I was coming to this? I move my mat a few inches to the left, hoping she won't spot the clear stretch of Marley flooring next to me, but she runs over. People stare and pretend they aren't. Whiskey floats off Dom's breath. Her eyes are insane. Going everywhere, pin-balling around the room.

She greets me loudly by name, in case anyone missed that we know each other. Then she slaps her mat on the ground and struggles to straighten one leg while bringing the opposite foot flush with her thigh. She wavers, grabs my upper arm for balance, and we both fall.

We lie in a stunned tangle for a moment before I attempt to shove Dom off of me, but my wet palms skim her naked shoulders like koi gliding through still water.

The instructor is on us with much concern, so much fear of a potential lawsuit. She offers water bottles, warm washcloths, ice packs.

"I'm fine. We're fine," I say.

"This is killing my workout," I hear Gemma whisper under her breath. Tree's stare thickens the humidity.

I commandeer a shower stall in the changing room as soon as class is over, stripping out of my soaked clothes. I fold them on a bench outside the shower and turn on the cold water. For the first time since I began using the HEBE cream religiously, the urge to bite is there. I press down hard on my upper arm with a rough konjac sponge, but it's not as sharp as synthetic fibers and it simply gives like a mound of soft clay.

There are no mirrors in the studio, not even in the bathroom.

I dry off and dress, certain that they must have all left. I hold my spine straight and very long. My serene palm on the slatted bamboo, the door parting. Eyes blinking in the buttery light; voices. *Oh, there you are!*

In a circle: Gemma, Emily, Marigold, Tree. Dom.

"I can't believe you've been holding out on us. Dominique was just telling us that you're her *best, best* friend and *room-mate.*" Tree's pupils, two inscrutable pebbles, are all I see.

I look at Emily, who plays with her phone. So she didn't tell Tree Dom and I are friends. Interesting; I assumed she would. Dom hands me my backpack. I don't question how she got it. Class seems to have cleansed her. Her Reporter Face, identifiable by a pinch to her lips and a feline slimming of the distance between brow and upper eyelid, is set on her like a mask. She takes us in, and though I am angry, I also worry she can sense that I am ashamed to be seen with her.

"Excuse me," I say.

Back down the small corridor and past the showers lined with heavy ecru curtains that rustle in a sourceless breeze to the bathroom. There's a girl with dark eyeliner and a messy ponytail waiting outside. I recognize a kinship with her slouched, insecure posture before I see that she's chewing on a hangnail. Angry zits on her chin, erupted pus drying around the reddened craters. Unshowered, she smells briny, like the sea.

Her gaze burrows a dent between my brows. I massage the crease and try to smile. The girl continues to stare. A drop of blood beads her lower lip. I used to bite my lips like that too. I'd sit in class working at a slab of loose skin until it came off and landed on my tongue like a tab of acid, probing the tender spot until I winced, gave in, and removed the pressure.

I stopped when Mona caught me and said, *No one will ever want to kiss that bleeding mouth.*

I reach for my bag's buckle closure only to find it's unhooked. I can't remember if I left it that way, but the pressure of the girl's dead eyes puts the buckle out of my mind. I feel around the pocket until I find a tube of lip balm.

"Here." I gesture with the tube. "Have some of this."

She eyes the HEBE logo on the side. "Are you trying to poison me?"

"Take it or don't," I say.

She unscrews the cap, rubs balm all over her cracked, Juvéderm-stuffed lips. Then she tosses the tube into her soiled *New Yorker* tote, and I am so shocked that I don't argue or say anything at all. Then the bathroom door opens and the instructor comes out, barely smiling on her way down the hall. My companion steps into the bathroom and the door slams. Suddenly I really do have to pee. Bladder pressing the walls of my abdomen to a pregnant swell.

When the girl leaves, she does so without a second glance. *You're welcome*, I think bitterly. How nice life would be if I were so ugly and entitled.

The bathroom is shockingly dingy. Even nice places need one ugly room, like a junk drawer in a beautiful house or a rotting molar inside the mouth of an Instagram model. I wonder if Tree has a room like that. If HEBE does. Graffiti on the concrete walls has been poorly painted over; I can just make out a dick with a shock of cum illustrated above the toilet paper dispenser. Diptyque candles clustered on the sill below the single window work to combat the diluted atmosphere, the artificial lemon verbena shit spray.

The death mask under the single sickly light bulb is my face.

I find the jar in my purse and unscrew the lid. It's empty. The walls licked clean. I rub my finger around the curves and smear the oily residue on my cuticles. With the backs of my nails, I scrape the inside of the jar until it loses its slip.

I stare at my reflection, at the furrow between my brows, while I scrub my fingers until they are nearly dry.

SCRATCHING IN THE middle of the night. I roll over, thinking it's Richard snoring. His side of the bed is empty. The ruffled sheets remind me that I can't remember the last time I saw him. More scratching, like a key digging into plaster. I follow the sound to the nightstand. There, my hand works at a crack in the wood usually covered by a vintage Hermès scarf, another Dom castoff. The scarf is on the floor. The opening in the veneer is about three inches wide and an inch deep. Toothy splinters spring out of it. One shard of wood is jammed under my nail. Pain radiates from the spot. Flakes of Himalayan Salt polish, a pale salmon that mimics the precise shade of those lamps sold in every home décor store in the city, dust the wood.

I dip my fingers into a glass of lukewarm water on the night-stand to quell the sting. Wide awake now, I idly stir the water while scrolling my phone with the other hand. Late at night, the color drained from my room, I am one of the last people on Earth. Cars hush down the street. The occasional shout from First Avenue maximizes the apocalyptic atmosphere, and as shadows slide over the walls and the phone's blue light blares ever brighter in the oncoming morning, I sense myself floating, moving backward in time. My fingers travel a familiar pattern to Mona's ancient MySpace profile. Her mother never had it taken down, or didn't know it existed. Mona's favorite bands and movies from 2007 codified in the list of "Friends." Her complexion is blotted sheet-white by the camera flash, crescents of eyeliner making the whites of her eyes stand out in every photo.

I click faster through the slideshow of old profile photos, following those shifting eyes around the screen. I'm in many of them, a faded wraith blurring the middle ground. We hang on a swing set, giving the camera the finger. I remember this one being taken. We snuck into the playground at midnight with a group of boys from a neighboring high school who promised weed if we went to their usual spot to smoke it with them. My tights ripped as I hopped the fence, which was low and crowned with sharp twists of metal. The boys scattered, swinging from monkey bars and proffering lit joints as they took turns on the slide, embers tracing patterns in the dark. Too big for the equipment, their gawky teenage limbs jutted in all directions. Mona and I retreated to the swings. It was early fall, she was going through a French phase, a beret jauntily perched over a semi-teased bouffant, buttoned into a navy peacoat she found at Goodwill. Using her patent leather crossbody purse as a shelf, she rolled a spliff while I nursed the scratch beneath the hole in my tights. The metal hadn't broken the skin, but I felt a raised welt where it scraped.

Then a flash went off, temporarily blinding us, and when it cleared, we saw the artsy boy, his name lost to me now, clutching a digital camera.

"You look like models," he said. He raised the camera again. This time we anticipated the flash. Shielded our eyes, hands as visors, middle fingers thrust against our brows.

Fifteen years later, alone in the hush of my bedroom, the result, a juvenile fuck-you to the male gaze, strikes me as insincere. We rejected his fantasy so easily precisely because we conformed to it so well. When the photographer lowered his camera, he laughed, as if to say *you love it*. Later, Mona Spiderman-kissed him while he dangled upside down, legs lashed over the monkey bars, death-gripping her hair.

2008

The day Mona passed out, I waited on the corner of her street like I did every morning since middle school, but she never showed. I walked alone to school. She was missing from our first period homeroom, so I didn't see her until gym class. Two out of the three Ashleys changed out of their cheer uniforms in the locker room—game day—and Mona came in late, pushed them apart and marched to where I sat on the bench tying my sneakers.

"Watch it!" Ashley Mick snapped, too late for it to have real power. She was as stunned as any of us. More, because she wasn't used to being treated as if she were invisible.

Mona hurled her backpack into an empty locker. It rattled the whole row. She ripped her shirt over her head and I heard the threads tear at the seams.

"Are you okay?"

She wheeled to face me. I noticed how thin she'd gotten, ribs and collarbones pressing at the underside of her epidermis like desperate hands trapped beneath fogged glass. Ghostly, a vision from the horror movies she watched when her mother was asleep. Her mouth was ironed into a flat, angry line.

The muscles around her eyes softened as she regarded me frankly. "Yeah, I'm fine."

Near the end of the year the PE instructors had given up and let us roam the track like feral cats as long as it wasn't raining. Mona and I liked to walk laps. Sometimes we shared headphones and listened to some spitting male pop punk band whose lyrics expressed our rage at being loveless and bored in suburbia in terms plainer and more brutal than we, as girls, were permitted. Our music was violent. It spoke of revenge, of the desire to hurt, to humiliate. Retaliation by way of heartbreak. I felt it thrumming in my stomach, that burning urge to lash out.

Today, when I offered my iPod and a slippery pair of Skullcandy earbuds that I brought to school in place of my dad's Sonys because they were cooler, Mona shook her head. We paced in silence, lapping the Ashleys as they shallowly rehearsed the halftime routine for the lacrosse game, and the overly competitive boys who reeked of body odor, and the immature weirdos with greasy hair and elastic tattoo jewelry playing tag on the football field or singing showtunes.

The air held the sharp, urinal scent of the horse track across the street, home of the Triple Crown's least famous leg. You could just make out, over the chain-link fence bordering the field, the green roof shielding the stables. We'd gone there on a class trip each spring of elementary school, and the stable hands let us feed the horses fistfuls of hay.

"Hey, remember when we got the jockeys to sign our caps?" I asked Mona.

She aimed a hazy smile into the distance. "I still have mine," she said.

"Me too," I said. "Never wore it, though."

"We really thought we were going to be jockeys even though we didn't ride."

This had been in the third grade; after that year's trip to the racetrack we begged our parents for riding lessons. I'm not sure how they afforded it, but they managed to pay for a summer's worth. We were awful equestrians, Mona and I. Me, I was terrified, far too timid to take control of a horse. But Mona, she was so wild. She had no interest in leading, tossed herself like old laundry over the hump. She let herself be steered until she was nearly thrown off.

The sun beat down on us, gilding our hair and warming the track so that it gave under our sneakers. I held the two Monas at once in my mind. Sixteen-year-old Mona, a pale blade of grass rolled in the wind, and the nine-year-old version, strident atop a magnificent beast, duetting black manes flying with the force of their gallop. One of those prism-trapped moments out of time when you sense yourself, decades older, looking back.

I looked at the Mona of now. A tuft of hair had fallen over the eye closest to me. I reached to brush it away, so familiar we were to each other that I didn't think twice, and she surprised me by shifting back. The hair slid, exposing her petal-smooth neck.

Where the strands had been pulsed a shining, livid bruise. It came alive on her skin, like a just-birthed eye first opening.

Mona had had hickeys before, but she'd never had a secret. I felt a chasm widening. I wanted to reach out and grab her before it was too late. The last vestiges of innocence were escaping us, and I found that I, once so eager to be done with childhood, wanted to hold on with all my might. But I took the coward's path—I pretended that I didn't see.

AP US history came next. Ashley Mac was in the middle of pronouncing racism over now that Barack Obama, the senator from Illinois, was a serious presidential contender, during what was supposed to be a discussion about Martin Luther King Jr.'s "Letter from Birmingham Jail," when the fire alarm went off. We stayed in our seats for a beat before joining the throng in the hallway flowing outside.

My class filed to our allotted emergency location. The tense energy dissipated, took on a playful edge, as it became clear that there was no fire. The Ashleys braided each other's hair in a daisy chain, "accidentally" flipping their cheerleading skirts at the knot of emo boys with chunky black bangs and jutting lip rings, laughing. The emo boys rolled their eyes and pretended not to stare at the Ashleys' exposed bloomers.

Commotion, originating from the tangle closest to the side doors, rippled through the student body. Deep-rooted intuition pushed me forward. I broke through the wall of my history classmates to get closer to the disruption.

I saw her. Limp on the stretcher, a fallen dahlia, body so small she barely made an impression. Paramedics wheeled the stretcher around the corner and out of sight. I noticed, too late, the red lights blinking against the sad smattering of trees trimming the parking lot.

I stared at those trees as everyone else filed back inside. I wanted to scream at my peers until my throat was shredded. They had done this to her, I decided. They hadn't seen her, hadn't loved her, and she'd tried to disappear.

A hand fell on my shoulder. Mr. Wilson, my history teacher, stood next to me. Our proximity was jarring. The pores on his nose, the meaty sweat gathered under the arms of his cheap polyester button-down. His tie was a vintage world map like the one that hung on the wall in his classroom.

Mr. Wilson squeezed my shoulder and gave a small, sad smile. "Take your time coming back to class," he said. "You won't miss much."

And he left me there.

6

Screams. High-pitched and keening, they could be from a woman or a dying animal. I listen as the elevator doors part, then close, Tree's peephole fixes me in its cyclops gaze. Twisting the knob, unlocked, I step into the foyer.

I thought I was dreaming when I got the text from Marigold inviting me to lunch at Tree's apartment. I turned my phone off, paced a lap around my bedroom, and turned it back on, but the text was still there. Twelve-thirty on Wednesday, 125 Delancey Street, 26th floor.

The sound is louder here, and clearer, a metallic grind undergirding the squeal. Abruptly, the noise stops. Starts again, runs for a shorter burst, starts again. Not screams—a juicer.

Tree's foyer opens onto a spacious dining room with a view of the East River. Walls white as the driven snow, as Grandma Lucy would say when looking at my upper arms in a sleeveless top. She always said it with a mix of revulsion and reverence, which is exactly how I take in this room. It doesn't look like anywhere a person could live. More like a dollhouse. Gauzy mosquito netting on the windows makes the water and the sky, the buildings, flicker. Silver frames above a mirrored credenza hold white canvases splattered with intermittent red paint, like squares of plaster carefully removed from a crime scene.

Footsteps. Tree appears in a cream cotton dress with tiny blue flowers. A perky bow sits between her small breasts, which puff out the smocked bodice. Her hair is crimped into a subtle wave. The screeching has stopped, an unnatural silence stuffing my ears. "Hi there," Tree says.

My face gets hot. "Sorry, I didn't think you'd hear me knock over the—"

"No, please! You're more than welcome. Come into the kitchen, I'm finishing lunch."

In the center of the white kitchen, a juicer covered in verdant drippings. Two tall glasses filled with the liquid sit on the counter.

Tree hands one to me.

"You didn't have to make me anything."

Tree turns her long, muscled back and opens the refrigerator. While she is not looking, I dip my tongue into the smoothie. One sip coats my mouth with a grassy film.

"What do you think?" She is facing me again, placing a foil-covered platter on the marble, and I am surprised at the naked want for my approval on display. Her desperation leaves hyperpigmented splotches on her décolletage.

"Tastes like citrus."

"It has lemon, kale, mint. Some almond milk in there, too. Oh, and wheat germ! I got the recipe from Go Green, Girl. Do you follow her? Delicious, isn't it?" Tree disassembles the juicer, drops the pieces into the sink with a loud clatter, and dries her hands on a French linen towel, which she lets collapse to the floor, then steps on with an onion-hued house shoe.

She yanks the foil off the platter and crumples it in her fist. On the plate is a ring of mangled vegetables. Carrots cut into blunted matchsticks. Frayed celery stalks with browned edges circling a metal container of lumpy hummus.

The liquid salad I've been nursing out of sheer hunger settles in my teeth as I swallow. Tree takes a sip, and I mirror the way she drinks, rabbity lips pursed over teeth so that only the tiniest squirt is allowed to pass into her digestive system.

I wait for Tree to explain why she has summoned me here. What could be so important that we can't discuss it in her office?

She ushers me into the living room. We perch on Ligne Roset loveseats identical to the ones in the HEBE waiting room.

"Tell me, how did you meet Dom?"

I moved to the city at twenty after two years of community college. Railroad apartment in Williamsburg that I found on Craigslist—four recent City College grads searching for a fifth roommate to offset the rent further. Besides my roommates, I knew no one. Anonymity was a pleasure I'd never enjoyed before. I moved invisible through crowds. Three months passed this way, then four. I would ride the subway, getting off at random stops to walk neighborhoods I hadn't explored before. I got a job as a barista at Think Coffee off Union Square, thinking it would be temporary. Some days I spoke only to my customers. I spent the meager earnings on movies at the Angelika, drugstore sunscreen, dollar slices, curbside falafel, second-hand clothing from Beacon's Closet

and Buffalo Exchange. Six months in love with my own company. Rudderless, attempting to learn who I was by process
of elimination. Catching my eye in the windows of banks,
curtained restaurants, boutiques lit so brightly from the inside
that the blank-faced mannequins stared as if they were my
own reflection. Biting my nails, the skin around them, to
pieces in every corner of this city.

But winter came. The labelless coat I bought in the opti-
mistic sunshine of September had holes in the pockets for the
air to rush through. The material I'd assumed was wool felt
more like rough polyester when the bone-cutting wind rolled
in from the river. The homeless man stationed outside the
coffee shop called me Joyce. *Joyce,* he would say, *Joyce. Don't
run on the stairs! Joyce, did you finish the shopping list? Joyce, time
for lights out!* It charmed me, at first. Who was Joyce? I made
up all kinds of stories while frothing milk and pulling espresso
shots for hours. But then I caught myself forgetting my own
name. Staring at *Sophia Bannion* on the credit card offers in
the mailbox like, *Who?* I stopped giving the man free coffee
and loose change from the tip jar. Kept my head wrapped in
my scarf as I rushed to the subway. I didn't know what kind
of woman I was, but I knew what woman I never wanted
to be—the one who wore everyone's face. The one who was
no one so therefore she was your wife, your mother, your ex.
What I needed was an identity.

What I needed was a real friend.

I went online. Explored forums for everything: makeup
addiction, parenthood regret, every stripe of celebrity, from
A-list actors to C-list felons. It was on one of these celebrity
forums that I first discovered Dom in a thread about social-
ites. Example post: *Maybe if this bitch stopped focusing on what*

foundation holds up best during a coke binge long enough to get her ass to rehab, we could all quit stalking her and cure cancer instead.

I recognized something of myself in these commenters, a wheat germ holiness. I found myself scrolling the forum for excerpts from Dom's blog. Her writing moved me, and we soon bantered back and forth in her website's comments. From the first time I sat across from Dom at Think Coffee and watched her tip a flask of whiskey into her chai latte, I saw she had something I lacked and craved. A sense of adventure, a controlled careen.

I tell Tree an abbreviated version of this story. She nods sagely, then changes the subject.

"You're wearing gloves."

I ball my hands into fists, tuck them at my sides. The fabric grates my stripped cuticles. "I ran out. The biting is worse than ever. Could you give me some more? What *is* it?"

"It's a top-secret proprietary formula we are testing for HEBE. I call it youthjuice. I can't tell you exactly what's in it yet. What I need from you right now is your testimonial: the notebook, please."

Tree's palm is a runway. The lifeline extends to infinity. I look toward the backpack on the floor by my feet. The notebook is not there. I haven't seen it in days. The buckle slips through my fingers like a snake and I root through the stiff compartments for what feels like an age.

"I'm so sorry. I don't have it."

"What?"

"The notebook. It's not here."

Shadows crater Tree's features. She looks as though she might strangle me with her bare hands. I flinch involuntarily,

and stammer, "At home. I left it at home. On my nightstand."
I pause. "I really thought I put it in my bag."

Intensity builds behind Tree's green eyes. She draws her
palms together, and smiles. "That's okay. You can show me
once you have it." As Tree speaks, her focus flits about the
room, glinting off crown moldings, the pictures in their
frames. Then it settles on my face. Her palms unfold like a
paper fortune teller's. "Let me see your hands."

I hesitate, then remove the gloves. Tree takes my flayed
fingers in her warm ones; she examines them from every
angle, bending forward and back, plucking each digit. The
skin is pickled and moist as the flesh beneath an old Band-
Aid, sticky and shining from the Vaseline I slathered on this
morning.

"Women," Tree begins. "Women are full of so much hurt.
You can see it in all of us if you look close enough. You can
tamp it down, but the hurt has a way of releasing itself. I felt
it the moment we met. I thought, this woman has a hole in
her heart. I can't fix whatever is missing from your life, but I
think I can help."

Shaken, frankly weirded out, I return my hands to my lap.
"Can I use your bathroom?"

I pee, then wash my hands for a long time. Scrub between
each finger and under each nail. The soap stings. I brace
against the counter. Aloof marble meets my hips. Cold air
bursts from a vent near the floor. My breath tightens inside my
chest. There's a spray of red on the floor. A haphazard pattern
of droplets, as though someone flicked a paintbrush above the
tile. I rub my big toe through the spots. They smudge.

I wipe my foot on the bathmat, which is in the shape of
a woman's nude torso. Breasts, belly button, and pubic bone

outlined in black, no limbs, no head. I wash my hands again and rejoin Tree in the living room.

She starts talking like she never stopped. "Are you happy with us, Sophia?" Tree asks. She hasn't called me that in weeks. I've adjusted to Soph. Quite like it, actually. My full name puts me on guard. *Joyce.*

"I have never been happier. I love working for you."

"I can tell. You do such good work. A visionary in training, that's what I told Marigold." A dry laugh. "She didn't like that much."

"Marigold is . . ."

"A bitch? Come on, just say it. I would be nothing without her, but she's a monster."

"She's not the warmest."

"No. Which is why she'll never amount to much more than a glorified secretary. Don't get me wrong, Marigold is a world-class executive assistant. If she ever leaves me, I'll die. But she doesn't have what it takes to succeed on her own merit."

I revel in the subtext: *She doesn't, but you do.*

In high school, my parents took me into the city for an aptitude test. They worried about my idleness; I could spend whole Saturdays staring at the ceiling fan. We took the Long Island Railroad to Penn Station, the 1 up to Lincoln Center. Rode the elevator to the eleventh floor of a gray building that smelled like the underside of a rug, where a woman in a beige skirt suit led me to a small room furnished with a metal folding table and chair and a black box resembling a recording device. My mom waited outside while the woman in beige administered odd tests. She left me alone with the black box. I was told to listen for a beep and press the button when I heard it. Next, I recorded whether a voice sounded "masculine" or "feminine." I drew spirals until a fuzzy tone signaled me to stop. The tasks felt meaningless, but I was overcome with the desire to do them correctly. I had the sense that the woman was watching the whole time, though there was no two-way mirror, no visible camera.

At the end of the day, my mother and I filed into the woman's office. I sat in the leather chair. Her beige suit creased around her compact body like an envelope. My mother hovered at my shoulder. I felt as though I was about to hear a bad diagnosis. Could they, I wondered, detect cancer based on when you heard the beep?

"Is my daughter good at anything?" Worry lifted the end of my mother's sentence.

The woman smiled wide. "Of course," she said. "Everyone is good at something."

What I am good at, it turned out, is observation. I am the one who notices. The one who sees you and your boyfriend fighting at the edge of the party, who takes note of you spitting your food into a napkin under the table. "Leave it to you to avoid any *practical* aptitudes," my mother said as we left the office. We joined my father on the street, where she informed him that he should stop bothering to save for college because his daughter was *as good as useless*.

I want to explain this to Tree. She's like an older sister, a wise and worldly babysitter. "I love working for you," I repeat. "It's a dream come true."

Tree smiles and it's nothing like the smile of that beige woman. Hers is a warm hug from behind. "With," Tree says. "You love working *with* me. I'll be right back." Tree gets up, and I am alone in her living room.

A bookshelf covers one wall. I walk over to read the

fragmented poem the titles make. The books are glossy, unblemished. Naked women who've never had a sunburn. Spines uncracked in a cool gradient from cream to salmon to sky blue. Wedged into the corner of a shelf is a photograph in a Waterford frame, the only bit of personal ephemera in the room. Tree and Gemma at a college party, arms crooked around each other's necks. Blazing smiles, glossed lips. They are so innocent and happy. A white smudge in the upper left draws my eye and I pick up the frame. It's a face blurred by the flash.

Breath on the lone stretch of spine moving from my collar to my hairline. Turning, I am nose-to-nose with Tree. We nearly kiss, that's how close our mouths are. I present the photo. "This is cute."

"Ah, yes. Wild nights with Gem."

"And Marigold. That's her in the background, right?" I point to the smudged face. "She has the same hair."

"You're right, that is her. I forgot she's in this picture, too."

"I didn't know she went to college with you guys."

Tree takes the picture and puts it back on the shelf. "Marigold has always been around," she says. Then she grasps my forearm, presses something into my hand. A jar.

2008

An overdose, they said. An overdose of what, no one would say. Turns out a freshman boy found her convulsing in the science wing, panicked, and pulled the fire alarm.

She'd been taking more pills lately, white or blue pearls that she'd sneak with gulps of water or coffee when she thought I wasn't looking. Pretending I didn't see was easier than I would have liked to admit. As long as she was walking around, speaking in complete sentences, she had to be fine, I figured.

Clark's bell jangled. My hands shook and sweat gathered around the curve of my bra's underwires. I'd never cut school before. Mona did, sometimes, but never bothered to invite me. I was prudish, she assumed, which was true. What she didn't realize was that I would have gone in a heartbeat if she'd asked. There wasn't much I wouldn't do if Mona asked.

I stayed on the football field after Mr. Wilson and the others had gone inside. Listened to the sirens kick up. Ambulance lights whirled against the drab familiar edges of the building. Walls I knew better than those of my own bedroom. The crack in the brick along the library window, the lick of ivy lapping the foundation, nature's attempt to reassert its dominance.

My whole life, active shooter drills and stranger danger and razorblades in the Halloween candy, had led to this.

Invisible in grief, I walked off the field and squeezed through a gap in the fence. Instead of following the traditional path through the battered metal doors, I turned into the parking lot and kept going downtown with a runaway's determination. I had almost nothing with me but a nearly empty backpack. I thought longingly of the books I'd left behind when the fire alarm went off, of the normalcy they signified. Only once the blackened windows of the bars on the avenue came into view did I realize where I was headed.

In civilian clothes, Chase seemed smaller. Black T-shirt with a faded skull in the center. Black jeans washed gray at the knees. Earbuds necklaced across his collar. Hat pulled low over his eyes, a stiff bill pointing back.

"Hi." He tipped his chin toward the wizened man at the counter. Benjamin Clark, the owner, narrowed his eyes as Chase steered me outside with a forward-pulsing energy and not his hands, which were shoved deep into the pockets of his jeans. We walked to the corner, made a right at the diner. In the municipal parking lot, Chase stopped at a blue car with tinted windows and a dented fender, and took out his keys. I hesitated near the hood as he climbed inside.

He paused halfway into the vehicle. "You coming?" he asked.

"How do I know you're not going to murder me?"

Chase laughed. "You don't."

A wall of sound hit me in the face when the engine started. Chase lowered the volume and I was able to make out the bitter growl of a vaguely familiar song. Drums gathered in my gut and I felt a surge of defiance.

"I hate this song," I said.

Chase twisted the dial until the music faded to a low grumble.

Fat silence stewed in the car. Streets glided across the windshield. Warped, as though I'd never seen them before. I wondered where we were going and, as I thought it, Chase pulled down a side street and parked. For a long time I stared out the passenger window at a small brick house with dead plants in the window boxes. Tried to shake the unsettling déjà vu that flooded my nostrils. Then, I remembered.

"My babysitter lived on this block."

Chase drummed his fingers on the steering wheel while he waited for me to say more.

"Mona—my friend who I came with the first time, when I spilled the Arnold Palmer? Something happened. She's in the hospital, I think?"

"Is she going to be okay?" Chase had been facing straight ahead, but now he turned as much as he could in the seat, straining the seat belt, knee jutting over the console.

"They said it was an overdose, I guess. I just left. I couldn't be there anymore."

I was babbling. Words flowed like an unstaunched stream from a fountain. The vanishing line of cars parked down the street wavered, and I realized I was shaking. My body displayed all the signs of cold—goose bumps, chattering teeth—but I was not aware of the temperature. Everything felt theoretical, and very far away.

"What hospital?" Chase said.

"I don't know. No one said. I didn't know who to ask."

Droplets from the ceiling, landing on my cheeks. "Your car is leaking," I said, but the words sounded textured and wet, not a leak at all but tears spouting from me so hard and fast that I barely felt them.

Chase stretched his arm across my lap and for a confused instant I thought he was going to push the door open and force me out, but he unlatched the glove compartment and produced a rumpled fistful of napkins stamped with the Clark's logo.

I blew my nose into the pile. The car's recycled air swallowed my sobs. A propulsive fishy gasp rattled my chest. Chase checked his phone, fiddled with the radio dial, pulled a thread from a hole in his jeans. Flicked it onto the floor. Eyes everywhere but on me.

When I regained some composure, I padded my damp eyes with the soiled napkins. "Can we get out of here?" I said, staring at my lap.

Chase maneuvered onto the road with a touching level of care. We drove for ten minutes. Glided out of Nassau County, over the invisible threshold into Queens, then he pulled into a diner's parking lot. I'd passed this place a million times on the way to Grandma Lucy's, which was only a few blocks farther down the boulevard.

I had the sense of sliding backward in time upon crossing the threshold. The diner had that old-fashioned Americana style that made one long for a past that never really was. I half expected to glance over and see Chase in a leather jacket, hair a molded toothpaste swoop, hard and shiny with gel. To feel a poodle skirt circling my heels.

We slid into a booth under an arrangement of framed photographs showing the same large, ruddy-faced man in a grease-splattered apron and navy baseball cap posing with minor celebrities. Actors who played the culprit on a single episode of *Law & Order: SVU*, cable news hosts, television chefs. One medium-successful pop star who had a top ten hit six years ago. She was fragile under the fleshy man's arm, made of glass, and her top (shiny, pilled, rhinestone-studded) seemed cheap.

A waiter dropped off two menus. Chase left his flat on the table. He was comfortable here, he fit the scenery. He seemed like a regular. No one acknowledged him with familiarity, and it occurred to me that this might be my fault; maybe he brought different girls here all the time. Perhaps the staff knew him so well that their lack of warmth was by design. Strategic, so as not to tip me off.

I didn't particularly care. Chase could have five thousand girlfriends. He was here with me now. With me, and all I craved was comfort food, something I hadn't eaten since childhood, before the realization that carbs, dairy, and sugar could ruin a woman, could stop her before she began.

Two inches of dark roots showing under the waiter's fried blond hair, her blue-black cat wing liner a deformed mirror image of Mona's signature. I ordered a tuna melt, fries, coffee, and a vanilla milkshake. Amused, Chase asked for the same, and a side of pancakes.

I had stopped crying in the car, but my cheeks were stiff, wrong, as though a too-small mask had settled over my face. I massaged them with the pads of my fingers until the skin hurt and the coffees arrived. Chase and I emptied plastic packets of half-and-half, discarding the containers on the speckled linoleum.

"Do you want to talk about it?" Chase wiggled a spoon through his coffee.

"Can we talk about literally anything else? Truly anything. Like, how long have you worked at Clark's? I've lived in that town my whole life and I've never seen you before."

Chase removed the spoon from his mug, set it down on a napkin, and sipped the coffee with unexpected delicacy. "I've been there a couple months."

"Do you like it?"

"It's okay. Easier than my last job, which was at an Applebee's."

"Do you remember the birthday song?"

"Do I remember? I sing it in my nightmares."

"When I was a kid I wanted to go. My parents would never take me," I said.

"Most people hate it. If you want to find out who you really are, have someone surprise you with the birthday song at Applebee's. That's when you'll discover your true nature. Old ladies punching their middle-aged sons in the face, soccer moms barricading themselves in the bathroom, three-hundred-pound dudes sobbing like their dog was just run over by a truck right in front of them—I've seen it all at Applebee's."

"I loved the idea of the whole room singing just for me. Like for those forty seconds, my birth was the best thing that had happened. The fucked up thing is that we'd eat there other times but never on my birthday. It's like my parents knew it would make me too happy."

The food came, and we ate without talking. My phone vibrated in my purse. I let it ring out. Probably my mother, or someone from the school, wondering where the fuck I'd gone.

"Did you go to my school?" I was still trying to figure out how old he was, and where he had come from. If I had to guess, I would have said he was maybe two years older, possibly a student at a nearby community college.

"Nah," he said, and offered nothing more.

Chase ate his pancakes with systematic precision, cutting the stack into neat squares and using the side of his knife to depress melting whipped cream into the sponged holes. He popped the soggy mess into his mouth. Packets of butter and syrup remained untouched in a small bowl next to his plate.

Between bites of tuna melt I dipped fries one by one into the vanilla milkshake. My mouth puckered from salt and sugar.

Though I longed for facts about Chase, to shape a version of his past in my mind, I appreciated that his lack of curiosity kept us suspended in a timeless vortex. We could simply exist in this diner booth, sharing this meal, no *before* or *after* marking us with permanence.

After came. The check was dropped, and Chase snatched it, a chivalric gesture that caught me unawares, without time to reach for my wallet. I mumbled gratitude and stayed put as he paid at the register, then returned to place a few dollars as a tip. The cash was so vulnerable and exposed on the cracked tabletop that I covered George Washington's grim portrait with the saltshaker as I slid out of the booth.

Doomed evening clouds settled over the parking lot. The air smelled like rain. A few large drops landed on my shoulders. We made it to the car as the sky opened up. Chase turned on the wipers and the heat, and we sat and watched the glass fog as it poured. I had the sense of wanting something but not being sure how to make it happen. The fact that we had already kissed did not create the ease or flow I'd imagined. Leaning over, taking his hand. These were the logical actions, the building blocks for physical intimacy I hadn't needed to perform before. Other boys didn't give you the chance. They plunged forth with all the grudging determination of a prince slicing his sword through a thicket of thorns on his way to rescue the sleeping princess.

These were the steps that needed to be followed, the one thing that would lead to the next. *Slice*—an arm on the shoulder. *Slice*—a closed-mouth kiss. *Slice*—the jab of the tongue. *Slice*—hand gripping breast. *Slice*—shirt sliding up.

Chase was different. He sat on his side of the car with his hands in his lap. Then he slid his gaze over to me and watched, stunned but not unhappy to find me sitting in the passenger seat. The look on his face, that snagged grin, lit something within me. I lunged over the seat, put my hands on his neck as if I were about to strangle him, and kissed him as hard as I could.

He wrapped me in a hug, pulling me over the hump of the seat. My thigh hit the stick shift. In Chase's lap, I scrambled to undo his belt. He put his palm on mine and moved my hand away, which touched me so deeply I started to cry again, or maybe I was crying already and that's why he stopped me.

We kissed desperately for so long that my mouth and jaw began to ache, the salt of my tears mixing with the heat of our spit. I put my head on his chest. Tears puddled around my mouth and dripped onto his shirt, disappearing into the dark fabric. He patted my head, the fingertips a lingering pressure against my temple. I breathed into the ache.

"I'm losing her," I said, mouth mashed into his pectoral muscles. He pushed the hair away from my face. I mistook his tenderness; I believed it was about me. I didn't think that he too had lost something that day.

7

Smoke billows, obscuring the interns in a veil of gauze. My eyes sting and fill with tears, but the tears are not connected to any emotion that I can access. I'm completely calm.

It's just that the bus is on fire.

I peer out the window, head heavy with fumes, as the driver pulls onto the shoulder.

Interns shove to the front. Screaming gets louder, a frenzy of knife-like elbows and knees traps me in my seat. Inhaling, I feel high. Better than the turmeric pods, forgotten in the inner pocket of my bag. Better than biting.

The bus could explode and I wouldn't notice. I might die here, behind a wall of skinny rich girls greased-up for a HEBE shoot, skin melting off their bones, jeans sloping off their hips, and the smell of burning crayons all around.

The doors open and a pressure valve releases. It takes me a moment to register the empty space in the aisle, the fact that I can stand, I can step out of my seat, place one foot in front of the other. The fact that I haven't gone up in flames. Yet.

I go down the steps onto the side of the expressway. The

bus has released us onto a thin strip of pummeled grass. Tufts of soot-colored smoke pour from the open windows. An orange aura heats the vacant blue sky. Flames smoldering, about to burst. The sour-hot smell of burning metal and rubber makes me retch. I feel particles of exhaust clinging to the film of moisturizer and sweat on my face. A ritualistic circle of litter surrounds me: a punctured Marlboro carton, a flattened strip of gum oozing like snake flesh from between the cracks in a foil wrapper. Tree's town car is parked in front of the bus, the back door thrown open. She's half out of her seat. I see the shaky rise and fall of her chest from here. Sunglasses lowered down the bridge of her nose, she looks over the rim at the smoking bus. Her ice-gray eyes ooze over me. Her white-hot hair is caught in the sun.

A sedan almost hits Marigold as she climbs from the side closest to the traffic. Cell phone pressed to her ear, she yells into the mouthpiece. The interns cry into their phones. Parents, boyfriends, best friends, nannies. Crude, nebulous sounds spill from their mouths.

I spot Jamie leaning on the rock face. Staring at her phone but not talking on it.

I take my brush with death, turn it over in my hands, and am met with indifference. There was a moment on the bus when I was trapped in the seat, and as I waited for a toxic blast to pummel me from existence, I was a bubble floating in space. I closed my eyes and waited. Now, I recall what pulled me out of this half dream: the gentle, urgent weight of a hand on my arm. And then I was running too, struck once more by the base urge for survival.

My senses return one by one in the improbable daylight: sight, sound, taste, smell, touch. Relentless, like standing on the sun's surface. I wish for an eye mask, an occlusive layer.

Everyone is typing or talking. Richard would make too big of a deal. He'd insist on picking me up. My parents would be confused. *But if you're all right, why are you calling?* I imagine my mother's voice ringing from the speaker like a flicked crystal. Dom is most definitely sleeping.

Jamie looks unmoored as she watches her fellow blubbering interns circle their dust-clad tennis shoes in the dirt. We lock eyes. I roll mine. She smiles. Several feet from Jamie is another intern with rose gold bangs. She throws her phone into a Celine Nano and announces to the swirling exhaust: "You know what he did when I told him I almost died? He *laughed*. And then he asked if someone left a curling iron on. Swear to God, I deserve better."

Rush hour traffic oozes down the expressway. Sunset on the windshields. Everyone on the planet moves away from me, vanishing into the horizon.

Tree blocks my view. She puts her hands on my shoulders and squeezes. Her skin is cold despite the heat and the smoke. "Are you *okay?*"

"I think so." I touch my face, making sure that it's still there. The cheeks give and slide upward, revealing the hard ridge of my gums. Tree pulls me into an unbalanced hug. Embraces me like a gust of air-conditioning. I stumble when she lets go.

She moves down the line of flustered employees. Laying on hands, arranging her mouth and brows into a facsimile of concern. Marigold trails in her white Oxford and black pants, like a first-chair clarinetist in a high school orchestra. The interns wilt against the backdrop. Faces a little too shiny. Smudged lipstick extends the corners of their mouths and mascara crumbles onto their cheeks. Outfits askew with twisted hemlines, collars pulled aside, fading tan lines and lace bra straps unmasked.

A fire truck pulls up behind the smoking bus. Firemen pile out, lumbering slow-motion astronauts in heavy gear. The largest of the men, hose looped around his neck, swaggers to the rear of the bus, where the driver gestures to the luggage compartment.

The fireman shakes his head, and the driver throws up his hands.

Then the bus driver stalks over to confer with Tree and Marigold. Tree cranes her neck above Marigold's shoulder. Whispers into her silk hair.

The remaining firemen face us. It's a middle school dance: boys on one side, girls on the other. If I listen hard, I almost hear the dulcet strains of "Eternal Flame" through the snarl of traffic. A car horn blasts, cutting the tension, and I realize the music is real, it emanates from a passing truck's open window.

I am liquifying, coming apart. The air and my body are one. A veil of heat shimmers.

Tree addresses us with her brightest *don't-sue-me* smile. "Whew, that was quite a scare! Apologies for the wait while we figure out what's wrong with the bus. Unfortunately, it's still out of commission."

Rather than continuing on to the shoot as planned, we have two alternatives: we may expense a cab ride home, or we may expense a cab ride to Tree's apartment, where she will treat the team to dinner.

Then she appears right in front of me, a mirage. "You're coming with us," she says.

I follow her into the town car, which has been idling all this time. The air is sweet and perfumed, the driver effectively invisible. A tin of Altoids and a baby-sized water bottle rest in the cup holders between the seats. Gemma, Marigold, and Starla fill out the back row.

Tree sighs and leans against the headrest. "If you guys weren't on the bus, I would have considered it an act of God."

"But if they'd died like that, they'd be useless," Marigold says.

I stare out the window as the car chugs through traffic. Soon we take exit 46 toward Manhattan/Randall's Island, inch onto the FDR Drive. The AC is up too high and I am damp with cold, fishy sweat. I take out my phone to seem important. No new emails. On Instagram, a DM from daddy1201, a profile with zero followers and a stock photo of a Wall Street type in a '90s-era pinstripe suit. *Be my baby 4 cash?*

We come to a stop. Potted plants shaped like spirals flank the entrance to Tree's building. The doorman tips his hat. In the car, Marigold had placed an order with a vegan Mexican place in Tree's neighborhood. She sends Jamie and a lilac-haired intern to the bodega for disposable plates, utensils, and napkins. Tree wants the compostable kind made from potatoes. The food comes before they're back. Containers of black bean enchiladas, guacamole, dairy-free horchata. Marigold leaves the covers on until the girls arrive. The interns don't wait for a signal. They take plates and stand in line. An horchata ends up in my hand, the drama of the day melting with the ice on my tongue. Everything in the room is so shiny with life. I can hear every heartbeat.

Gemma and Starla sit on the cerulean chaise lounge, juggling plates on their knees. Tree's finger grazes the back of my hand, the shock of bare skin pinging through the ulna and radius. She gestures with her horchata.

"Beauty is possible," I say. The sweetness dries my tongue to a husk. I move it around against the walls of my mouth, trying to draw moisture. Tree floats off for small talk with the interns, their trauma forgotten in the excitement of entering Tree's world.

I meander to the window, the East River a ream of black satin washing the lip of the city. I press my forehead to the glass. Inhibitions lowered by my brush with death, I poke out my tongue. Lay it flat against the window, which tastes like hard water and soothes my thirst.

"Whoa," goes a voice. The reflection of an intern, hair in double braids, gapes, and all I can do is laugh, tongue still attached to the window. Saliva gathers in the crevices of my mouth. I see myself, up close and crazed. I withdraw my tongue and swallow the excess liquid.

My head starts to hurt, a steady drum behind the eyes. The life inside me, it's too much. I'm conscious of every cell.

"Are you okay?" the intern asks, but she's not even looking at me, she's staring at the starless sky through the giant windows. Or at her own baby pearl face looming over the beyond.

"Yeah, just a little tired." I sink into a plush armchair, the floral upholstery ugly enough to be impossibly cool. "I'm going to . . ." I lean back. Blink. *Rest my eyes.*

CHURCHLIKE SHADOWS CANOPY the ceiling. I sit up. The lights are off, but there are no curtains, and the walls catch the coin-bright moon. Tree's apartment is off-kilter, like a picture frame knocked slightly out of place. Humiliation spreads down my chest when I spot a puddle of spilled horchata on the pale, expensive rug. Rising from the couch, I walk toward the kitchen, intending to search for baking soda to treat the stains, but pause when I hear something. A wet glug. Water runs somewhere in the apartment.

The walls rock; I am Rose rushing through the shifting lower deck of the sinking Titanic. I move toward a sliver of light poking under a closed door. A shiver spreads up my leg. I put my hand on the doorknob and twist.

A CLAW-FOOTED BATHTUB anchors a pristine bathroom. Larger than the bathroom I used last time I was in Tree's apartment. Cavernous. My eyes follow the pale tile to the shocking water filling the tub. Pink froth gathers around Tree's sun-speckled shoulders, collecting in the wells of her collarbones. The red, a relief after all that white.

She doesn't hear me come in. Her head, encircled by a lavender HEBE-branded terry cloth headband, dawdles on the spire of her neck in a lazy rocking motion. Her limbs and spine are protracted. Her hair is electric platinum, swept up in a stylish messy bun. Tendrils snake down and catch the vibrant water. Her hand grazes the lip of the tub, a collection of rings reflecting the candlelight.

Tree shifts, rippling the water, which moves with uncanny thickness. I notice a sharpness, like menstrual blood soaking through underwear or the taste when you bite the inside of your cheek. Tree sits up straighter. Thin red seams striate her freckled back like scratch marks. I understand, all at once, what I'm seeing, what I always should have known. The impossible takes shape before me.

It's not water. It's blood.

She turns. Our eyes lock, and she smiles, no teeth. I've seen this look before. It's the one she gave me when I showed her my healed, gloveless hands. It says, *Ah, I knew you'd come.*

"Finally," Tree says. She stands up. Rivers of blood spill down her breasts, drip onto her ribs, pool in her navel and the V-shaped muscle between her hip bones. She reaches for a towel draped on a ladder-shaped shelf, wraps it around her sinewy body.

Unlike everything else in Tree's world, this towel is filthy. Ratty edges loose with strings. Muddy stains marble the fabric. I am rooted to the floor. Tree takes her time dragging the towel down one skinny arm and then the other. Next she does her legs. Stained nipples bloom on her taut chest. Tawny residue covers her skin. She is oily and bronzed like an Ancient Greek statue.

Tree drops the towel onto the floor and cinches a satin kimono-style robe etched with flowers. I notice how revived she appears, as if her top layer has been scrubbed clean off, revealing fresh, supple skin.

"Is that blood?" My voice sounds underused. It doesn't belong to the conscious me, but to some hidden creature that dwells in my head.

Tree laughs. "Of course. You know that."

"But . . . why?"

"Because it works. Fuck Botox, screw retinol. Blood is the ultimate elixir of youth." Tree forks a splotched hand through her hair. Her eyes are glassy and wild. "And it's non-invasive."

"That's disgusting."

"Oh, sweetie." She laughs. "What do you think was in that cream I gave you?"

youthjuice. How it makes my hands flicker like light bulbs in the dark. Vanishes the scars. Goes deeper and dissolves my will to bite and pick until I am pockmarked with the damage, the evidence of my interior ugliness writ large, mapping the pain on my body.

I gag. Touch my face to calm down, but my hands are the cream, and I can only picture slaughtered pigs dangling above a vat of moisturizer, and hear animal screams of death.

Invisible hangnails sting to life on each finger, standing on end like fine hairs.

"My methods are unorthodox, but I am going to be beautiful forever. And soon I'll be able to help others stay that way too. Imagine looking like you do now well into your sixties, seventies, eighties. When you can't tell how old anyone is, age will become obsolete. And then, how many steps are there between perfect skin and eternal life?"

I look at Tree, pink-streaked as a piglet. The ends of her silver hair are clotted with blood and matted, the texture of straw. But still beautiful. I envy even this repulsive, murder-soaked image of her. Envy is what keeps me from running.

"So, you—what? Have Marigold in some laboratory strangling chickens with her bare hands? Where does it come from?"

Tree's expression deflates. She seems sad, like I've missed the obvious, and she doesn't meet my eyes when she says what comes next. First, I think I can't be hearing her right, the horchata was drugged, I'm still asleep, I'm dead and locked in the eternal dream.

But she repeats herself, and the words are unmistakable: "The interns."

Interns. The ones who leave. No one sees them again. Gemma and Tree, going on about how replaceable they are, how they are only good for one thing. *I would have considered it an act of God.* I assumed the one thing they meant was fetching coffee.

But now I see how badly I misunderstood.

The one thing is their youth. The cream of their skin. Their drum-tight stomachs. Every part in its rightful place.

And I hate to admit it, but I'm inching closer to Tree, closer to the beating heart of the tub, my fingers creeping into the bathwater, grazing. The blood clings when I pull my fingers away.

"Go ahead," Tree says. "Hop in."

IT'S SO WARM. Hot, actually. Boiling, lightly bubbling up around me. Comforting as childhood. Colors pulse before my eyes. Alternating red and blue and purple flashes that run over my eyes in soapy swirls. I feel a stir, as though my layers are renewing themselves. I'm like a snake writhing out of its old skin. Full-body exfoliation.

Tree must've diluted the blood, or mixed it with some kind of chemical, because it's runnier than it should be. There's much more of it than seems possible. It can't have come from just one girl. I try to pick out who it might be, but the interns are one watercolor of blissful inexperience. Their faces run through my mind like runny eggs. Uneven eyes, yoked noses, candle-melting lips.

I repeat lies about why I'm doing this, my favorite being the one that says I'm here to let the wrongness settle over me, to understand what I'm up against. I'm here to do the right thing eventually. The ends of my hair dip into the blood like so many gruesome paintbrushes, splattering the porcelain. The swirls in the tub clear and my knees crest the fill line. Under the violent liquid, they take on the hue of death. I slip down until the blood touches my chin, and then I keep sinking until I'm submerged. Holding my breath, I count to twenty, fifty, one hundred. Then I break the surface. Gasping and open-mouthed, I taste metal. Liquid such brilliant red it's nearly black.

I press my tongue to the roof of my mouth. The remnant of simple syrup. The sour, dehydrating bite.

Cupping my hands, I gather blood. A thin skin ripples. I raise the blood to my face and take a tiny slurp through my teeth. I want to find out what foreign blood can do to my insides, whether it turns me over, reworks my organs. The only blood I've ever known is mine. A constant source of fascination. I used to examine the flowered end when I changed a tampon before tossing it. And then there was the biting: iron taste spotting my tongue, staining my teeth, dirtying me. Not like this young, innocent, cleansing blood, so sweet and earthy, tasting of roots. What if this is the cure for cancer, capable of knitting cells together? More than just skincare? Maybe what Tree is doing isn't so bad. These interns, they aren't good for much, it's true. They get spray tans and manicures on the weekends; they spend Mommy and Daddy's money; they shop as though Nordstrom and Saks are nonprofits that would go under without their generous donations. They lack both artistry and structure.

These girls, they are a waste of their own blood.

Normally, I sleep in the bath. Something about the heat and the candlelight. Something about the womb. But I'm wide awake. Brain bouncing off the walls. My whole body is buzzing with life. I am a sack filled with bees, alive in a way I haven't been since Mona and Chase. Since I initially discovered the high that comes from ripping into your own flesh with your own teeth.

As I lie here, my hands shake with power. I turn them over. Remembering my gloves, relegated to a flea market jewelry box with a lock and key in my underwear drawer. Shameful lace skin.

Blood pools in my nail beds. Otherwise, the skin is smooth. No hangnails. No scars. Cuticles primly tucked. Each nail a crisp ivory arc shining like moonstone.

TREE SENDS ME home in an Escalade with blackened windows. The blood turns crusty on the ride and washing it off in my shower at home is difficult. The water runs purple, then pink. I linger until I start to prune, then I shut the tap and step onto the heated tile. Newly clean, my entire body is like the underside of a kitten's chin. Birth is the miracle of life, but what is rebirth?

Beyond the mirror fog I shift in muted blobs, a dark splotch for my hair and a larger, pale one for my body. I clear a circle with the side of my hand. The skin under my eyes where the faintest traces of crow's feet had started to appear is bright and plump, smooth as an ice rink at the beginning of the season. Touching the spot where a pimple formed on my chin yesterday, I find the tell-tale tenderness of a surfacing breakout has vanished. I am so pretty that I want to cry.

In fact, my eyes do water. Ridiculous. I staunch the tears with the heels of my hands. I feel my eyeballs slide back into my head. Still, it's better than rubbing. Eyes are gentler than tissue paper, and the windows to the soul, always.

AT SOME POINT, Richard bangs into the apartment. I'm on the couch, watching television, which I rarely do unless it's with Dom. Primary-colored bears dance somewhere in outer space, the landscape odd with a sun that never sets and ochre hills rolling into eternity. This is the channel the TV was tuned to when I turned it on. I haven't blinked since I can remember; my eyeballs are dried open, and I don't look away from the screen until Richard's muscled physique blocks the red bear pirouetting over the cratered horizon.

Cocking my head, I attempt to peer around his inverted triangle chest at the bear ballet unfolding on a sandy, faraway planet. He steps closer, completely obscuring the screen. His face is a mask of displeasure. He takes his hands off his hips and balls them into fists.

I find the remote and mute the TV, blinking as I wait for him to speak. He blinks right back. "Well?" he finally says.

"Hi?" Did we have plans? I check the time on my phone: 4:45. Too early for dinner.

"Hi," he says, in a very not-hi way. *Drinks? Was I supposed to meet him for drinks?*

"Hiiii . . . ?" I wave. I catch sight of my hand in the television's blue light. Scabs have reopened and a massacre of blood rivers down the fingers. I blink. When I open my eyes, the hand is perfect.

Richard scoffs. Actually scoffs, and crosses his arms. "Is that all you have to say?" he asks.

"Ye . . . es?" I know immediately that it was the wrong thing, because his face is swallowed by shadow and his shoulders seem to hulk higher and higher until they reach his earlobes.

Lately, Richard has been something of a phantom in my life. The sound of water hushing the shower tile in the morning. The missing wedge of cashew gouda scuffed from the wrapping. The polished work shoe I almost kill myself tripping over on the way to the bathroom. We were not always like this. Once we talked on the phone the nights we didn't spend together, falling asleep against hot speakers, exhaling into each other's dreams. We sent photos of lunches, shared random musings about philosophy and stupid memes. What happened to us?

Richard shifts, scattering the shadows. His anger is curdled worry. But I feel no remorse as he takes an exacting circle around the living room, placing one obsidian shoe in front of the other, before sitting on the edge of the couch and scraping his hands through his textured hair. His exasperated sigh is nearly paternal.

"Why didn't you text me? It's been over twenty-four hours. Where were you?"

The bears roll like candy down the hill, appealingly primary-colored. Cheeks so round they sink their little bead eyes.

Richard still wears his shoes, black socks bunched tragically around his skinny ankles. Those ankles. I might never see those ankles again. We might be breaking up.

"The bus caught fire," I say.

"What bus? You don't take the bus."

"We took a bus to the shoot."

Richard scratches his knee, bunching the leg of his khakis. He seems like he wants to ask more questions. He says, "What are we doing here, Sophia?"

"Sitting on the couch," I offer.

"Sophia. I texted you like a dozen times. Last night, this morning. I called Dom. We were thinking about getting the police involved."

Dom would never have called the police. "My phone was off. It died, or something. I don't know." I rub the seam of the couch cushion until I locate a tiny hole. "It's complicated."

Richard reaches for my shoulder and turns me to face him,

dragging my eyes from the television. His swimmy irises say, *I'm breaking up with you.*

Indifferent sadness tugs like dull pain fighting through a numbing agent. I could plead with him. I almost want to; I will miss him if he's no longer in my life. But something has severed us. I'm not sure when it happened. It could have been last night, when I slid into the bath. It could have been earlier. The day I walked into HEBE for the first time; the day Mona left me for good; the day I cracked from my mother's womb and parted my lids to the world.

"Sophia," Richard says again. I don't think he has said my name this many times in the history of our relationship. The longer you're with someone, the less their name means. It's just a sound. "We've been together for a long time now. You know I love you." Richard takes my hand. "The guys from work are all getting married."

I cross my arms and slide toward the arm of the couch so that I am facing Richard at a slant. His hand sits on the cushion where my body was like a limp pillowcase.

There was a time not long ago when I believed I would marry Richard. When I thought that's what I wanted. We joked about whether our kids might have his sense of humor, my skill for secondhand shopping. He had recently begun pointing out rings when we were shopping. I started to imagine an easy life of opulent comfort. A society-pages life.

"I don't want to get married," I say. Under the flashing light of kindergarten-colored bears who are best friends with their planet's two suns, I realize that it's true. It's not Richard; I don't want to be married to anyone. I want to be like Tree; an ice-island of a woman.

"Look, Sophia." My name, like it's a talisman, like we are

on a teen drama. "I'm almost thirty years old." It's there, a silent reminder: *And so are you.* "I need to think about my future. I need to be with a woman who has lifelong partner potential."

Lifelong partner potential. As I ruminate, Richard's face is the last I see hovering before me in the moving dark. First, I picture Mona, then Dom, flickering like the ghosts of Christmas Past and Present.

And there is Tree, Yet to Come. Her pearlescent complexion startles me. I press farther back, folding my knees and placing my feet on the cushion between my body and Richard's. He lifts the hand that previously held mine as if to caress my face, but doesn't lean forward to make contact. Instead the hand hangs, caught in an invisible net. The downturn of his mouth tells me that if he leaves, he won't come back.

I'm sad, but also irritated. I want to see what happens next.

"I guess that's it, then," I say. "You better go find her."

He throws up his hands, kisses me on the forehead, and leaves. I don't get up to see if he left his key to the apartment behind.

I turn up the volume. The bears hold hands in a circle and coo at the blazing sun.

8

Dom is in a good mood. Calmer, the vibrational shimmer of her muscles quieting, her breath ironing out. Downers, maybe, or just a little weed. A publicist in sensible round-toe flats, a self-important headset vined around her ears, checks Dom's name off a list, and ushers us into a warehouse on Grove.

"Greenwich Village. How vintage," Dom whispers.

The room throbs, a beating heart seized in a rhythmically tensed fist. Women with newscaster waves hold purses double the width of their torsos like shields. In the center of the room rises a majestic ice sculpture of a penis. By Aria, the artist Tree hired for the HEBE goblet. The scrotum gleams silver under the hot lights.

The bar is set back against a graffiti-splashed wall, a line of neon cocktails at the front and a mostly-for-show bartender who pretends not to check his phone as we approach. Dom takes a green cocktail. The Wicked Witch, proclaims a framed sign on the bar.

I catch a whiff of menthol as she knocks the drink back. I ask for water. The bartender slides a plastic cup over the bar.

Dom looks at me funny, a little too lucid for my liking. For an heiress who spent a summer at the same New Canaan psych hospital that Edie Sedgwick once attended, Dom can be remarkably perceptive. She finishes her drink, ditches the empty cup, and picks up another Wicked Witch. The beverage gleams, a split glow stick, as she knocks it back, alien juice pulsing into her waiting bird mouth.

I glance around the crowd. "Where's the murderer?"

Jason Red had been a famous club promoter until he killed his PCP dealer, an El Salvadoran immigrant nicknamed the Saint, in a fit of rage during a financial dispute. Then he preserved the Saint's body with formaldehyde in the bathtub of his apartment on Tenth Avenue and Seventh, left it there for a week, carved it with a meat cleaver, zipped the parts into a Louis Vuitton trunk, and took a cab to the Chelsea Piers. He so charmed the driver that the man later testified that he helped Red heave the trunk into the Hudson. That same night, Red covered himself in fake blood and glitter for a guerrilla party at the McDonald's in Times Square, where he told anyone who would listen that he'd just killed a saint on a sign from God.

Gossip columnists reported on the rumors, but no one believed him until Saint's parents, who settled in New Mexico after leaving El Salvador when Saint was five years old, contacted the police after growing concerned when their reliable son missed three Sunday afternoon phone calls in a row. Red's claim that he heard the voice of God ordering him to kill Saint was used as evidence for the insanity defense his lawyers employed to garner a more lenient sentence, with time served in a psychiatric facility.

Now he circles the warehouse party shirtless, his fanged

nipples exposed and a floor-length sateen robe winging from his upper arms like a cape. Even now he's aggressively handsome beneath a mask of glitter and white face paint, with a dimpled smile and sly eyes. He ambles like a maddened ringleader, a manic grin cleaving his face.

As he rounds the corner and starts toward the bar, I am struck with the conviction that I cannot look Jason Red in the eye. If I do, he will see right down deep into the core of everything I try not to think about. The soft pink pillow in my gut where I store my shame.

"It's a unisex makeup line," Dom is saying. I haven't been listening.

Projected onto the wall behind Dom's head there is footage of horses slow-motion running through tall grass. The film mesmerizes me, a sort of liminal space within the larger liminal space of the party. Their manes make me think of the rainbow of hair colors on the HEBE interns. I feel slightly sick.

Dom edges a sharp elbow into my ribs. "Are you gonna pass out?"

I shake my head. Give a smile that feels like a wince. For a while we inhabit our bodies at the bar, observing the party. These bodies from which we perpetually seek escape, plying them with serums and lotions, microneedles and cold jade stones, seaweed wraps. Softening and firming in turn. Everyone in this room is searching for the same thing, and now I have it within my reach. All I have to do is grab it.

My rib cage inflates and compresses. The murderer is getting close. I sense him as an essence, then a shadow, then a person. What is a person but a vase for blood and mucus and bile. Music thumps in my heels, my head spins.

I crane my neck, gaze stopping at his collarbone.

Dom steps in with a gracious double kiss on both of Red's cheeks, an *oh-my-god* squeal. They seem to have met before. She compliments the products, which we have not touched. She inquires about the penis sculpture.

"Isn't it brilliant?" Red says. "When I found out that I'd be throwing my first rager on the outside, I just had to hire Aria. Did you know she studied under Triple X? We used him *all* the time at the clubs before I went away. His art is so provocative."

Red pauses, and I can tell he's studying me. I reach for my glove cuff and am met with the clammy skin on my wrist. Of course. No need for gloves anymore.

"What is it that *you* do?" Red asks.

I finally meet Red's gaze. He's no clairvoyant; he's a sad man, Ben Nye Clown White settled in his crow's feet, a naked patina of guilt hardening his features, which up close I see have been cut, stretched, and stitched into a new orientation.

"I work at HEBE."

"With Tree Whitestone? She's a legend. I'm only a little jealous." Red cuts a mirthless laugh. His bloodshot eyes lose focus and slide aimlessly over the crowd, bovine tongue briefly visible as he licks his lips. I spot a waiter circling a tray of nutty brown avocado toast triangles. My mouth waters.

Red's eyeballs make their way back. He grins. He bores into me, and I wonder what dark waters he sees. Then he grabs my forearm. Brings my hand up and peers at my curling fingers. Lifts up and up. Pulls me closer. He smiles wider. "Nice nails."

A publicist appears at Red's side and says something in his ear that makes him drop my arm, and sends him skittering off like a bug.

"I hate these things." Dom's words are slurred and hazy at the edges.

"But you love the free shit." I'm petulant and tired. I want to be home massaging youthjuice into my hands while the television natters in the background.

"Everyone loves free shit; it's Darwinism or something." Dom gestures with her sloped chin to the gifting table by the entrance. "Shall we?"

The horses twitch like a great rainstorm. We collect gift bags from a new publicist stationed at the front. I cast a look into the crowd, but I don't find Red anywhere.

"What's in this, a fucking bomb?" Dom paws at the tissue paper inside her gift bag, holds up a tube of lip gloss. Thick liquid globs from one side to the other as she shakes the container back and forth. It reminds me, unfortunately, of semen.

DOM'S BEDROOM MATCHES her demeanor. Cobwebs have been cleared from the corners, clothes folded and put away. Color rises in her cheeks, and a modest shine lacquers her hair. She has changed into a silk robe, a T-shirt of the sort of thin gray cotton that only A-cups wear, and cashmere sweatpants with drawstrings at the ankles. We sit on the bed. Dom orders a pizza and salad on her phone from our local place. Pizza used to be my comfort food. As a kid, I would pull the cheese off with my fingers and shove the lacteal globs in my mouth, scraping the soggy part of the bread with my teeth. It's never tasted that good since.

The salad tastes bad, flavorless lettuce soaked in acid Italian dressing, salty olives. But a trapdoor has opened in the pit of my stomach, leading to a cavern so deep it can't be filled by food alone. There's nothing down there, a bottomless pit, a dark well, the walls purpling and crawling wet. As soon as the plastic fork hits aluminum, I'm nauseated. Dom stares at me over the ridge of her crust. The remaining pizza in the thrown-open box on the floor resembles an exposed mass of guts. Tomato red runnels cracking through pustules of mozzarella.

I bolt into Dom's en suite, accidentally kicking my backpack over on the way.

I just make it to the toilet. Vomit drags itself out of my body. Bile claws my throat. Once my stomach is empty, I flush, then wash my face and hands with Dom's Aēsop soap.

The scene in Dom's bedroom is just as I left it. Only there's one small change: the enormous pearl clutched at Dom's clavicle. The jar must have rolled out of my backpack when I knocked it in my rush to the bathroom.

"What are you doing?"

"It fell out of your bag. Is this what you've been using on your hands?" She reads the label. "youthjuice . . . It has to be good, they look amazing."

I wrench the jar away from her. She holds the lid, concave side up.

"I'm testing it for work." I try to be casual about it, holding a shrug in my voice, but Dom clocks my desperation and latches on, a tick burying its head into the epidermis and preparing to suck.

"A new HEBE launch? Come on, lemme see. This is what I do!" She stretches toward the jar. I pull away roughly and her taloned nails, painted like a neon chessboard, scour my inner wrist. The jar slips and gives a tiresome bounce on the rug, cream oozing over the lip. I hurl myself after it, pawing the mess into my cupped hands and back into the jar.

Studying me, Dom tips her nose beneath the rim and sniffs.

"What's in this shit? You're acting like me when I've been out of coke for a week."

"It's under embargo."

Dom's liner wings pinch down, retracting into the belly of her eyeballs. "You're honestly so weird lately. What is going on with you?"

"I've been really busy. We're working on, like, three campaigns right now."

"Yeah."

"What's that supposed to mean?"

"Yeah. It just means, yeah, you're busy. I know. It's pretty much all you talk about these days, if I can get you to talk at all. Ever since you started that job it's like nothing else matters. You were never this obsessed with work before."

"Because I worked at a fucking coffee shop! Serving people like you all day."

"People like me."

"Oh, you know what I mean. Rich people."

"Don't do that."

"Do what? Remind you that you have way more money than I could ever dream of and that if you wanted to quit your little vanity project blog tomorrow you'd still be set for life?"

"Yeah, I get it, eat the rich, whatever. You never seem to mind when you're paying hundreds below market value to live here and stealing my clothes so you can look cooler than you are for Tree Whitestone and her cronies. Typical part-time fake-socialist bullshit. Don't act like your problems are my fault." Dom flexes her lime-green toes. "Those HEBE bitches are poisoning your brain."

She leans over, unzips her Alexander McQueen bag, and pulls out a notebook. My notebook. The HEBE logo is embossed in the powdery lavender cover. She tosses the note-book on the floor. It lands pages-down at my feet. Relief gives way to cold shock as I remember Dom holding my backpack after yoga, handing it over like a favor. Not a favor—a betrayal.

Dom puffs air through her nostrils and kicks the notebook. "That place is doing something to you."

"Paying my bills?" I push and push, saying everything I've always believed about Dom but never had the courage to admit. "You think you're so clever. You're just an heiress with a pill problem and a glorified diary."

Dom rears back as if physically struck. "That's funny," she says.

"Please, tell me what's *funny*."

"You think you're better than me because you're quote-unquote 'poor.' Like you don't have your own addiction." She points to the jar of youthjuice.

"Whatever," I say. "At least I'm not killing myself."

Dom's laugh is a knife through a balloon, an ugly mylar pop. "Okay, sure. Enjoy your daily allotted four hundred calo-ries of tofu. If you're going to act like a bitch, can you get the fuck out of my room? You're ruining the vibe."

She uses a long-stemmed lighter on the windowsill to light a row of candles.

"Don't burn the place down when you nod off later." I slam the door. "Blogging is dead!" I scream, and scramble down the hallway to my room like a mad spider, pounding the wall with the side of my fist.

Sitting on the floor, I open the notebook. The first few entries are coherent. I vaguely remember writing them. Notes about the consistency of the cream, and the results. But sev-eral pages in, the handwriting becomes loopy and borderline illegible. Then it launches into a string of nonsense. The paper is creased and dented, the marks heavy, as if I wrote with all my weight concentrated on the pen. Rips here and there where I pressed down too hard. It reads like I wrote these pages in my sleep. Spirals and fireworks and tornados like I used to draw in the margins during class, immature doodles. One entire page reads: *beauty is possible. Beauty IS possible. Beauty is POSSIBLE. BEAUTY IS POSSIBLE!!*

I consider the possibility that Dom filled the notebook herself. If she did it while high, she might not even remember. I've seen her take Adderall and stay up all night painting and writing blog posts she'd later delete. And that slogan is on HEBE's website and social media profiles. It's not a secret. The more I think about it, the more it makes sense. She's gaslighting me. Maybe she's even jealous. I have my life together. I work for Tree Whitestone. I'm part of something bigger than myself. And she has been going extra hard lately. Her sheeny, unfocused eyes. It's hard to reason with her when she gets like this. On one of her binges.

Satisfied, I close the notebook. Rest it on my knee for a second, staring at the cover. Then I tuck it into my bag and put it out of my mind.

2008

I didn't visit Mona in the hospital. The word itself—hospital. That compact, tooth-clicking row of syllables. It sounded too final. But she was out by the weekend. I found out when her mother called. "She'd kill me if she knew, but she needs a friend."

I went straight to her house after school. I circled the block three times, gathering the courage to ring the bell. Mona's mother must have been waiting by the window; she answered before I fully retracted my finger from the button. Her dyed-black hair fanned off her face like dark magic, and her eyeliner collected in the well of deep wrinkles beneath her eyes.

She stepped aside to let me into the foyer.

Mona's living room was cramped and floral. The whole house smelled of cats. They had three. Shoes were not allowed, and the carpet had a gritty texture, which I assumed was litter collected in the pile.

We never spent much time at Mona's house, but of course I knew the way to her room, which was on the first floor, down a yellow-lit hallway branching from the living room.

She was propped up in bed, surrounded by pillows. Delicate, like a feather dropped from a great height. Her eyes were closed, but I could tell she was only pretending to sleep because she stiffened as I perched gingerly on the edge of the bed. She seemed breakable; I did not want to touch her or breathe too forcefully in her direction.

As I entered, she turned into the light from the window and her face disappeared, creating an unsettling void. I gave up on all pretense and stretched out on the bed next to her. The twin mattress was too small to comfortably hold us both, and my right leg dangled toward the floor, grazing her daisy-shaped rug.

I nestled into Mona's neck. She smelled sour, like old medicinal sweat, but it wasn't unpleasant. I inhaled deeply. "I missed you," I said to her hair.

She sighed and opened her eyes. "You bitch," she said. "Why didn't you come visit me?"

"I was scared. I didn't know what happened to you." She scoffed and turned away again. "But you're right; I should have come."

She cracked a smile. "It's okay. I was pretty out of it till I got home anyway. Pretty much slept and watched *Jeopardy!* the whole time."

"You hate *Jeopardy!*."

"Yeah, well. There isn't anything good on network TV during the day. It was that or *Judge Judy*, which I hate more. Plus, I didn't know how to change the channel. I had to ask the nurses anytime I wanted to watch something else."

This comment sent us into a fit of stupid giggles.

Catching my breath, I said, "Don't they want people to gather the will to live in the hospital? Mind over matter and whatever? The least they could do is spring for a decent cable package."

"Shit is too expensive for the dying, I guess."

Dying. That was the only confirmation I needed that things were exactly as bad as I'd feared. She almost didn't make it.

We were quiet for so long that Mona's breathing slipped into a deeper rhythm that told me she might really be sleeping this time. And this, the knowledge that she might not hear me, gave me the courage to say what I'd been too scared to earlier: "Why did you do it?"

Her breath quickened and she shifted toward the center of the bed, pushing me farther to the edge. "It wasn't on purpose. Things got out of hand."

What got out of hand? I wanted to hear her say it. It felt like we were grasping at some shared truth, but we each had only some of the pieces and the meaning was muddled.

"I kissed that boy from Clark's," I said.

Mona sat up a little, forcing me off her chest. I reorganized until we were facing each other, the time-honored stand-off of teenage girls about to gossip.

She smirked, but it didn't reach her eyes, and her voice was flat when she said, "Damn, girl. Good for you."

Mona's reaction puzzled me. Perhaps she had tumbled too far in a new direction, an adult dimension home to larger concerns. Usually, she was more interested in my dating life than I was, pushing for the details as if she were trying to meticulously recreate the action in her mind.

But now she simply asked if I would get her a glass of water. I retreated down the hall into the kitchen, opened a few cabinets until I found the glasses, pulled one down, and filled it under the tap. The sounds of the television filtered in from the living room, where I was sure Mona's mom sat in her tattered house clothes, staring blankly at *Judge Judy*. Mona's distaste for daytime network television sprung from her own living room.

I kept the water running after pulling the glass away and stood there listening: a woman suing her ex-boyfriend for car payments, and something about a dog. A sniffle too loud and wet to be coming from the television.

Turning off the tap, I returned to Mona's room to find her actually asleep, chin tucked into her neck and a delicate snore feathering from her parted lips.

I put the water on the nightstand and left without saying goodbye.

9

"I can't have an orgasm, I've moved my forehead enough today." Gemma is across the table from me in the left Ovary, trying to pout without wrinkling her face. Below the table, the notebook comes alive on my lap under tented fingers, a vital organ. It burns a hole.

"Soph, help me convince Gem not to cancel this date tonight," Tree says.

"Hm?"

"Tree is trying to set me up with one of her investment banker friends. I keep telling her I'm getting too old to show emotion, so I need to schedule one of our treatments first."

"We don't have enough for that," Tree says.

You think you know someone and then a new dimension reveals itself. Moments ago, I would not have pegged Gemma as someone who needed a date to be arranged. I pictured men flocking to her like appointed angels.

Today she is haggard. From certain angles, a sag beneath the chin. Her future face overlaying her current one in nightmarish compilation, a funeral slideshow. The women of HEBE exist for me in a shimmering bubble, a mythical nowhereisland. Before my eyes, black spots of mold form on the bubble's cool, opalescent surface. Gemma wearing her age sends a sick dread from the crown of my head to the pit of my stomach. I called the meeting, but the reality of Tree and Gemma in the room has me reluctant to begin. I spent all weekend reading the notebook, pacing the apartment, hiding from Dom, who left sometime on Saturday and never returned. Bruises up and down my thighs from bumping furniture. I press one, a dull pleasant ache that starts deep in the muscle.

I have to tell them about Dom.

"You wanted to see us?" Tree says. Her pretty face falters, a flash of displeasure.

I clear my throat. "Um."

"Honey, what did I tell you about vocal fry? You have *got* to work on that or no one will take you seriously in a boardroom. Remind me to send you the link to my voice coach's YouTube channel, her exercises will change your life." Tree runs a finger from the hairline to the center of her forehead and presses down. Closes her eyes and massages in a circle. Her forehead ripples like a lake that calms when she pulls her hand away. Her eyes spring open.

"But please. Tell us what's on your mind, Soph."

My throat feels stuffed with cotton. I smile smile smile at the Ovary's salaciously curved walls and try to remember what I rehearsed.

"What about the FDA? And the cops?" Not how I planned to begin, but good enough.

"Is that all this is about? You're worried about the consequences! The FDA is a joke. We can put mercury in our moisturizer and they'd never know," Tree says. "And did you know that cops only solve two percent of crimes? I read that in *The New Yorker*. Don't be fooled by all their flashy equipment— they're eye candy. Soph, remember—we're going to lean heavily on you when we figure out the branding."

All I can think to say is: "I'm excited to be part of the team." Beaming faces all around, cheeks crawling into eyes, smiles growing.

Gemma, scooting out of her seat, says, "If that's everything, I should bounce. My Pressed Juicery order will be ready."

Tree stays seated, tapping her tablet. I move to follow Gemma, but Tree calls my name as I'm reaching the exit. "Please. Sit with me for another minute."

The universe bonds to her will. I sit. She touches her tablet again, slides it to one side, and that's when I see it underneath: a newspaper clipping. Slightly yellowed and crisp. Almost fourteen years of weather captured in the paper.

I don't need to read it, but she turns the page anyway. I angle my face upward as she slides the clipping across the table.

Tendons in my eyes strain not to look, but a memory jogs loose. Not about the end. An earlier memory. For years Mona said her mother's lasagna was better than any restaurant's. "Better than Carbone," she liked to say, though we'd obviously never been there. We'd heard the restaurant referenced on a show about Upper East Side teenagers, and it had become our shorthand for the best of the best. I was fourteen before I tasted the famous lasagna; it was a special occasion. Her mother had received a promotion at the hair salon where she worked. I starved myself for a full twenty-four hours in anticipation. I drank too much coffee, which made me jittery, and lay in the basement with the lights off, watching MTV and then a spate of sitcom reruns, moving as little as possible. Whenever

I shifted positions my stomach would growl. At four o'clock, I got ready. A few swipes of my mom's Maybelline Great Lash, Vaseline rubbed on my lips to fill in the cracks. My skirt was blue and white paisley with a lettuce hem. I couldn't decide what to do with my hair, so I pulled it into a tight ponytail and brushed mousse along the temples. I walked the fifteen blocks to Mona's in stiff white patent flats with buckles. She lived next to a bar where a gaggle of men sat like boulders on the sidewalk. They were prehistoric—they never moved. I self-consciously clutched the heart-shaped rhinestone at my clavicle as they gawked. The buckles cut up my ankles.

Mona's mom answered the door in a black nightie passed off as a regular dress. Sheer, vulgar panels around the ribs gave it away, and the dainty satin bow between her small breasts. Candles sparkled in the dining room over a white plastic tablecloth and the good plates, a set of scalloped lavender glass dishes that I coveted. The nicest things in the house. Mona's dress was baby blue satin, lace trim and a velvet bow; she bought the slip at the one good thrift store and added the frilly details herself. Some threads were visible where she'd done a less than perfect job concealing her stitches. Her mom said grace before we dug in.

The lasagna was disgusting. Overcooked, tepid noodles buried in watery, oddly sweet sauce. The cheese shreds were not completely melted. Flavorless knots of ground beef caught in my gums. I'd feel them for days afterward no matter how many times I brushed my teeth.

This scene from the past plays on the Ovary ceiling. I could draw the newspaper clipping from memory: the school photo they ran, the tiara tucked into her Courtney Love hair and the despondent chin-in-hands posture she refused to change, going so far as to threaten litigation when the photographer went to adjust her. A wave of nausea swells, and the room runs like paint thinner. I blink, and a single tear escapes my lashes, races down my chin, and lands on the page.

It's only then that I look. I grasp for the paper, thumb blotting her face. "How did you know?" I ask Tree. "They never used my name."

"We run extensive background checks on all our employees."

"But—"

"Extensive. But there is such want in you; I would have known there was something anyway. It's like you are constantly on the verge of confession. Go ahead—tell me. Why did you call me here today?"

Warm light comes down and bathes her in a halo. She is my holy and divine savior, the most beautiful way out. My hands on the notebook, baby smooth like a second chance. My heart races. On my phone, in my pocket, is an email Dom sent the morning after our fight. Girls' names and coordinating dates, the interns that have gone missing since I started at HEBE. I unlock the phone with my thumbprint.

The email is open where I left it.

"Read it," I say, handing my phone to Tree. Her profile remains placid as her thumb glides down the screen. She claws a hand through her bleached bob. Her wide mouth is a solid line. She slams the phone face down on the table.

"You need to take care of this," she says.

"She doesn't really know anything."

"She knows enough. Only a matter of time before she connects the dots."

"But there isn't . . . we don't . . ." Words continue to run from my open mouth. I am a leaking faucet. I'm not making sense. Because she is right, of course. Dom will figure it out. Even if she doesn't reach the whole truth, the impossible, uncanny truth, she will land close enough to inflict damage. The air has a sour, metallic taste. The taste of soot and memory.

I nod. "Okay. Tell me what to do."

TREE MEETS ME at the apartment. Her shirt has a high neckline and when she shifts to hand me the baggie of heroin and a syringe, a scaled psoriasis patch on her neck becomes briefly visible. The bag is slippery. Plastic brushes my fingers like an eel, and I almost drop the baggie. Then I do drop it, and Tree says, "For God's sake," under her breath. The walls throb in rhythm with the headache ticking the tendons of my eyes.

Tree takes the drugs and the syringe into the kitchen. I hesitate, then follow.

I remember a passage from my Thích Nhất Hạnh phase about washing dishes. This was when I thought living in the moment would stop me from biting. You're supposed to be fully present, attendant to each dish. It's how we stop time. I'm trapped in that exercise against my will. I would like for it to be tomorrow. I would like for the sun to rise on a new world. I will shower and blot my night-wrinkled complexion with serum and exfoliate death off my arms and legs. There is coffee to drink, and a nail appointment to be kept. Did I wash the silk pillowcase? I dream of a cool silk bath on my neck and Tree expertly spills poison into a spoon. Expertly because, I realize, she is an expert. She doses our girls. Doses them with drugs until they are dizzy with want of the end. Half in the afterlife already, and delirious, eyes wide to knowledge.

The girls are not particularly smart, and Tree gives them the gift of omniscience. They alone have cracked the mysteries and secrets of humanity. They hold the key to the meaning of life, which is never dying—or dying in the face of the greater good.

I feel the girls watching like bugs in the dark. They are in the cabinets and on the ceiling and one grows from the back of Tree's thoracic spine, a deformed twin with nose and mouth and eyes parting the curtain of her hair.

She turns to me, spoon in one hand and a lighter in the other. Just one of her now. She sighs. Takes my wrist and holds it out, palm up. Then she puts the lighter in my hand, closes the fingers around it. "Light it."

I flick the lighter and Tree holds the spoon above the flame. The powder has been mixed with a bit of water. We stand there watching the powder turn liquid in the bowl of the spoon. It feels like it takes forever. I focus on the flame's blue tip—*I am washing this plate; now I am drying the plate*—until Tree finally removes the spoon and picks up the syringe.

"I should've had you practice," Tree says. Her back is to me, and I can't see what she's doing. Checking the time on her phone, maybe. Answering an email. "There's not enough time. You'll be great. Just go for a juicy vein. One that pops right out."

"Me?"

"A child could do it." She hands me the syringe. "Careful. Now, there. Go for a juicy vein and push. You got this."

The digital clock above the stove says we have ten minutes before Dom arrives. I texted her last night, lured her home with the promise of an explanation. I appealed to her sense of charity. *I need you*, I said, *you've made my life worth living.*

Ten minutes. It might as well be an hour, or a year.

Off the pantry is a small bathroom. I go in and lock the door. The syringe wobbles in my hand. I stare at the fine point and consider expelling the drugs into the sink. I consider dumping them into my own bloodstream. The easy way out.

I put the needle on the edge of the sink and vomit in the toilet. I haven't eaten in a few days so it's mostly water and mucus, dry heave, but still it goes on and on until I'm wrung out like an old washcloth. Then I straighten. Smooth down the pleats of my high-waisted shorts, which are Dom's. I run a tuft of mousse through my fringe. Tap along my browbone and under my eyes. Inhale for a count of six. Exhale.

Tree summons me with a soft rap at the door. "Two minutes," she says.

Dom is never on time. Maybe she won't come. But her key scrapes the lock and we are squared off in the foyer. Dom has deteriorated in the last few days. Her hair springs from the side of her head in clumps. One side is shaved unevenly, baring the lumpy, planetary surface of her skull. Old makeup clings to the pitted surface of her cheeks. Black crust lines her eyes.

"Hi," I say.

"Hi." Dom coughs into the crook of her elbow. She tries to smile, but it's gruesome. The smile drops from her chin. Her eyes bounce like Skittles. "You wanted to talk?"

"Yeah, uh. Let's sit in the living room."

She follows me, scratching her arm through a gash in the sleeve of her lace kimono. The living room is empty, and I wonder where Tree is hiding. No trace of her. A curtain ripples, and I startle. Could Dom have seen? But no, she's hovering by the couch. Where she scratched behind my ears and oiled my

hands. Where we passed afternoons and nights. Where I realized she was maybe the only one who loved me since Mona.

She's scanning the room, bouncing on her heels. Not the
twitch of suspicion, but the twitch of an addict.

"Are you okay?" I can't help it. She's still my best friend.

She blinks at the gap between the couch seat and the floor.
She is meek and trembling. If I could persuade her to drop
her investigation, convince her she's crazy, and that she needs
to get clean, I could get Tree to back off. Invite Dom to work
with us, even. She'd be a great addition to the team.

"Dom—"

"Tell me what's going on." She is alarmingly lucid all of a
sudden. It slaps me in the face like raw salmon, and the fantasy drains away. There is no way out of this.

"It's not what you think."

"Tell me, what do I think? You always seem to know." A
reversal, a dizzying inversion. All the moments with Dom
throughout the years laid out, the perspective altered. My
chest feels curiously empty, scooped out with a melon baller.
We are all strangers to one another. Perhaps no one is stranger
than the one we think we know best. Mona taught me that.

But I seem to have forgotten. Fourteen years is a long time
to remember.

I reach into the back pocket of my shorts. From here, everything happens so fast. Tree lunges from nowhere and tackles
Dom to the ground.

"Sophia! What the fuck!" Dom says. Muffled, her mouth
pressed to the parquet. I will need to Swiffer when this is over.

They are both yelling for me now, Tree and Dom. Dom
and Tree. My name sputtered and spit and swallowed. I might
be screaming. I don't hear it, but my throat is scraped.

Tree pushes Dom's arm into the floor. She forces it straight. The skinned-over veins in her inner elbow shine like the inside of a shell. I can hear the ocean in her.

I am holding the syringe. I am washing the next dish.

Dom worms under Tree, pinned by her palms and knees, her skirt tears, revealing a burnished thigh dimpled with bruises.

"Who is this crazy bitch?" Dom screams. "Wait, is that . . . Tree Whitestone?"

"Sophia, what the fuck are you waiting for, please?" Tree says.

My mind rejoins my body. I lower myself. It's like prayer. Kneeling and supplicant, hands gathered with the syringe between them.

Forgive me, Father. Whose Father? Certainly not mine.

The needle's point slips into a jumping vein in the crease of Dom's elbow. I am sinking the syringe, I am depressing the plunger. I am drying the dish.

Euphoria breaks across Dom's face like fresh winter sunlight. "Soph . . ." It's the last sound she makes, like that of a door creaking shut.

Tree falls to the side. Hair sticks to her forehead in sweaty clumps. Her headband has been knocked out of place and her chest heaves with the effort of wrestling Dom, surprisingly strong for an addict who does not exercise. Dom, who shakes. A woozy half smile flits over her face. My hands still grip the syringe's plunger. We make a holy tableau.

For a long time, the only sound is the round of our breathing. Three pulsing inhales; three puffed exhales. A siren outside.

Then three becomes two, and the world falls quiet.

JULY

2008

By the time Mona was back at school, everything had changed. I had been meeting Chase during her absent afternoons. Some days I walked to Clark's after the last period. He'd have a coffee waiting. Milk, no sugar, the way I liked it. I'd drink the coffee near the back of the store and flip through lewd magazines, fielding Chase's questions between customers. Then he'd lock the store, and we'd spend his break kissing and sharing a joint in the alley.

On his days off he'd pick me up from school. We'd drive to a diner or a coffee shop in a different neighborhood, somewhere we would not be recognized. Once we went to the mall to buy a suit for his cousin's wedding. We trawled the men's department at Macy's holding hands. He looked extremely handsome in the tepid department store lighting. I noticed faint lines around his eyes when he smiled in the three-paneled mirror.

I rarely let myself wonder how old he was. When I day-dreamed about his life outside of me, I pictured college. He never spoke of classes, but he said little about anything. That day at the mall, he seemed adult enough to scare me. Like I knew we could be nothing more than this: an illicit day spent shopping, play-acting coupledom.

There was never a question of whether I'd go with him to the wedding, but in the coming weeks I daydreamed about it constantly. I pictured organza. Lily of the Valley. Slow dancing under a canopy of fairy lights. I had never been to a wedding.

Another time we went to the movies. A boring Western epic with long shots of the desert spliced with fight scenes. What Mona would have called *a boy movie*. At that age, I chafed at the suggestion that I would not like the same things that boys did, but truth be told, I dozed on and off, waking in occasional fits and starts to the sound of gunfire. My body was sideways in the seat, so the first thing I saw when I opened my eyes was Chase's face in silhouette. He was enraptured by the dynamics playing out on screen. The son, some up-and-coming actor far too moisturized to have recently journeyed through the desert, knelt before his bleeding father, an aging heartthrob who was still very sexy despite (or because of) his grizzled appearance. Sunset blazed behind them.

Chase fumbled in the dark for my hand, took it, squeezed. I closed my eyes again, pretended I was still asleep.

There were so many things we never discussed. We talked around our lives instead. Stories had a never-shared intimacy. I told him about my second-grade skating lessons, how I slammed my head on the ice during free skate and blacked out for a full thirty seconds. Chase told me about the year he drew a lightning bolt scar on his forehead every day after he got home from school, "So I could pretend to be Harry Potter."

He was probably older than I realized. I didn't know his last name. I wanted him to meet my mom someday. I had the date of his cousin's wedding circled in pink Sharpie in my school planner, nursed fantasies of him showing up in a limousine, whisking me to the reception and showing me off to his family. Pictured him in the audience at graduation next year, clapping louder than anyone when I walked across the stage with my diploma.

I was in love, or a form of love. The kind of love that you can only have once, when you are very young and understand little about the realities of other people. But at sixteen, what we had was enough. I felt blessed. I'd waited for this day to come, and now it was here: I belonged to someone.

Mona changed the subject when I mentioned Chase. We saw each other less and less. She was thinner each time. Older looking, too. Lines formed around her eyes and her lips developed a dissatisfied pucker. We had been plunged into a future neither of us could have imagined when we were just two girls playing Barbies in my basement.

I didn't know how to handle it; I turned away.

10

I'm staring at the glob of spinach between my mother's front teeth. This is our bimonthly brunch at Uva on the Upper East Side, the only part of the city in which my staunchly suburban parents willingly set foot. They regard the wedding cake townhouses, the women in yoga pants trailing Bichon Frisés from jeweled leashes, with awe.

Every other month I take the 6 uptown and sit across from my parents in a booth, spitefully drinking three cups of black coffee against my mother's repeated assertions that I will stain my teeth. By this time she will have finished her updates on the neighbors' adult children: so-and-so's son is starting a residency at New York-Presbyterian, someone else's daughter has joined the Peace Corps, another daughter's wedding to a hedge fund manager was featured in the *New York Times'* Vows section.

I never hear about the burnouts, the ones with grease-slicked hair playing video games in their parents' basements, the ones with babies they didn't want and can't afford. They exist, though. I saw them all the time when I was a teenager, on the edges of the grocery store examining bags of lemons like they were some unimaginable delicacy, sitting in the park watching Mona and me drink beers wrapped in paper bags and cackling at nothing funny with haunted fallout shelter eyes.

But my mom, she can't acknowledge them. She's too afraid that I will end up as one.

When the bill comes, my parents hesitate. Dad dissects every line of the check to make sure not a cent is out of place. It's funny. I never noticed before that my mom has the Dianna Smart hair. Black as midnight with a tuck under the chin. Intelligent hair. Hair that can't be bothered to worry about itself. Mine falls down my back in wild tangles, snagging buttons, catching zippers and the soft rubber between subway doors. Worrying clumps tearing out in the shower. It never dries the same way twice.

After brunch, we cross to Central Park. A balmy day. Heat builds in oppressive columns between the buildings. It's climbing toward a hundred degrees. We sit on a bench by the Alice in Wonderland statue. Children scramble on Alice's huge legs, their tiny feet and hands sliding dangerously on the brass.

We watch them play for a minute and then I say, "We're on the edge of a major anti-aging breakthrough at work."

My mother's demeanor suddenly brightens. She's aging well, but she's vain, despite the hair that desperately tries to convey that she is not, and the stubborn line between her brows has deepened since our last brunch. She doesn't openly condone injectables, but mainly because she can't afford them. Dad seems curious, too. He washes his face once a day with Ivory soap.

"How does it work?" he says, taking on a classic masculine posture of questioning.

"We can't discuss the details just yet."

"Who is *we*? I only see my daughter," Mom says.

"You know what I mean, Mom. I'm not allowed to discuss the specifics of the product."

"When is it coming out?" my mother says. The *you're not getting any younger* is silent.

"Again, I'm not at liberty to discuss the details."

"If you can't tell us anything, why did you bring it up?" Dad checks his watch.

"I guess I thought you might be interested in what I'm working on."

"We are interested, but you don't have any information. What exactly is your role in this project? I thought your job was to look at pictures all day."

"My job is to drive the aesthetic of a multimillion-dollar beauty brand that about a billion women of all ages use daily. I created the imagery for a major campaign launching next month. You should be *proud*," I say.

"Proud is for jobs that make a difference. Doctors, lawyers. What's to be proud about? You play with makeup."

"Lawyers are crooks, you say that all the time."

"Crooks who make serious money," Dad adds, picking at an abandoned *New York Times* on the bench. He props it on a crossed knee.

Mom snatches it out of his hands and tosses it on the ground. "You don't know where that's been," she says.

I tell them I have plans with Richard, whom they love, give them each an affectionless kiss on the cheek, and leave them with their sunglasses flashing against the dull afternoon light.

MIDSUMMER BAKES INTO the fabric of the city without warning. Moving is like pressing through standing water, bacterial and heavy. Either I'm sticky with sweat or shivery from air-conditioning. We shuffle somnambulant between desk and kitchen, kitchen and bathroom. Interns huddle under blankets in the Ovaries to gossip and paint their nails. Their numbers swell, reaching a peak. *Hunting season*, Gemma and Tree call it.

Otherwise known as summer vacation.

Us full-timers track the interns like peacocks ready to breed. We learn their names in order to itemize them: Hanna J. has ideal cheekbones that give her face the distinction of fine Art Deco architecture. Lisbeth's riotous curls spin a glamorous tornado off her scalp. Brixton's lips are plush satin pillows, always slightly damp with a mist of spittle. Hannah with an H could take your eye out with those spears she has for nails that never break. Sara with an A has Kate Moss hips and Marilyn Monroe breasts.

We compare notes in closed-door meetings. Our priorities are different but the same: to be natural, to move with the grace of youth. To never worry about decay.

My evenings spread in lonely spirals now that Richard and Dom are gone. If I don't follow Tree to the bar, I take meandering walks around SoHo and watch my reflection bounce from store window to store window. Sometimes I take myself to dinner, three-course vegan meals with oat milk cappuccinos and almond cookies for dessert.

When I finally unlock my apartment—mine alone, now—it's to a haunted emptiness. My eyes skip over the door to the half-bath by the kitchen as I pour lime-infused water into a tall glass, add a wedge of fresh lime, and drink it standing over the sink, idly wondering if building management will eventually notice that Dom no longer lives here.

In the half-bath by the kitchen, the syringe I shoved into Dom's arm rests passively in the sink. The theory goes: if the door is never opened, the syringe was never there.

Dom's bathroom is a bigger problem. I can't think about Dom's bathroom, so I turn the TV on as loud as it will go, and pour myself another glass of lime water. I order tofu and sriracha salad from my third-favorite restaurant, where the food is good enough but healthy, and massage youthjuice into my hands while I wait. I spend a long time dragging the fatty substance the full length of each finger. Taking extra care at the cuticle, where a spear of pre-pain tingles if I press hard enough.

I know I should spread it around, onto my face and neck. But what I want more than eternity is to be whole again. Complete and not at war with myself. I'm addicted to smooth hands. A woman's hands show her age first.

Jamie is the intern I fixate on. We all have one, a pet. An unsullied version of ourselves. Jamie is mine. Kind of a muse. At a shoot last week I watched her crawl on the floor like a worm, slathering the models with moisturizer and oil. Perfect hands greased, she slipped when she tried to rest them on a pillar or a table. Smeared grease onto her stovepipe jeans. I asked the photographer to take a few close ups of her kneading a model's knife-sharp bronzed calf. The concept for the shoot was typical: naked women, physically unimpeachable but for a single sexy flaw. One with vitiligo splashing her cheeks and neck. One bulging with pregnancy, another an hourglass size-fourteen. My favorite girl had a teardrop-shaped scar like someone with a sharp nail had opened the skin beneath her left eye.

Tree was bored by the final images. Frankly, so was I. She asked my opinion and I glanced from Tree, to Gemma, who had created the mood board, then back to the monitor. "They feel familiar. Like I've seen them before."

"Familiar. You mean like nostalgic?" the photographer asks.

"No. Familiar like played out. Here, can we take a look at the ones I had you shoot before? I'd love to see how they turned out."

The photographer pulled up a close-up of Jamie's buttery hands depressing the skin on a model's slim, browned calf.

"I didn't okay these," Gemma said.

Tree tilted her face toward the monitor. "Shut up, Gem. These are perfect. I want more of them."

Gemma's anger manifested in a wriggle of the nose that pushed the upper half of her face toward the hairline. I didn't say anything; she really should be proud. I am what every boss wants: a worthy successor. She looked to the side and closed her eyes. By the time she opened them, she seemed settled. Eyes where they should be, forehead wrinkles gone.

Then Gemma gave me a fake smile. "Good work."

I took the compliment, however hollow, like flowers gathered loosely in my arms. "Thank you, Gemma."

Behind us, the camera bulbs flashed.

Dom's bathroom throbs, a wet black heart, calling for me from the core of the apartment. *Ba-dum, ba-dum, ba-dum.* I raise the volume on the television. Primary-colored bears babble. I change the channel. Blond brides-to-be dab their misty eyes as mirrors hedge their virginal reflections brimmed with lace and tulle, and they say, *yes!*

After the shoot we went to a biergarten so unlike Tree's usual spot. Long, splintered tables and drum-heavy music underscored by a sizzle-pop-clatter chorus of bottles opened and potatoes fried. Tree's hair had grown a few inches, fritzed ends grazing the collar of her striped men's button-down. Her silk jacket was balled in her lap, and her chest was smooth, no trace of the bristling dried skin I saw that night with Dom. She sipped water with a twist of lemon, silver bracelets clinking on her wrist.

Gemma, down at the other end next to the plus-size model and across from the one with vitiligo, listened as they swapped battle stories about a photographer they'd both worked with who was currently on trial for assaulting a supermodel on the set of his most famous shoot. I know the photos, which appeared in *Blonde* magazine, though the model is stubbornly brunette: her nipples protruding like knotted cherry stems from the sparse fabric of a soiled wife-beater, his hairy knuckles creeping into the frame to grasp a milky ankle, a microphone's netting caught between her teeth and smeared with pink lipstick.

Tree bunched her cocktail napkin hard and rolled her eyes when she heard the photographer's name. She is the kind of woman survivors dread—a self-proclaimed feminist who does not quite believe you didn't ask for it.

Because she would never let it happen to her. Because anything that happens to Tree Whitestone happens because she wanted it, at least a little bit.

I touched the toe of my shoe to Tree's leg and, when her eyes met mine, I rolled them. I noticed Jamie watching and instantly felt sort of bad, like maybe I went too far. Women supporting women and all that. I should set a better example.

"You did a *great* job today," I said to Jamie.

Jamie's nose stud winked. "I couldn't have done it without

your direction. The concept for the shoot was genius. I mean, *interns* with models. I love how it subverts the viewer's expectations. How did you come up with it?"

My hand floated next to my temple, as if to say I plucked the idea from the literal air like such low-hanging fruit. "Honestly, I had the idea while I watched you prepping the models. It just looked . . . right."

Tree glanced up from the mangled napkin in her hand. "That's the way to do it. You have to look for inspiration everywhere. It doesn't pay to be too rigid. When a concept is staid, you have to pivot. And that's what you did today. I'm really very proud." She dug her nail into the wood, where someone had carved A+M4Ever on the tabletop, and ran her index finger over the A's first diagonal repeatedly, deepening the groove.

I unconsciously mimicked the gesture on the leg of my jeans.

Jamie peered into her tonic water. A large ice cube hit the side of the glass mid-sip, splashing her mouth, and she sputtered and laughed. Her laughter made me laugh, and that spurred her on. Jamie dropped the glass with a gentle clatter and put her face in her hands. Her shoulders trembled and heaved. I bit my lower lip, my chest vibrating.

When we regained composure, I invited her outside for a smoke.

On the sidewalk, Jamie gratefully accepted my vape, and we passed it back and forth for a few minutes. The ground shone black like a mouth from rainfall, the air was light and cool, a rare treat of a summer night. I almost wished I had a sweater.

Jamie handed me the vape and kicked at a crack in the sidewalk with her black suede creepers. I flinched as the delicate fabric hit moist concrete. Suede was forbidden in my house growing up. Too expensive, my parents said. Too impractical.

"Nice shoes." I took another puff.

Jamie studied her feet. "Thanks."

"There's always a waitlist for those."

Jamie shrugged, making it clear she's never had to wait in all her life. "My brother got them for me. He's a sneakerhead. Thank you again. For today. It was a great opportunity."

Tempting, the idea of telling her the truth. That my burst of inspiration was rooted in her humiliation. I wanted to see her on her knees, scrubbing. Cinderella in the ashes. Getting her hands dirty. Porny, the product like lubricant or engine oil, a slick, tanned substance inviting the viewer into a private moment.

In that way, I was no better than the pervy photographer with one hand on the camera, the other on his dick. I might as well have been masturbating with my tongue hanging out, that's how much I enjoyed seeing Jamie suffer.

But she thanked me for it, and I felt like a genius or a god.

She started rambling about how she looked up to me, how I was like the older sister she never had. The street shrunk around her and pulsed with a white time-travel light, and then it was Mona puffing on my Juul, older than I ever saw her, the baby fat flushed from her jaw, the bones of her knuckles more pronounced.

She pulled her hand from her mouth. The shift in motion caused a shift in time. The music from the biergarten returned, and it was Jamie again, Jamie and me. Jamie, the one who survived. And I hate to say it, I do, but her eyeliner was perfect. The wings slanted from the center of her face, elongating her features, shaping her feline and adult.

The guest bathroom intrudes on my thoughts again. I'm back in the living room in the television's infinite blue light.

One episode and then another. The brides are all the same. Their frozen foreheads strain as they squeeze out tears. Their mealy décolletage turns red against spoked lace. Accompanied by aunts, mothers, cousins, best friends who are interchangeable. Like stale HEBE interns, they flicker on the screen and out of my memory.

I chug a lemon water and burn through three turmeric root pods in a row. My heart rate slows. A car honks outside, followed by a siren's low and mournful moan.

MY PHONE GOES off inside the couch cushions. It's late, past midnight. I've been napping in front of a crime show, the show dripping into my dreams, giving them a vividly sordid, noirish flavor.

I pry the phone free from the couch. It's Emily from work. *We live in the same neighborhood, right? East Village?*

On the screen a grizzled cop, slope-shouldered, describes the moment he walked into a murdered woman's house. *Guts on the walls. Guts on the ceiling.* Emily texts again immediately. Asks if we can meet tomorrow. She drops a pin: Tompkins Square Park.

In the morning, I walk over to the park. Emily isn't there yet. I enter and sit on a splintered bench near the perimeter. A blond boy, like a rugged, dirty Justin Bieber, lies on the opposite bench. He at first appears to be asleep, but he shifts when he spots me and smiles. His teeth are unnervingly bright.

I'm reminded how vulnerable I am, a woman alone. Veins visible on my arms and legs. He could rip me apart, turn me inside out.

I pull my phone from my bag, open and close various apps. The boy gets bored, drapes an arm over his eyes. I study his lusterless mop cut, the torn collar of his yellow and black checked shirt. Within seconds he is snoring.

Fifteen minutes pass, and still no Emily. She hasn't texted since she told me where to meet her. The park is ominous, the circumstances strange. Emily isn't part of Tree's inner circle; she doesn't know what she does to stay perfect. But maybe, I think, she does know.

I take a lap around the park, passing calcified heroin addicts, homeless teenagers, NYU students, chatoyant and loud, their motions echoing with the click of a metal credit card hitting a table. I round the path toward where I started, the bench now occupied by another young woman that I initially assume is Emily, but soon enough realize is blond and loose to Emily's prim brunette. It's Tree.

On instinct I duck behind the nearest tree trunk. Bark flakes onto my shirt.

Tree crosses, uncrosses her long legs. Dancer's legs. She wears a short floral dress with absurd pleats. A small bag sits on her hip, the chain strap nestled on her bony chest. From this vantage, she could be a lost child. Tree opens her mouth. Says something I don't hear to the boy, no longer asleep on the bench.

Abruptly she stands, steps onto the path, cuts a diagonal through the park. Pushes a signaling hand through her hair. The boy trails her to a tuft of bushes, where a third figure emerges, positioning himself in Tree's way. She stops. The figure is male, wearing a purple sweatshirt, hood up, white cords pulled around his chin.

Ninety-five degrees in the park and I'm sweating through

my shirt, linen sticking to my torso. Laughter filters, a sound like crystals on a chandelier rubbing together. Whoever this is, Tree has met him before. From the pocket of his hoodie he pulls a shiny, floppy object. Tree reaches for the jewel-like thing, a bag of some sort, and the man twists his arm overhead, out of her reach. He turns and walks back into the frill of bushes lining the park. Tree glances over her shoulder in my general direction and then follows him out of sight.

I think of the parks Mona and I hung out in as teenagers. Suburban parks with thin ruffles of trees through which you could see the hunched beetle spines of cars parked on the street, the knots of kids loitering outside the church after Friday evening youth group.

Here, in this park, a needle is near my toe. Somewhere, a barking dog. Somewhere, snoring. Somewhere, Tree, raped or killed.

I feel infected just standing here. I want to wash my clothes. Scrub between my nails until they bleed. Last week, a college girl was beheaded in Riverside Park. A Columbia student in search of drugs, or a better view of the river. Nature is the most dangerous thing for all it promises and all it conceals. And the park is the closest thing you get to nature around here.

Peering around the rough column of bark, I watch what must be a transaction between a boy with stringy bangs and a tan girl with gold gladiator sandals lashed up her thick runner's calves. She looks as nervous as I feel, yanking her too-small outfit, which I can tell she wore in hopes that her sexiness would garner a discount on the pills the boy hands over in a cloudy Ziploc. The girl shakes hair out of her eyes. Their bangs are mirror images, the boy's and the girl's. If they stood side by side, their hair would make a heart. The popular girl and the sad, weird boy who likely hopes the drugs will mix up her serotonin in such a way that she falls accidentally in love with him, the boy who provided the high.

She looks like an Ashley.

More bark flakes off, landing on my skirt, my shoes, my pristine shirt. Tree reappears, smoothing wrinkles from her pleats. Dabbing the corner of her mouth with a napkin. The man comes up behind her and walks in the opposite direction without a goodbye. His backpack is dotted with patches and there are holes in his jeans.

Tree's eyes telescope around the park. There is fear there, yes. She is wondering if she's been caught. Cataloging, taking stock. It's possible to imagine that she knows I'm there, that she has spotted me and chosen to let me remain hidden. That this is something she wants me to see. She reveals herself to me in ways that are beyond language.

I see you. I want to shout it. *We are the same.*

But she's closing for the night, a garage door sliding down. Her body language is contained, and she doesn't face me. She gazes toward the sidewalk. Beyond this park, the Village and, further, the whole city. Tree's city. She walks off, and soon is no longer visible. On the bush she crawled out of there's a white spot standing out against the leaves. A piece of Tree's skirt tangled in a thorny branch, torn.

I retrieve the fabric, tuck it deep into my bag. There, I find my phone. Emily, I remember. No messages from her, or anyone else.

2008

School ended on a sun-splashed David Hockney afternoon. I stood from emptying my locker to find Mona next to the industrial garbage can I'd wheeled over. She'd lifted an English test off the top of the papers I'd chucked into the trash and was reading my responses to the short answer essay questions from the English lit midterm about *Lord of the Flies*.

"Huh. So that's what the conch symbolizes," she said, and tossed the sheet aside, not into the garbage but onto the floor. It skimmed the linoleum, as if buoyed by a small wind, and landed in the path of a startled freshman who then stepped on it with a neon-yellow flip-flop.

"What's up?" I said. I tried to keep my voice steady, as if it wasn't a surprise to see her there. As if everything was the same between us.

"Come to the pool with me? I'm fucking crawling out of my skin." Mona flopped against the row of lockers, rattling them like pills in a plastic bottle.

We stopped by my house for swimsuits. We traded wardrobes like chips from the same bag. Mona was taller, but my clothes were nicer. I let her wear my favorite sunflower bikini and chose a boring striped option. Chase's attention had made me benevolent. I smiled at strangers now. On a family trip to the city, I placed a five-dollar bill in a homeless woman's wicker basket outside Macy's. I entertained the idea of volunteering at a women's shelter that summer. And I felt especially generous toward Mona in the bland 3 P.M. cavern of a recently kicked-off summer vacation.

At the pool we tossed our cutoffs aside and splayed on two coveted chairs under a large umbrella. Most of the young children were home for snacks and naps, and the frenetic energy of the earlier afternoon had given way to a laconic sparseness. If I focused on the junction of jewel-blue water and sandblasted tile, I could teleport to a cubed glass house in the Hollywood Hills. Inevitably some ungainly, over-tanned limbs would soon splash into the frame and remind me exactly where I was. But for the time being, it was bliss.

Mona was a dream, laid on her stomach, hands stretched to the floor and sunglasses perched on the end of her nose. Her beauty could not be denied, though her ribs poked the skin on her back and fading bruises littered her legs.

Questions percolated my diaphragm, scraped at my throat. Oh, how much easier it was to say nothing. I mindlessly chewed a handful of chips, salt and vinegar blighting my taste buds. To wonder is the natural state of the teenage mind—or at least it was for mine. Asking was the impossible step; truth was, I didn't want answers. Answers shut you off from the possibility that everything was fine.

Mona rolled onto her back. Sunglasses slid down the bridge of her nose to settle against her face. She exhaled through her mouth.

I turned my attention back to the pool. Three blond heads bobbed in the shallow end. "The Ashleys are here," I said.

Mona sat up, eyed them like a shark. "Ew. Don't they have a food court to terrorize?"

Mona hated the Ashleys with an intensity I couldn't muster. To her, they symbolized injustice. Systemic oppression. Class warfare. Mona and Ashley R. had been close as kids. They were neighbors, their moms were friends. Before Ashley R.'s mom quit working to stay home and bake cupcakes with her Valium collection, she worked at a pharmacy three days a week. Mona's mom watched both girls in the mornings before her afternoon shift at an Irish pub down the street from Clark's. Photos of Mona and Ashley R., plush as stuffed animals fresh from the toy store, decorated the credenza in Mona's dining room, a reminder of their brief brush with glamour. My favorite showed them in an inflatable kiddie pool. Ashley sat in the water holding a rubber duck. Mona stood and shielded her eyes against the sun, little face screwed up like a raisin.

When I asked why Mona's mom held on to the photos even though she hadn't spoken to Ashley's mom in years, Mona said, "She wants to remember what it was like for us to be them. The golden girls."

Months after the pool photo was taken, Ashley's mom quit her job, Mona's parents divorced, and I met Mona at day care. History has a way of slotting you in your place.

The Ashleys, shielded by bug-eyed shades, zeroed in on us. The pool was their territory. We rarely came here, preferring to idle the hours in the park. The Ashleys' faces rose with the kind of amused curiosity that comes before a bitch-storm.

As they climbed out of the pool, hips ringed with towels,

Mona and I busily debated who was hotter, Pete from Fall Out Boy or Adam from Taking Back Sunday. The conversation was just for show; we already had an agreed-upon position. Adam was more classically attractive, but Pete had that energy. Like he wanted nothing more than to eat you out for hours.

I thought, fleetingly, of Chase. We hadn't had sex, but I felt us building to it the same way a train seems to gather speed just before it slides through a tunnel.

We ignored the Ashleys as they formed a half circle around our chairs. I liked having an audience. Each sentence took on a performative double meaning. My voice slipped up an octave. We felt the Ashleys grow agitated the longer we refused to acknowledge them. These girls were not used to waiting.

Suddenly, Ashley R. sat down on the edge of my lounge chair. I was positioned sideways with my legs dangling, facing Mona, so when she sat, Ashley R.'s knees grazed my thigh. Her skin was very warm, like freshly baked bread. She smelled of Banana Boat and vanilla body spray. Girlhood in a bottle.

She reached over, plucked my sunglasses from my face, dropped them on the deck, raised one flip-flopped foot, and stomped.

I held my breath as the lenses shattered.

The five of us remained suspended. Time bent and twisted to catch us at once in the moment before, during, and after the assault on my Ray-Bans. It must have been only a minute, but it stretched to fill an hour. Mona broke the collective trance; she lunged at Ashley R. and their bodies rumbled onto the concrete.

I lost track of myself, and then I was standing up, clutching Ashley Mac's arm to my side. She didn't shrug me off, but reached up and squeezed my hand, our flesh white with tension. Beside us, Ashley Mick yelped and covered her mouth.

Mona and Ashley R. scrabbled, inching closer to the pool. The lifeguard's whistle cut across the grounds, clear and crisp as a gunshot. Neither girl reacted. They were lost in their hatred, a hatred extra fierce because it came entwined with ancient, rooted love.

The two girls gained momentum on the damp stone. Ashley Mac's nails sunk into my palm as we watched the alien mass of their bodies, one girl with too many limbs, crack the jeweled surface of the pool.

Time slowed as the water fractured, crowning them in reflective shards. The lifeguard puffed on his whistle again, producing a weaker sound, and dove in after them. Splashes all around, filling the sky. Ashley Mac dropped my hand, and there was no one there to yell *no running!* and, gleefully, we ran closer to the pool's edge. The lifeguard, the oppressor of our childhood summers, was otherwise occupied in a feeble attempt to pry our friends apart. In the bliss of the water, they spun like dancers.

The lifeguard wedged between the girls, wrenching them in opposite directions. Mona and Ashley R. surfaced, chests puffed, skin waterlogged. Hair plastered to their necks. Mona's sunglasses floated by like a child's toy sailboat. A bruise bloomed on Ashley R.'s cheek. Her bottom lip, swollen and distended, resembled an engorged caterpillar. Mona, winded, was otherwise unscathed.

Pool dwellers had scattered during the fray. Now they clung to the tiled rim, too stunned to move. Mothers ferried the few children who remained, pulled their still-dripping bodies into their clothes, wrapped towels around their small heads in lopsided leaning towers, shoved them toward the parking lot, hissing warnings.

The lifeguard, a muscular, top-heavy senior boy named, in all seriousness, Rick Hardback, spoke in low tones. Mona rolled her eyes, collected her sunglasses, and dragged herself against the panicked current to the pool ladder.

"Let's go," she growled. I felt the burn of the crowd's stare as we collected our towels and errant clothes from the loungers and began the slow march to the gate.

I shrugged on my oversized flannel, but Mona flagrantly displayed her soaked bikini. Taut, high ass cheeks and flexed haunches. She was too thin, but always stunning.

Mona walked ahead until we reached the end of the block. Then she roughly pulled on her shorts and collapsed on the curb. She rested her forehead on her knees and began to cry. Hard, like an angry child. Snot and tears ran down her face.

Big, obvious displays of emotion made me uncomfortable. I hugged myself, tried to get small while I waited for Mona to tire herself out. Eventually I sat down next to her and rested my chin on her shoulder.

"This isn't about the sunglasses," I said.

She lifted her spine slightly so she could see me while angled downward, a troubled comma. A treble clef of pain.

"You can tell me," I added. "Whatever it is, you can tell me."

Mona stood quickly, causing my teeth to clamp from the force of her pushing into my jaw, and started off down the street. Gnarled fingers of wet hair hung limp and scraggly down her back. Her knees overextended in a childish convex as she walked.

I hesitated. But I knew that if I didn't follow, it would be the end of something I was not yet ready to lose. And so, I went.

11

The interns swell and shrink in numbers. Right now they fit on one side of a conference table. One morning I ask for a coffee and no one appears. When I look up, the intern table is empty. Minus Jamie, lost in her laptop.

Emily hasn't been in since the day she stood me up in the park. Jamie has been filling in for her role, taking on additional tasks pertaining to the blog. The other interns, what's left of them, resent her for being singled out, but lack the drive to do much about it. Mostly they slump on their exercise balls and frown at their phones. Or they groom themselves. File their nails, sweeping keratin dust onto the floor. Tweeze their eyebrows.

Today Jamie is wearing a knitted midi-length House of Sunny dress with an abstract lily pad pattern, skinny straps, and three oval cutouts on the back. Her shoulder blades jut from the fabric, stretching the knit. She must be cold, but she doesn't show it. On her feet are clear jelly sandals like the ones I wore in third grade. Her hair is held off her neck by a tortoiseshell claw clip. Every part of her outfit could have come from the dollar store. Her movements, however, drip with money. There is weight to her demeanor, solidity. She walks like she knows there is a place for her, wherever she goes.

I invite her to join me for a matcha since there is no one to make my coffee. We drink them on the steps outside a boutique on Howard Street. Mannequins in the window with featureless faces.

On her phone Jamie shows me the profile of a robot who is also a model. The bio: "Robbie. 19. Model/robot."

"A little on the nose," I say.

Jamie shifts her thumb and a pert, freckled face fills the screen. Space buns on either side of her head. Chunks of blue glitter fill the part. Her skin is eerily plastic, and her torso has a boneless Gumby twist. Too long and stretched. Like a factory floor accident.

"That," I say, "is extremely fucked up."

"Do you think so?" Jamie stretches one leg down the steps, the other bent toward the sky. Her dress fans over her lower body, phone resting in the hammock between her thighs. "I think I'd like to be a robot. No aches and pains. Ageless forever. Being eighty but looking twenty-five. I think it would be wonderful."

Clumps of matcha graze my tongue as I finish the latte, set the empty cup on the next stair. The irony is not lost on me. "I'd rather be a vampire."

Jamie bounces her phone in the cradle of her skirt. "But you'd have to drink *blood*." She waves her fingers on either side of her head.

"You'd get used to it, if that's all you could eat." Something about it even appeals to me. Not the blood so much as the singular drive for sustenance. The ability to survive with one type of nourishment. The end of choice.

Jamie wrinkles her nose; the stud protrudes. "Download my brain to the Cloud and make me an AI. Much cleaner that way." We drop our cups in the trash and head toward Lafayette. "Hey, I was thinking. Wouldn't it be cool to use Robbie in a shoot?"

"One of our shoots?"

"Yeah. I just heard Tree talking about an anti-aging formula the product development team is testing and it's like, what better model to use? She literally doesn't age."

My pulse ticks in my ears. "I didn't realize you were interested in creative direction."

"I'm interested in everything," she says. Her all-the-time-in-the-world nonchalance enrages me. Tempting as it is to tell her I hate the idea of using Robbie to advertise youthjuice, that I think it's tacky and misleading, in service of the impossible desire to live forever, I can't bring myself to say it. Because maybe it's a good idea. Maybe it's genius.

NYPD is parked in front of the HEBE building. Jamie and I share a loaded glance and move silently through the downstairs lobby and the elevator to the third floor. The office is unusually quiet. Always zen, now held in suspension. Starla guards her post but doesn't greet us. When I approach the desk, I see the cordless landline balanced between her cheek and shoulder. Jamie and I split off to our respective tables without speaking.

My desk mate, a quiet web developer named Amy, leans over and points with her thumb. "The cops are in Tree's office; they're talking to everyone."

"About what?" My hands twitch.

"They didn't say. Starla brought them straight in to see Tree. Gemma is in there now."

Marigold's posture at her desk betrays religious fanaticism. She opens a drawer, takes something out. Stretches a rubber band between her hands. She pulls so hard it snaps, then she sees me see her wince.

The door to Tree's office opens. Gemma is followed out by a uniformed officer with stocky shoulders and a trim waist. Military haircut. He could be a stripper, if not for the substantial gun rattling at his hip. He could be an action figure. The cop deposits Gemma in an Ovary and confers with Marigold, who levels her gaze at me. Slowly, the cop starts to walk. His measured gait strikes the floorboards. Everyone stares as he pauses at my side and glances at my laptop screen, the innocent grid of my company email. I have the urge to slam it shut.

"Are you Sophia Bannion?"

"That's me." I try to keep it light, with a nervous chuckle that only makes me feel guiltier. I'm ready to confess to anything. Even things I haven't yet done.

He's unamused. "We'd like to ask you a few questions."

"I'm sure I can't help you."

"Don't be so sure. Most people don't know what they know."

I stand and present my arms: *after you*. Marigold pointedly does not look up as we pass.

The room feels off. It's two things: Tree's absence, and the way the furniture has been subtly rearranged to hint at interrogation. The chairs that are normally opposite Tree's side of the desk are now positioned in front of the couch. One chair is empty, the other occupied by a different officer. This one is a woman, tan complexion, pulled-back hair, with a gentler demeanor than her partner. This observation feels sexist, but also true.

The fact that they are both uniformed comforts me a little. If this were about a serious matter, like dozens of murdered interns, wouldn't there be a detective? Someone in a suit, gun hidden by the folds of a Brooks Brothers blazer. These cops have guns proudly displayed on their belts like fanny packs.

The first officer positions me on the couch and takes the empty chair. "Thank you for agreeing to speak with us, Ms. Bannion," the woman says, sliding a strand of hair behind an ear decorated with two tiny gold hoop earrings. She can't be much older than I am.

"What's this about?" My palms itch. I keep them pressed into the couch cushion.

"How well do you know your coworker Emily Russell?" The man's beefy hands dwarf a tiny notepad and pen, poised to take notes.

"Not super well. We're friendly."

"Her family has reported her missing. Did she tell you where she planned to go?"

I hesitate. Then I begin to describe the last time I heard from Emily, how she made it sound urgent and ditched me at Tompkins Square Park. There's no point in hiding it; if they find her phone, they'll find our exchanges and figure out that I lied.

They ask a few more questions, poke my story for weak joints. The man's miniscule pad strains under the weight of his meaty paws. Since he won't cross his legs, presumably due to some innate rejection of perceived femininity, he's hunched precipitously over the notepad.

Once the officers decide I'm no use to them, the woman walks me to the door. Up close she looks even younger than I am. After she's done here, will she meet friends for a drink?

Does she have a date planned? She shakes my hand and gives me a number to call if I remember a detail that seems relevant. I joke about how I thought all cops could be reached at 911, but she doesn't smile. I feel her watch me return to my desk, force myself to sit down and check my email like everything is normal. I wait until the woman summons Marigold, who puts up some resistance at the idea of abandoning her post, then gives in and charges into Tree's office, slamming the door.

I struggle to stay calm while I go into a small bathroom down a vacant corridor. This is where we direct VIP guests who stop by for coffee meetings. Employees rarely use it, unless they don't want to be overheard.

I grip the sides of the sink, turn the knobs as far as they will go, and vomit directly into the spray. Clotted acai and raspberry from breakfast floats in the water. Mealy swirls of matcha. A gruesome, muddied rainbow. My reflection shimmers and jumps. A ghoul, strings of brown hair clumped with sweat and a toothless purple mouth, stares back. Behind her is a younger girl. Face sickly green like a healing bruise. She parts her cracked lips and a mess of pastel pills spills out, dissolving easily as sidewalk chalk in the rain.

At the same time my mouth is opening and I'm vomiting violet foam into the sink, my eyes are leaking fluid. The room rattles, shapes stretch and repeat, and then it is just me in the mirror. Me, and the green sconce on the wall behind me that I thought was a face. Water is still running. Huge wet spots plaster my shirt to my torso, skin pink through the transparent linen. I lift my hands, trembling, but whole as two lilies birthed from the dirt.

I start to laugh, and the laughter morphs into a hysterical cackle. Tears spill down, drip off my nose and chin. I hiccup and eventually catch my breath. Stick out my tongue. Then I rinse my mouth and stand under the automatic dryer, blasting hot air onto my soaked shirt. Pain behind my eyes and in my throat from vomiting. Faint scratches I don't remember making highlight my throat. Like I tried to claw my larynx out. I take stock in the mirror. Shirt a rumpled mess. Forehead pinched. Two frown lines carved on either side of my downturned mouth. Over-washed, like a sad sweater wrung out of shape.

Leaving the bathroom, I expect a receiving line. It seems impossible that I went undetected. But there's no one; the office is preoccupied with the loftier drama of a missing coworker. Interns stage-whisper behind ice-flat curtains of hair.

"Are they interviewing everybody?"

"I hope the hot cop asks to see me."

"That's not how it works. They're, like, both in there."

"Whatever, she's hot too."

"It's a police interview, not a porn shoot."

"Why not both?"

"Ugh, do you think she's like . . . actually missing? Or did she just run away?"

"On detective shows they always think the girl ran away. But it's always a murder."

"Who's gonna be next?"

"What if it's you?"

THE GUEST BATHROOM beckons from the bowels of the apartment. My apartment. A shifting, wet sound from behind the door. Like a soaked towel slapping the tile. I turn the television volume as high as it will go and take my Baggu totes full of groceries into the kitchen. Unloading the ingredients for dinner, I listen to NY1. Fill a pot with water from the tap, add a sprinkle of Kosher salt, and set it on the burner.

"A young woman from Westchester County was reported missing on Monday. Authorities say she was last seen leaving her apartment on Saturday afternoon."

I drop the jar of nutritional yeast I'm shaking into a mixture of miso paste and cashew butter for vegan cacio e pepe. A favorite dinner of mine that I made for Richard on special occasions. He claimed to love it, but he moved his tongue critically as he chewed, his palate searching out the ways that the sauce wasn't thick or cheesy enough, the hint of cashew he swore he couldn't taste.

"Just like the real thing," he said. But it wasn't, not even close.

The news report about Emily drones in the background. They don't mention me or HEBE by name, but refer to a coworker who was supposed to meet her in Tompkins Square Park. "This is the latest in a slew of young women's disappearances." A conservative talking head dials in and rants about a rise in crime.

I slam the flat side of a long knife onto a pile of peppercorns. Pungent air tickles my nose hairs and I sneeze. I focus on the clouded water as I stir the spaghetti. I'm fine. Everything is fine. Only there's a smell, the tangy, mulchy bite of decay. Nothing a bit of palo santo incense can't fix. Dinner is ready and I pour yuzu seltzer into a glass, I'm going to eat in the living room, but another girl is missing, one I don't know, nothing to do with me, but I'm walking away, down the hall, and into the second bedroom. The door is there, light flooding the gaps around it. The light pulses and shudders. A bang followed by a steady, moist pulse. The beating of a heart. I hold my breath and open the door.

She's there, in the tub. Her limbs are arranged wrong. Like a Barbie whose arms and legs were ripped off and reattached off-kilter. At least somewhat well-preserved thanks to the formaldehyde I ordered on Amazon and shot into her veins. I owe that trick to our friend Jason Red. How long it will last, I have no idea. I haven't been able to do anything else with the body. Dom's body, the angel-blue husk that used to be my best friend. I'm starting to think I'm not capable of having friends, not really. As soon as I get close to someone, I rip them apart. For a while my hands were enough. But I need to face it—this is who I am.

Dom is easier to talk to like this. Sober as a judge, she sits perfectly still and listens. Her patient eyes stare at the ceiling while I perch on the toilet lid and tell her about Emily's disappearance between bites of cacio e pepe. Pepper crackles between my teeth.

Just saying it aloud makes me feel better. Convinces me I haven't done anything, not really. I helped an addict down her chosen path. I used a product my employer gave me. It's not my job to ask questions.

And I really don't know what happened to Emily.

Scraping the tines of my fork through the creamy sauce at the bottom of the bowl, I cast an appreciative gaze at Dom's profile, tilted to the heavens.

Even dead, she's still my best friend.

TREE IS ABSENT for two days. Otherwise, it's business as usual at HEBE. On the third day, Tree comes in at ten-thirty. Newly tan, the color strange and fake against her white-blond hair, she seems well-rested. She swans through the office, touches the top of Marigold's head, and they vanish into Tree's office. Five minutes later, Marigold returns to her desk.

My computer pings with a new email. A calendar invite to an all-hands meeting.

HEBE files into the right Ovary. Staffers take the fiberglass seats around the table, interns forming an asteroid belt around us.

Tree marches in and Marigold closes the door behind her.

"Team." Tree regards us as her children, hands cradled at her abdomen. She's wearing a satin headband and a plaid wool dress. Schoolmarmish, and wrong for the weather. She sits on top of the conference table like she owns it, which she does, she owns everything in this room, including us. Especially us.

She thanks us for our cooperation with the NYPD. Though, ideologically, she doesn't condone the police state, HEBE will do everything it can to support the search for Emily. There are currently no updates on Emily's case, but Tree will share new information as soon as she is able. Then she opens the meeting for questions.

Blinks around the circle, and finally an arm quavers upward.

This intern's black hair is arranged in a series of elaborate braids like a medieval crown. Earrings dangle around her neck. "Does this mean there's an open position?" A pause. The intern loses confidence, slumps in the chair. She tries again: "Emily's job?"

Such audacity I never would have suspected from an intern. Then again, it isn't all that surprising, is it? The way these girls barrel through the office, through the city, stomping on the rest of us with their designer shoes.

Tree squints. She's deciding how seriously to take the inquiry. Then she says, "Emily's job will be here for her. If— when—she is ready to return, HEBE will welcome her with open arms."

ANOTHER MEETING FOLLOWS. The Storytelling team and the product development department are planning for the next launch, a line of glossy lipsticks named after famous murder victims. Tree's idea is to reincarnate them. Worn on a living woman's mouth, these dead girls could experience things they never had the first time around. Our customers will breathe, eat, smoke, kiss, curse in their places. Classic blue-red is "JonBénet." Dark mauve, "Black Dahlia." Peach nude, my favorite shade, is "Sharon."

Marigold wonders how recent we can go with the names while toeing the line between provocative and déclassé. Gemma thinks it's a moot point—if we're doing it, might as well do it all the way. Debate ensues over whether the victims have to be dead, have to be women. We need six more names to round out the twelve-piece collection, thirty percent of which, Tree declares, should be women, or at least not cis-het men, of color.

Shades are assigned to each of us, handed over in unmarked plastic tubes. I uncap mine. A soft peony that, when swiped on my inner wrist, creates a near translucent stripe, as though I peeled back a rectangle of flesh to reveal the younger layer beneath.

Back at my desk, I navigate to an old social media site and surprise myself by typing "Chase Montgomery" into the search bar. I hadn't even been aware he was on my mind. Maybe it's a need to recall what it was like to feel so strongly about another person that I verged on evaporation. I don't recognize him among the collection of profiles that load on the page. None are an exact name match. A hazy mirror selfie, the face blocked by the flash, comes closest. But I can't be sure that it's him.

At times I honestly wonder if he existed, or if Mona and I conjured him in our collective teenage fever dream. Google yields nothing but a single hit on a people-finder database that lists an address. That's the only sign I can find, so unremarkable as to cast doubt on my own recollections. My memories are unfocused. There's the outline of his over-long hair against the gray interior of his ancient car, the smoky scent of his perennial black T-shirt, the amphibious movement of the fish tank in his bedroom, lit by the blue light of the television, his turtle, Ralph, a dark boulder weighing down the bottom.

I feel the details of his face slipping as I try to retain them, an ocean wave teasing rocks on the shore. He might not be a person at all, but a mirage from the past. I spend the afternoon searching for him out in the annals of the internet. Has he changed his name? Is he hiding from the government? He had a whiff of a serial predator about him, dating me when I was only sixteen. Even back then he seemed to have studied the art of grooming, plying me with vodka and making me feel smart with the weird little art-house movies he'd put on in the background while we were making out, forever steering my chin away from the screen.

I switch to googling victims. Paging through forums for unsolved mysteries and conspiracy theories, I jot names in Notes: Hae Min Lee, Madeleine McCann (too young?), Natalee Holloway. Missing and murdered. Mona fills my mind instead, a thousand incarnations. A child in a sandbox, lace-trimmed bloomers mushrooming her chubby legs, shoveling grains and dumping them on top of a naked Barbie doll; thirteen and sullen in a Nirvana T-shirt cut into a crop top, folding paper fortune tellers in the school cafeteria; sixteen and sucking a Blow Pop at the pool. And the last time I saw her is there, hovering, hovering.

I can't let it in.

I TALK TO Dom, and Dom talks back. Her fish-gap mouth doesn't move, but her voice bangs in my ears. Her voice and her heartbeat are my favorite songs. Around us the smell of Om-Mi-God patchouli and almond dust incense hide the creeping odor of death.

Since losing Dom I'm like a loose tooth rocking in someone's mouth, nervy and swollen. The slightest touch makes me cry out, a bump from a stranger's elbow on the train, a brush of a jacket on the sidewalk. I watch endless television. Sleep on and off on the couch while the fulgurating screen charges me like a battery.

In my head, Dom takes care of me. She scratches my scalp with checkerboard acrylics. That the fine-as-glass nails really belong to me doesn't matter. She feeds me granola bars, whisks the crumbs from my stained sweatshirt. Coaxes me into the shower. Rubs oil on my hands. She cooks elaborate recipes from my collection of raw vegan cookbooks. Stirs adaptogenic powder into my coffee. Blends concealer onto my face. Loving me the way I can't love myself.

But it is me. All along, it's been me. Dom is gone. There's no one left.

The fever breaks on a lonely weekend. I'm in the kitchen blending fresh nut butter in the Vitamix. Dom nowhere to be found. I don't sense her presence the way I did before. No ticking from the heart of the apartment. No phantom nurse-maid delivering me to health. I feel better than I have in weeks.

The following day, head clear, I go through Dom's purse.

Duane Reade receipts, dried husks of lipstick, a layer of sand and dirt on the bottom, and a tightly rolled joint. I take the joint outside. It's so hot on the fire escape that my hairline immediately begins to sweat. I have no idea what time it is, but the position of the sun indicates that it might be early evening.

I take off my sweatshirt. Underneath I have on a pink camisole, circa 2005. The lace trim stretches and gapes around my breasts. The tiny bow that used to sit between them has fallen off, leaving behind a few loose strings. Ugly red creases on my chest from lying in the same position, in the same shirt, since I got home from work on Friday. The tank top reeks of old perspiration, the body's foul perfume.

Suddenly Dom is back. Exuding health and fitness, color returned to her cheeks. Smelling fresher than ever. She lights the joint, puffs, ashes into a cracked terra-cotta pot. Then she presses the soggy end between my lips. "Breathe in."

Smoke constricts my lungs. I cough once, hard. Dom slaps me on the back and my nostrils burn. Then, an opening in my body. More space between my bones. An unbearable lightness. My ears seem impossibly far apart.

"You okay?" Dom floats in front of me. The city is a cardboard set piece, and we are the only real part.

"Sesame Street," I say.

Dom laughs. Hits my knee with hers. "There she is."

We smoke, her ghost and I, and we watch the street. Nothing much happens, but I laugh easily. At the hilarious shade of yellow when a taxi turns onto the block. At girls in bikini tops and cut-offs drinking from a bottle in a brown paper bag. I laugh at the darkening sky, I laugh at the lights coming on in the buildings, I laugh at the strange, improbable lives unfolding all at once and on top of each other at this precise moment in time.

I laugh at my dead best friend, alive beside me, smoking but not breathing. I laugh at the memory of Tree aflame with blood. Lit up like a rose. Baring her fangs.

And then I scream.

THE ALARM GOES off at the usual time. Alone in my wide bed, surrounded by striped sheets. Paranoia kept me up half the night, clawing at my face and shaking on the bathroom floor. Tree calling from every corner—behind the shower door, down the toilet's long throat. Bottles in the medicine cabinet rattled with the quiet boom of her voice. Blood gurgled from the faucets and striped the walls. The veins surged through my skin like interlocking highways. I clenched my fists to keep from tearing them out.

The colliding blades from the coffee grinder hurt my ears. I drink a large glass of lukewarm water from the tap. Rub my temples. Coffee is suddenly unappealing. I go into the bathroom and stare at my face. Ghastly. Puffy and gaunt. Shiny like an irritated wound. Lines trace my forehead, between the brows, the corners of my mouth. I can't remember when I last washed my face.

But my hands—they are perfect. Whole. Unbaked dough resting in a pan.

I shower, dry off, and open the medicine cabinets. The HEBE bottles, mashed from my fists, logos and names partly rubbed off, mock me. The jar of Tree's cream catches the light in the room, beams out like a flashlight.

I count to ten. Unscrew the lid, claw some moisturizer into my overgrown nails, and mash it onto my face. Closing the medicine cabinet, I catch myself in the mirror. I still look like shit, but shinier.

Then I go to work.

STARLA GREETS ME with a nod. I attend meetings: about the victim lipsticks, about a self-care serum the product team is developing in conjunction with a panel of mental health experts. Tree mentions an innovation she plans to unveil within a few months and smiles at me when she says it. Afterward, I scout girls online. A fifteen-year-old with an androgynous name who has gone viral for dancing hip-hop routines while yodeling has our look: freckles, sunshine smile, glossy lips. Natural as a heroine on a teen drama.

She's a decent dancer and an incredible yodeler. The moves look easy, lots of hand gestures and isolated hips tossed off like an afterthought. Her ribs are insane and her diaphragm visibly jumps as she sings. I scroll down to the beginning of her account.

In the first few videos there is no dancing, only yodeling. These have much less engagement from her followers. When she starts shaking her hips, that's when the metrics explode. Most of the comments are from men, but the ones from girls and women really stand out. Full of yearning, they say things like *i wish i was you* and *you look just like me when i was seventeen.* I bookmark her as an option for the lipstick campaign. We're using "real girls." I'd argued that it was too much. That we were courting controversy. At the very least, I added, a portion of the proceeds should go to a victims' rights organization.

Tree tapped the stylus for her tablet on her chin, worrying a red line, and considered. Then she said: "The victims' rights movement is very pro-law enforcement. This is more of a statement about misogyny in our culture." Which seemed to settle it.

I close the app. There's a new email in my HEBE inbox. Another update about Emily. The message is from Marigold's address, but the statement is signed by Tree. Actually signed, with an electronic version of her lilting signature. I skim it first, then go back to the top and read every word carefully, like I'm searching for hidden messages in the text.

Emily, it claims, purchased a one-way ticket to Prague the day she stood me up. I picture Emily in the shadow of the Astronomical Clock, shielded by sunglasses and tourists.

It's a nice fantasy.

"SUN IS THE number one cause of aging."

"I thought it was age."

"I use SPF fifty morning and night."

"At night?"

Resentment sets in, a nonspecific irritation. Every voice grates. A woman brushes my elbow with her puff-sleeve, and I want to wring her neck. Someone laughs too loud and I black out for a second, coming to with the polished edge of an end table gripped between my hands, tempering white-hot rage. Snippets of inane conversation come at me.

Two women sip sparkly, sugar-free apple juice and compare hair removal regimens. "There's something charmingly primitive about a blade against your skin," one of them says. "Plus, the exfoliation can't be beat."

The women notice me, and I look away. I wish Dom were here. She would mock these women to their faces while making them love her. But I'm all out of sorts tonight; I'm not sure I can remember my own name.

There are a few men here, nothing special. Dozens of cheap hedge fund copies, like someone went wild with a 3D printer on Wall Street. They mostly hang by the vegan charcuterie platter under the satin HEBE four-year anniversary banner hung over the windows.

Jamie twirls over in a Reformation jumpsuit with no back. Triangles of emerald fabric conceal her gravity-defying chest. Strings are tied loosely at the nape of her neck. I feel the distinct shape of her bones as we hug.

She gestures with a pint of kombucha. "Quite the party."

The men in suits appraise her, face then breasts then hips then toes. I angle so that her sloping vase of a back is turned toward them and sip my virgin martini. The olive settles at the V of the glass like an eyeball. The men's eyes bounce from Jamie's suppleness to my narrow, pinched stare. They flush when caught. Rub at their sweat with French cuffs.

I am powerful in this moment, imbued with womanly magic. I imagine they are all Richard. He was used to a meek, petty version of me. He's not familiar with the new me, whose heartbeat thrums so loud and steady I feel it in my ears. Whose blood is thick, red and white cells peacefully coexisting, veins pumped to near bursting. I haven't plucked a cuticle in weeks.

I take Jamie by the wrist and pull her away. "Who were those guys?" she says.

"Investors, probably. Venture capitalists."

"I thought our investors were women," Jamie says. She scans the crowd like she's expecting a start-up fairy godmother in head-to-toe Theory to appear, waving her checkbook.

"Some. But most VCs are men, it's just the reality."

Someone yells, "I want to dance!" Commotion from the three interns. The music, twinkling classical fare, isn't lively, but they push into the crowd anyway, making their own rhythm. No one can begrudge them, these fluttery butterflies. They reach for one another; they rotate and cling, they laugh, giddy children for whom the world is just a dream. They spin faster and faster, holding each other up, clearing a space on the floor. And then Tree is there, gossamer in white, dancing with them.

A few onlookers pull out their cell phone cameras. The HEBE staff watches from under the brutalist chandelier in Tree's dining room. Bright-eyed and pulsing like rabbits, the interns hold hands and twirl.

Tree's limbs flow like water. Her hair bright as spun straw, freshly peroxided, an orderly Red Sea parted down the middle. Berry lipstick. Her arms taper a touch dramatically around the elbows. Otherwise, she is a vision in twist-front crepe with a plunging V-neck, long sleeves, and a high center slit high-lighting a white fishnet-encased leg and a clear slingback heel with a geometric crystal butterfly alight on the PVC toe box.

She is an ice sculpture, the eighth wonder of the world. Even guests who aren't looking twist toward her, chins and knees and shoulders sloped in her direction. I can't tell if I want to be closer or as far away as possible, on the other side of the planet.

"Soph? We've been looking all over for you." Gemma steps around the dancers and air-kisses next to my cheek. She regards Jamie. "And . . . you! Great to see you, too."

Gemma tugs me toward a high table occupied by Marigold and Starla. Marigold turns up the corner of her mouth, an attempted smile. She's not drinking her beverage, an apple cider tincture, but swirling the golden liquid, dispelling car-bonation.

Her eyes glaze past my shoulder and I follow them to where Tree now sits on the settee, animatedly telling a story to an assembled group.

"I'm going to get a canapé," Marigold announces, then departs.

"What's with her?" I say.

Gemma repeatedly crumples and smooths a lavender cocktail napkin stamped with the HEBE logo. The paper softens and starts to disintegrate. "What *isn't* wrong with Marigold is the better question. She always has a stick up her ass."

"I hate these things," Gemma adds. "Tree sucks up all the oxygen in the room."

"Funny, I thought you liked it that way."

Gemma lifts her champagne flute. "You're very funny. Like that little stunt you pulled at the body oil shoot. Classic."

I put my glass down. Hold up my hands. "I'm sorry about that, truly."

"No need to apologize. It was rather impressive." She folds the corner of a fresh napkin. "My first week at HEBE, I was one of two editorial assistants, and a little bitter about it to be honest, considering I was Tree's best friend and she had begged me to work for her. I was all set to start business school when she came calling. One afternoon, the other EA left this notebook on her desk when she went to lunch. I'd seen her scribbling in it during meetings, so I peeked inside. It was a list of pitches. Some of them were crap. Rip-offs from blogs like the one your friend runs. Faux edgy shit. But one was really good. I memorized it and pitched the idea before she could at the next editorial meeting. Tree loved it. The other girl was so crushed."

"What was the pitch?"

"The saddest thing is, I don't remember."

"Did she quit?"

"Tree fired her a few weeks later for—get this—being boring. She actually said that in the termination meeting. *You're boring, you have boring ideas.* We laughed about it afterward."

"Why didn't she call you out? She had the notebook."

"I've asked myself that question so many times over the last few years, I swear. And do you wanna hear the worst part? Now she's dead."

"Dead, as in . . . moved back to her hometown to go to nursing school?"

"No, dead as in buried. Heroin overdose in the 1 OAK bathroom."

The noise I make, somewhere between human and not, an inanimate, strangled squeak.

"I know," Gemma says. "*1 OAK.* Like, what is this, 2005?"

SOMEONE HAS TURNED the lights low and the walls perform a quarter turn. Shadows set me off-balance. My heart is in my throat, a throbbing muscle. Hiccups I can't tamp down.

It's been an age since I've seen anyone I know. I look around for Gemma, Tree, Starla, Jamie. Even Marigold. The crowd has swallowed them all and I'm alone out here. I go deeper into the crushed bodies, over to the floor-to-ceiling window. I think of falling however many flights. Diving into the cold seam of the river.

When I spin around, the room's occupancy seems to have doubled. Claustrophobic, I move through the dense crush and duck into a hallway. The music sounds louder, as if funneled and amplified by the narrow walls and the lack of muffling bodies. This song. I've never listened to this song before, though I've heard it a million times. It's about wanting to drink until you die. Drowning from the inside out. The vocals are spun sugar, autotuned beyond recognition.

In the safety of the empty hallway, I slide down the wall until I'm sitting on the floor. The music bottoms me out. My head is heavy, and I lie down on the ground. Ear to the floor, voices reverberate through the boards. Drumbeats and foot-steps pulsing. My dress rides up my thighs. Suddenly, I'm scared that someone will come along. I push onto my hands, crawl backward until I'm kneeling, then stand. I peer into room after room. Most have doors open and the lights off. The one at the end of the hall has the door mostly closed, a lamp on inside. Two long shadows stretch into the hallway. Pressing an eye to the crack, keeping my weight back so I don't nudge the door farther open, I make out Tree with her back to me, and Marigold sitting on a bed, legs double-crossed with one ankle pretzeled around the other. Her blue shirt is wrinkled. Frizz surrounds her hair and expands her head by degrees. Her arms gesture wildly as she speaks in climbing whispers. Tree's posture is rigid.

Through a break in the music, I catch pieces: *can't believe* and *endangering everything.*

Tree turns her face, features drawn so far inward she looks like a preserved skull. I pull back. Her eyes trace the ground. Something glints, light off the edge of a knife, and I spot the glass in her hand just before she pitches it at the wall above Marigold's head, where it explodes.

Shards land on the pillows. The paint is streaked with brown liquid.

When the chaos clears, Marigold is doubled over, her hair a protective shell, her hands gnarled into the mattress. She looks up, almost at me. I step back, slamming into a girl in a leopard slip dress and square-toed Doc Martens. I run down the hall and shut myself into the farthest door on the opposite end of the hallway.

It's pitch-black, no windows, and a strong smell like rubber skidding on asphalt. Blindly reaching for a light switch, my hand grazes something cold and heavy. Slippery as a dead fish. I recoil, a knob of hard plastic on the wall jabs my spine. Feeling around, I find that it's a light switch and toggle it upward.

Warm light bathes the closet, but I am so, so cold. The blood drains from my face, just like the blood has drained from the body wrapped in a plastic garment bag and hanging from the closet rod. It's a woman, naked and colorless. Smooth as a Barbie. Chestnut hair and open mouth mashed against the plastic casing.

Mona. After all this time.

Splotches of pink blur and I think I'm going to pass out. Oh, I'm going to pass out. My breath returns when I realize the pink spots are her fingernails. One acrylic has popped free and floated to the bottom of the bag, settling like sediment.

I take a hanger from the ground and use it to rotate the bag so I can see the corpse's face more clearly. It's Emily. She's beautiful. She is a revolving dress soiled by a good party, and I am hysterical, the laughter jerking and punching my chest until I'm on the verge of throwing up or crying. If I laugh loud enough, someone will hear. They will open the door, and see me, and see the body, and I will tell them everything. The words will come. And they, whoever they are, will not blame me. They'll understand that I was trapped until Emily freed me. I was a victim, too.

I hiccup, bile rising, and then I'm on my knees, vomiting a mass of baba ghanoush and seething kombucha next to Emily's slackened, plastic-sheathed foot.

I'm weak, my legs don't work. I force myself upright. Thinking clearly now. I need to leave before someone finds me. I turn off the light, slip into the hallway, which is mercifully empty, and shut the closet door. Keep moving, don't stop until I'm out the front door and the door is closed, the party secure behind me, revolving around the body in the closet.

Halfway down the elevator it dawns on me: I have my own body waiting at home. I am far from innocent in this. I am at its center.

There is a rattling sound that makes me think of a soul leaving a body, but it's only my teeth, chattering against each other as I mutter every prayer that I didn't know I remembered under my breath, and even the rats run into traffic to get away.

THE AVERAGE PERSON contains about one and a half gallons of blood. It's the effort I can't get over. The effort, and the preparation. You need a container, and somewhere to put it. You need to watch it drip. How badly must you hate someone to drain them? How badly must you want what they have?

I replay the image: Emily's sucked-dry body, brittle pearlescent skin shining blue under the sheen of the plastic, torso mangled and drooping. That dislodged acrylic, a final cry for help.

The memory makes me queasy. I climb into the bathtub and rest my head on Dom's chest. She has lost the power to shock. Looking at her suffocated face is merely like touching a hot stove with a dead hand. I spend the night like this, dissociating, damp in my underwear on the fiberglass, Dom's skin sticking to my cheek. I hold Dom's *The Future Is Female* T-shirt and inhale her tobacco leaf and pink pepper perfume. Dream with my eyes open of tanning-bed brides finding their dream dress over and over and over. The same episode on repeat in my head, a glitch in the matrix. When the bride morphs into the dead Emily, then Dom, then Mona, I'm far from surprised. She twirls in layers of chiffon, pearls against her shriveled décolletage, nose and mouth and lips molding in new shapes like a hunk of clay.

When she opens her mouth to say "YES!" dust falls out like a plume of feathers.

All the while I am thinking: *Beauty is possible.*

2008

I thought Mona would go home. We'd order pepperoni pizza with cash her mom left on the counter. Watch a movie on pay-per-view. Mona loved to order porn, hide the remote, and watch me squirm. Once, when we were fourteen, I cried until she turned it off.

Or maybe she'd be browbeaten after the fight with Ashley, would want to snuggle in front of *Snow White*, her favorite movie from childhood that she'd seen a thousand times.

I trailed her into town. When she didn't turn down her street, I figured she would stop outside our usual diner. Pause at the door and level her gaze at me. *Milkshakes and fries?*

She was almost a block ahead, and soon it became clear that she didn't know I was behind her. Instinct urged me to give her space. I hung back at a corner, let a green Volvo pass, then a red SUV. She bypassed the diner and approached the entrance to Clark's.

She hesitated at the door, then went in. This altered the calculus; I sensed I couldn't just march after her into the deli. Pausing, I pushed my cheek softly to the weather-beaten brick, ear whorls brushing the pockmarked surface, as if I could hear through it. I thought I heard a hinge creak, though I could not have really heard it, and turned down the side street.

The alley was accessible by cutting through a parking lot that serviced a row of shops and restaurants with slivers of sidewalk between. I started to round the corner into the trash-filled passageway and stopped when voices reached me.

They were unmistakable. These were the voices that scored my every waking moment. The voices that spoke when I was alone. Egged me on, built me up, knocked me down. I would know them in a crowded concert hall, in a disaster.

I hid behind a dumpster and looked anyway.

She was crying against the back door. Tears spilled into her mouth. Chase tried to hug her, but she pushed him away. He returned, arms open to her, bracing himself on either side so that she was trapped between his torso and the solid metal door. Desperation in his slackened profile. She wailed, tugged at the T-shirt he wore under his apron. From the color, I saw it was the same one he had on the day we found the ginger root in the dumpster Mona now kicked with the side of her flip-flop. The shoe flew off and hit Chase in the calf. He took advantage of the confused moment and pulled her violently to his chest. Her dirt-rubbed bare foot dangled.

Upon impact it revealed itself to me: he loved her, but she was inscrutable. He came to me. He marched right up to the edge of Mona, got as close as he could. I was the path of least resistance. And now I understood his reluctance to make a permanent mark. To do anything he couldn't take back.

I held my breath for so long my windpipe felt flattened. Blood drained from my face and I was woozy enough to grip the filthy lip of the dumpster, knuckles grazing a crinkled garbage bag. The alley, the town, the city beyond the bridge moved out in concentric circles and I was the eye of the storm.

Some life-altering moments are only recognized later; others you sense in the atmosphere as they are happening, like a fine mist shifting. Every molecule stirred, making me over into someone vengeful and disgusting with hatred. I watched them cling to one another. She sniffled, he offered words into her hair. Aware that I could leave at any time, I understood that it was necessary to put myself through this.

Mona abruptly pushed Chase. His arms dropped, the soft collapse of tissue paper ripped from a Christmas present, and his chest curved, a more dramatic concave than Mona's skinny forearms seemed capable of creating.

The grind of the thrown-open door and then she was gone into the deli, and we were alone with the rats and the molting garbage and the heat.

I wanted to go to Chase. I wanted to hit him, to rip my hair out, anything to make them regret hurting me. A minor car accident or a sudden-onset allergy; something to land me in the hospital, a small creature drowning in sheets, frail and cared-for. Mona would bring a bouquet of dandelions. Chase would sit at my bedside; he'd kneel on the bone-clean hospital flooring and beg for forgiveness.

I dug my nails into my palms. Chase stared at the closed door. Mona's departure hung like a curtain in the air. We were both lost in that vigorous haze. We could comfort each other so easily, if only I found the courage to walk down the alley, to show him I had been there all along. Mona would never love him the way I did. I was not sure she was capable of loving anyone. She had withdrawn so completely that I didn't fully see her as human. She was Godzilla meets Athena. A scaly monster in the dressage of a girl.

I left the way I'd come, bumping the dumpster with my elbow. A precarious pile of trash bags dislodged and tumbled down in my wake like stones bouldering the exit. I didn't stop to see if Chase was watching.

12

Am I beautiful? How can one tell the truth of their own face? There is a certain doll-like wideness to the eyes, a tuck of the jaw, a plump to the lips that can't be denied. If I spend long enough squared off with the mirror, these disparate attributes lose their sense. In junior high a boy I recognized from school but whose name I didn't know stopped me on the street. *You look fake*, he'd said. Years later I realized that was his way of saying I was pretty.

Emily's newfound beauty haunts me. Alive, movement had disrupted her. You could almost see her thoughts slither inside her head. Her forehead shifted with knowledge. She wore the inner workings of her brain. It's true what they say, then, about death and peace as bedfellows. In death, Emily is a fruit fallen from the vine, the last pure, ripe blush before the rot takes hold.

And the longer I mull on that, the less guilt eats at me. Maybe a short life is a favor.

Dom seems to agree. At least, she doesn't argue when I pose the idea.

But I am bothered. The battle for time is built to be lost. The deck is stacked against a girl from the second she recognizes herself in a mirror. She'll change until her very last day, and after she's gone, the flesh will flake from her bones. youthjuice is the only solution that makes sense. Sacrifice some for the good of others. Let the smartest and prettiest survive to become more so. Let the lesser ones rest.

A missing poster appears on a telephone pole near the office. It's not Emily, but someone I've never seen. Or, I don't think I've seen her. Ashley Allison. She has a low ponytail and a clean-girl coat of lip gloss that shines through the grain of the poorly photocopied image. Whoever misses her did not spring for the premium printer package at Staples. I have to admit, the shitty quality adds authenticity. A high-resolution photo with a glossy finish may well be an advertisement.

There are too many Ashleys, a veritable army of them. Oozing out of the woodwork in perfect lockstep through the revolving doors of offices in Midtown, SoHo, FiDi, Flatiron, on their way to upwardly mobile jobs in publishing, at Condé and Hearst magazines, design firms, galleries. Public relations. Not to change the world directly, but to apply gentle pressure to it, warm hands working dough into a new shape. You may never meet Ashley, but she is conducting your life from the sidelines. Telling you what to want, how to feel, who to be.

This Ashley is nineteen. A junior at NYU. All-American. Flannel unbuttoned at the collar, a silver Tiffany chain with the heart charm tugging coyly at her neck. Her smile strains credulity, each front tooth almost the width of my thumb. The rest descend politely into the corners of her mouth.

A ballet of firing synapses from my brain sends a manicured

nail to scrape off the tape affixing the poster to the telephone pole. Other signs advertise an alien-abduction-themed night at a club that is also an art gallery, a Cash for Your Warhol sticker, a shoe brand's sample sale in an abandoned storefront on West Broadway.

I've just folded the missing poster tightly and slipped it into my bag, between my leather wallet and the lavender HEBE pouch I stock for touch-ups, when someone calls my name. It's the female cop, the one who questioned me about Emily.

"Sophia," she calls again. Waves like we are old friends. She eyes the telephone pole, then smiles. "Officer Rodgers."

"Oh, uh. Hi." I hold my bag with two hands in front of my stomach. Aware that my body language is projecting profound discomfort, I relax my arms and shoulders. "Can I help you?"

She glances at the HEBE building. "I was just in the neighborhood." She laughs dryly. "It's strange, right? All these girls going missing who worked at your company. If it were me, I'd constantly worry I'd be next."

Oh. That's why she's familiar. Ashley is one of ours. "Yeah, it's . . . scary."

Officer Rodgers hooks her thumbs into her belt loops, drawing my attention to her bulging gun. "No bodies, no leads . . . it's like they vanished without a trace." Her eyebrows lift, forehead skin folding into the hairline. She'd be better with two or three units of Botox. "That doesn't happen very often."

"People do vanish," I say.

"Usually there's a reason. Sometimes it takes a while for us to find it, but usually there's a reason." Officer Rodgers rattles the handcuffs affixed to her belt. "A solution to every mystery," she adds.

"I wish I could help you out, I really do. But I barely knew these girls."

"Just promise you'll keep your eyes open and call if you see anything suspicious. You still have my card? All right, well, have a good night. Stay safe out there." She gives a two-finger salute but stays where she is, forcing me to concede. I take balanced steps to the end of the block, turn, and break into a run.

I get on the B train, heart pounding, find a seat by the door connecting the cars, and lean against the Poetry in Motion poster. For the whole ride I rest my hands on my bag as if holding the missing poster inside. I feel it through the nylon, hot against my hip.

At home I go into the bedroom, close the door, pull the curtains shut, and turn on the bedside lamp. I clear perfume bottles and jewelry trays to smooth the poster on the dresser. I force myself to look deep into Ashley's hazy eyes. Scan my body for any emotion and come up empty. This is not a person. It's a photo.

Even the real Ashley, Ashley in the flesh, was probably more image than human. But no matter how hard I try, I can't remember her.

And so, it is in this way that I am able to set the poster aside, to leave it face up and staring unblinking at the ceiling, and continue my night.

JAMIE. SHE HUGS my periphery. Charging into my personal space like, *Hey, hi, how are you, do you wanna get lunch/ have a tea/can I pick your brain?* Pick your brain. What a delightfully macabre little phrase. I don't want to be anyone's mentor. I picture Jamie hunched over the upturned bowl of my skull, slurping pink matter.

Eventually I cave and end up at the Warhol film retrospective at a theater on the Lower East Side. This is the kind of thing Dom always wanted to take me to whenever she was clean enough to sit still for two or more hours. We watch a man sleep, and then Edie Sedgwick in big earrings talks about her life while smoking a cigarette. Jamie is rapt. Reverence lifts her profile. The retrospective ends on a long shot of the Empire State Building.

We stay in our seats when lights come on while the other patrons file through the exit. I fidget in my chair, bouncing a knee and checking the time. Jamie's cheeks shimmer. She dabs at the tears with a crooked knuckle, smiles shyly when she notices I'm watching.

"Sorry. I didn't expect that to hit me so hard. It's not even the way those movies are meant to be seen. The real *Empire* is eight hours." She focuses on the blank screen. "It's so powerful," she mutters.

Is she kidding? "I wanted to gouge my eyes out," I say, and Jamie laughs. I could do anything and she would still adore me.

I'm prepared to go home, but Jamie wants a drink. We duck into the entrance of a new bar specializing in innovative nonalcoholic cocktails. She knows someone who works there. Jamie chatters about Warhol films while I sip my virgin skinny margarita. Strings of ginger and carrot get caught in my teeth.

"The whole point is there is no point," she says. "He wanted zero plot, no character arcs. Just people being who they were. That's why his films with Edie are so special. He just let her be herself and set the camera rolling. I would love to be that kind of artist."

I look at the other patrons crowding the narrow bar with their health-flushed cheeks and their coconut-scented hair.

"It's weird, isn't it?" Jamie says. I assume she's still going on about Warhol, but she continues, "The missing interns? You've seen the posters around the office, right? It's kind of scary. They all worked at HEBE."

More missing posters have cropped up like flower petals on the telephone poles of SoHo since I took down Ashley Allison's. I've collected more and hidden them in drawers around the apartment. Sometimes I take them out and lay them on the kitchen island. Look into their colorless, pixelated victim eyes.

"That can't be a coincidence," Jamie says.

"People go missing all the time. It's usually on purpose."

"You mean like Emily? 'Prague.'" Air quotes around the last word. "You don't believe that, do you? Neither do the cops, by the way. I heard they talked to Tree again."

I don't ask how she, an intern, could possibly know that when I don't. "Why not? I'd go to Prague. If I were running away, I mean."

"Emily isn't the running away type. She's way too intense. Color-coded spreadsheets for everything. You should have seen her filing system for product samples."

"No offense, but maybe she just didn't want to tell you about her travel plans. She was kinda your boss."

"Well, yeah. But did she tell you?"

"Tell me what?" I take a bracing sip of the margarita. Brain-freeze shoots from my teeth to my gums to my temples.

"That she was going to Prague. You guys were friends, right?"

"No. I mean, we weren't really friends."

Jamie takes a roasted chickpea from the wooden dish on

the bar and wipes chili powder on her black jeans. "That's not what she told me."

"What?"

"Nothing, it's just—she liked you, that's all."

"We were coworkers. Are. We are coworkers."

"She felt totally pushed out by Tree and them. They were always giving her the cold shoulder. Like she'd never be in the inner circle. That's why she opened up to me. She was excited when you started. She thought, you know—that you'd be someone she could trust."

"Why was she telling you all this anyway? No offense, but you're an intern."

"Something is going on at HEBE, that's all I know."

"High turnover at a start-up isn't unusual. Plenty of people don't thrive in a fast-paced environment."

Jamie wiggles her fluffy brows. She's decided we're in on this together. A rag-tag detective duo. "You're friends with that blogger from *MAKEUPSEX*, aren't you? We should get her on the case. She's, like, a real journalist."

The blood drains from my face, turning cold in my veins. "Leave Dom out of it, okay?"

Jamie's irises flash black and flat, an animal sharpness to her glare. "Ohhhkay. It was just a suggestion."

"Here." I shove two crumpled twenties onto the bar. "Drinks are on me."

"Wait, where are you going? I thought maybe we could grab dinner."

"I have a nail appointment."

HER NAME ON the whiteboard in Marigold's halted scrawl. Each letter spaced widely apart, so that the short word takes more space than necessary. The effect is that of yelling "Jamie!" down a well, the syllables returning elongated and vibrating.

Our weekly Storytelling meetings develop the cadence of a war room. Tree wants to go wide with the formula soon. I wonder how she can possibly pull off a public launch without getting caught. But she insists: youthjuice is the future.

And a new batch is needed. Emily's formula is being processed as we speak and soon we'll need more.

Tree mulls Jamie's name over as Marigold takes her marker off the board. She's a bit worn, the skin around her eyes purpled and collapsed at the edges, shadowed nasolabial folds. "Huh," says Tree. "You're sure?"

"I hadn't considered . . ." Gemma trails off.

Tree flicks her focus to the whiteboard. "Jamie is talented. Couldn't we use her? As a full-time employee, I mean."

"She's perfect," says Marigold. Her folded arms wrinkle her Oxford shirt. Tree looks at her assistant, lifts a threaded and re-filled brow. A long, silent moment passes.

Tree nods. "Okay."

Jamie. She has that spark. She could be anything, of that I'm sure. And that's the problem. That she could be anything. That she might find out the truth. That she might become an artist. I picture her in full cinematic detail, as she was at the moisturizer shoot. Pert nose buried beneath the swell of her eyes, collagen blighting her pores into invisibility.

The future and the past.

"Something's off." Tree studies a row of headshots. They've moved on to the shoot. "You don't like the models?" Gemma says.

"It's not that. They're great. But we need . . . more. A showpiece."

"I have an idea." I open Robbie's profile, turn my laptop around. Tree and Gemma huddle close to the screen. "She's an AI influencer." I channel Jamie's words and make them my own. "And she fits the HEBE look to a T."

"She'd be expensive," Gemma says.

"But a guaranteed headline-maker," I say. If I were to open Tree's scalp and peer inside, I'm sure her mottled brain would be mulling over the features, the interviews, the press. "And if you think about it, it's sort of great? Because the victims are dead, but Robbie can't die."

"Unless you pour water on her," Gemma retorts, but no one laughs. Tree's eyes are gleaming and I know that I've made an impression.

"Get her rates," Tree says, which means yes. Money is no obstacle.

Marigold wipes down the board with a rag, and we file out and into the office. An apocalyptic sun hangs in the west. Pressure builds behind my eyes.

I can't see Jamie from where I stand, but I hear her chirp, and it makes me want to wring her neck with my bare hands. Thumbs pressing into the windpipe, crushing it like dandelion stems. To feel her voice die in my grip.

2008

I ran to Mona's house, heart in my throat, ears on fire, limbs dissolving into the June heat. My phone was vibrating non-stop. Chase called three times, then four. He knew that I knew, then. He'd seen me fleeing the scene. I turned the phone off and threw it into a scraggly hedge. Creeping around to the backyard, I peered in windows. Too dark to see inside, my own face gawked back at me, feral. I looked pitiful, like a lost thing.

A decaying tree house loomed above the house in an old maple. Mona and I spent whole days up there as kids, drinking Gatorade and playing with a worn deck of cards. We didn't know any games besides Go Fish, and once that bored us, we invented our own. Our favorite involved throwing handfuls of cards on the ground, counting the value of the upward-facing ones based on an obscure scoring system. Points from our last game were still chalked on the wall in fading numerals. I rubbed at a seven with my thumb until it disappeared.

A splinter snagged. I stuck the finger in my mouth and

sucked, but the thin wooden shard was part of me now. I couldn't even feel it.

The tree house smelled of ancient wood and memory. Evidence that Mona had spent time here recently was strewn about—a checked blanket, a pack of Marlboros, an orange bottle with two large white pills rattling around. The prescription label said Timothy Wolford. Tim was a pimpled nonchalant sophomore genius in a hoodie, and the top contender for valedictorian in his grade. Had Mona stolen the pills, or was Tim exploring new commercial ventures beyond tutoring slacking upperclassmen in their final effort to get into college?

I couldn't pronounce the drug's name. Removing the plastic lid released a musty chemical smell. Pills rattled in the bottle. I shook them into my palm and gagged as I swallowed them dry. Then I sat in the corner, the old blanket pulled like a cape across my back. Shadows moved on the wall. The sun faded like an old photograph.

Time lapped and twisted. Overlayed photo negatives of the past: little Mona and me throwing cards on the floor and gathering them. Throwing cards, gathering them. She was pale with wavy black hair that hadn't been washed in a few days. I had toasted skin and light brown hair. Me, picking up the Queen of Hearts. Our highest value card.

Feminism, Mona told me, *is when women are better than men.*

We baked the ethos into our game. Kings were almost worthless. But find a Queen of Hearts and you win. Women, we believed, were always the heroes.

The younger me held the card out to Mona, who smacked it out of my hand, sent it fluttering to the floor in slow motion.

I felt a dull spike of fear in my gut. What had I taken?

The string of characters on the bottle was incomprehensible, generic nonsense. I figured the pills couldn't be deadly if Tim Wolford's doctor let him have them. But maybe I shouldn't have had both at once. I should have waited for the first to kick in.

Nothing happened after a few moments and the panic receded. I again lost myself in a daydream: Mona coming across my purpled body, my last cold breath brushing her face like an eyelash as she cradled my head and cried.

She'd feel sorry, and she'd never be able to look at Chase again.

Or she'd never find me, not until I started to decompose. I laughed out loud at the idea of my own face, pocked with maggoty holes.

"You're one sick bitch," I giggled to the stale tree house air.

The light shifted, stretching the floorboards, and my focus lifted until I could barely feel my haunches on the floor, or the moth-eaten fabric brushing the tips of my ears. I picked up the Marlboro carton. It was flattened and moist from humidity. Heavier than I expected. I lifted the flap. A blue Bic was nestled inside. There was one cigarette left, a bit crumpled in the middle but mostly intact. After a few false starts, I managed to light it. I inhaled, coughed, a gray plume billowed and burned my eyes. The cigarette slipped from between my fingers. A flare of heat on my ankles. I opened my eyes and saw that I'd been burned. The cigarette had rolled away, landing on the puddled blanket around my feet.

I stomped it out, and the embers sizzled a hole in the fabric.

Resting my head against the wood, I let an alternative afternoon play out on my heavy lids. The diner. Shiny red plastic beneath our sticky legs. Air conditioner blasting. Both of us a little dizzy, a little bit sick from the sun and the chlorine. The most I'd seen Mona eat in months. I'd missed the ferocious working of her jaw when she was hungry.

She stood up for me. She always had. And I was failing her.

"Do you think she'll have a black eye?" the me in my head asked.

Mona dipped a fry in her milkshake and chewed thoughtfully. "God, I hope so. That bitch." She cast a morose gaze at the milk bubbles on the surface of the glass. She looked like she might cry. "Those were your favorite sunglasses."

"We should go to the mall this week and get new ones."

"Yeah. Yeah, sure." She said it like *yeah, right*, sad and not sarcastic, the bite filtered out of her voice and replaced by a soluble gloom. I couldn't make her better.

In my imagination, I checked my phone. Three texts, each slightly more frantic than the last. Chase: *she means nothing; it's not what you think; i love you.*

I thought of my real phone, buried in the untamed plant matter guarding the house. A rebellious urge swelled. Most kids my age chafed at their parents' rules, but my parents gave me nothing, they were so bemused by my existence our conflict was meaningless. Fighting with them was like swinging for a punching bag that wasn't there.

It was Mona who had me aching for acceptance, then resenting that ache. It was as though she had raised me in her own image. And why should she get to have everything?

I was angry, and suddenly far away from the fictional diner. Fully present in the mildewed tree house, with the tickle of cobwebs and the pills thrumming my bloodstream.

Something else was there, too. Rage. A solid mass that started in my chest, traveled out through my eyes and took shape among the spiders on the ceiling. I saw it, dark and rolling like a rain cloud.

Mona had done this; she had hurt me. The more I thought about it, the more obvious it became that she did it on purpose. She brought me to Clark's, knowing he would be there. She saw the way I shifted like a flower, pellucid and fragrant, lingering in the sun of him. Saw how I lost control of my limbs.

Mona knew what power she had. She moved with witchcraft. She didn't love Chase, and she didn't love me. We were pawns.

The sky was dark; I had been in the tree house a long time. Nine o'clock, the earliest. Landing in the grass with a soft plunk, I turned toward the house, a crooked tooth amid the tousled garden. If you could call it a garden—it was a plot of tall weeds sprouting blooms. Mona's mom's car was missing from the drive. The only light came from the den.

Slowly, I crept to the edge of the bushes. Sounds came from the grass and I flinched every few seconds, imagining snakes and worms, rabid squirrels. Toads with warts for skin.

I heard my body working, like those frogs were in my ears.

She was silhouetted against the frame, bathed in the television's spiritual light. Muted, I was sure, the way she preferred when she was home alone. *Just to keep me company.*

I crouched below the window so I couldn't be seen and watched her lift her hand to her mouth and let it fall away. She seemed to be eating popcorn, but there was no bowl I could see. Shifting light from the television caught the sharp curves of her face. She resembled a prism, a stunning illusion. Lovely, opalescent, but childlike. Most people are children when they're alone. Each time she leaned forward, she briefly disappeared from view, then returned to settle in the curve of the couch. The throb of her throat as she swallowed. Eyelashes fluttering, she rocked her head side to side.

My foot crunched a stiff plastic shape under a bush. The plastic glowed. It was a Halloween mask, caked in dirt. I slipped the elastic around my head, adjusting the mask so I could see. Rain and snow and humidity from the past eight months had bent the plastic out of shape so the eyeholes didn't line up quite right. Gritty dried mud crumbled onto my face. The cramped nose trapped my breath and pushed it hot against my face. Sticky, carrying the salted whiff of the last thing I'd eaten, ages ago—vending machine chips that tasted like attic dust. It mingled with the mask's damp-cave smell and I gagged.

Touching the curves, I made out the mask's shape by feel. Two wide, moonlike crescents around the eyes. A dramatic sloping jaw. *Scream.*

I stepped as close as I could to the window, until my molded ghoul visage plinked the glass. Startled, I jerked, and fell. Heels of my hands digging into the moist and pliant summer dirt. Mona turned her head, but she did not come to the window.

I exhaled through my mouth.

The mask changed me, made me bold and blunted my humanity. I suddenly understood how people could be animals. I longed to crawl in the dirt, lift chunks of soil to my lips. I wanted to grip Mona by the torn T-shirt and shake her. Force her jaw open with clawed hands and shove Chase's Arnold Palmer–stained apron down her gullet.

I huddled against the house and watched Mona put something into her mouth over and over again. She wasn't chewing.

Whatever it was, she swallowed down in rhythmic succession. Pills. Of course. She was popping pills.

I imagined them filling her stomach. Her side-swiped bangs were crimped from the dried chlorine. That she hadn't showered after the pool wasn't strange; Mona often waited as long as she could between showers, typically three or four days, sometimes longer when it was cold outside. Not long enough to make her obviously gross, though if you spent enough time with her you would begin to notice a sour milk miasma hovering when she spread her legs or stretched her arms over her head. She would occasionally sniff the air and smile, as if satisfied with her own bodily function.

I was sure she'd relish the chemical burn of the dried chlorine, the film dried over her chest. She'd sleep that way, pool residue sinking into the sheets, and rinse it off in the morning.

It struck me how we'd come to an ending. The only way out was through. Someone had said that, and I wished I remembered who. No matter what, we could never go back to Mona and Sophia as we were. Everything had changed in the space of an afternoon. Change that had been building for a while. By the moment of recognition it was too late to reverse the flow. Something would push until we shattered. It might as well be me.

The mask amplified my breath like microphone static, and I stepped closer.

13

The invitation says: come in white.

It arrives as I'm powering down my laptop, massaging the stretch between my brows to encourage the softening of the lines I sometimes see sketched there in the mornings. I should use the cream. The fountain of youth is in my pocket. But I can't. Every time I reach for the jar, open the lid, the icing-thick substance winds up all over my hands. The place where my true nature is closest to the surface.

There's Botox for the face. Fillers and facelifts. Technologies that plump, doctors who can expertly staple the excess of you along the hairline.

But hands. They are the true windows to the soul. They sour first, with age or with hate. With the sun. I know who I am, but my hands show the world what I'm capable of. *If she can do this to herself,* the scars whisper, *imagine what she can do to you.*

So, in the mirror, a triangle is visible when I look toward matte daylight, as if finely illustrated with charcoal pencil.

Back to the invite. Eggshell white with burgundy font, each

letter faints into the next. Gentle, too-perfect cursive no human hand makes. The email comes from a burner account, but the address is unmistakable: Tree's Lower East Side penthouse.

PARTY NIGHT. HOME alone, the closet thrown open. Curtains drawn, Dom propped on my bed. Moving her was difficult, her limbs immobile and her skin like old rubber. Despite the formaldehyde, an abandoned subway station odor.

She doesn't answer when I ask about my outfit.

I take my time. Oil my skin mermaid's tail shiny. My hair is newly cut with a flirty French bang, wispy sideburns curling like snails around my ears. I apply pasties to my chest. My reflection in the mirror is seamless and nude.

I wonder if Robbie has nipples.

The dress is lemon-cream silk crepe with an open back that ties. Thin strings circle the low ribs and knot at the spine. Thicker ribbons are affixed behind the neck, trailing almost to the hem. In front is a high neck and two pieces of fluttery fabric that cross at the skirt.

I put on a pair of gold hoops that hug close to the lobe and a stack of gold rings on one index finger. A blotted red lip, champagne highlighter, three coats of mascara, and a small black purse to complete the outfit.

Twirling for Dom, I ask again if she likes how I look.

I order an Uber, wait until the car avatar turns onto my block before I leave. The backseat is hot. I roll the window down a crack, then up, then down again.

The lobby of Tree's building is empty, no doorman tonight, and the elevator yields to my touch. I wonder, briefly, if this is the rapture; everyone gone off to heaven but me, the world a cracked oyster for my taking, fat-hearted pearl beating at the center. This lobby, this building, is mine. I could open each mailbox with my mind.

The elevator dings shut.

An angel walks through the revolving door. She's in a swiss-dotted smock dress. Blue satin ribbon cups the base of her bun. Distantly familiar. Her mannerisms are from a movie I watched years ago and mostly don't remember.

Her identity surfaces when she says hello and smiles. Ah. I know her from the internet. She is someone I follow. I pass her photos as I'm scrolling, her white-toothed smile as intimate to me as the awning over the entrance to the corner bodega, the square of ceiling that greets me as I unshutter my eyes in the morning. She is part of my life's wallpaper.

"Did you get the invite?" the woman says.

But why can't I remember her name? "Yeah."

"It was so mysterious, I couldn't resist! Can you believe we couldn't tell anyone we were coming? What if we get murdered? Do you like true-crime podcasts? I listen to tons, I feel like I'd know what to do if someone came after me." The woman (what *is* her name?) presses the call button and the door springs open. We enter and the elevator closes us in.

"Dammit, what's the apartment number, do you remember? I'm sure I still have the email . . ." The woman scrambles for her beaded purse. I select the button for the penthouse.

She grins. "You're the best. So," she continues, "I know we're not supposed to question the other guests, but I'm just so *curious*. I've never seen you before; are you a content creator, or . . ."

"I work for a brand."

"How nice. I was in PR before I started my blog. It was such a great experience, but office life is just not for me. I really craved flexibility, so I went freelance. But look at me, giving you *way* too many details about my life."

Susannah. That's her name. "Your secret is safe," I say.

The elevator opens. Whoever wrote the invitation—Marigold, I'm sure—instructed us not to ring the bell or knock; the door unlatches immediately, and we are swept inside the foyer. It's eerie and empty, whoever opened the door has retreated into an unseen corner. Then a figure emerges. Marigold in a plague doctor's mask. She confiscates our phones, ushers us into the living room.

The magnificent view of the East River cradles a Grecian array, women and a few men, maybe twenty or thirty people in total, all stunning, all wearing white.

Faces come alive in the candlelight. Restylane-puffed lips and feline eyes stretched out of proportion, set into contoured cheeks, noses restructured so they point upward at the ends. No one here is the way God made them, and really, why should they be? Reinvention is the point of living.

I search for Susannah, but she's scooping a champagne flute with something bubbly from a tray on a tall table. The faces of the party slip by, taut and high-cheeked, resilient as Teflon.

I'm alert for Tree, but don't see her. Below, the river's dark ribbon pulsates. Wind batters the glass. On the water, a double-stacked cruise ship rides the current. Purple lights playfully glitter the waves. I picture drunk women in heels, falling. I picture someone vomiting over the railing. I picture flesh-colored makeup melting off an older woman like a second face.

And then there is a real face in the window. I startle, turn. Jason Red grins.

"Thought that was you," he says. Like he knows me. Like we are friends.

He is aggressively preserved so as to appear embalmed. I think of Dom in her current state.

Touching a cocktail napkin to his T-zone, Jason says, "Whoever is behind this activation is either a genius or a sociopath. And I should know! I'm both." He laughs devilishly, showing his dripping molars.

I give him my best game show hostess beam. This is work for me, even if no one else knows it. "I hope you're enjoying yourself," I say, then wonder if that was too forward, if now he will connect me with the scene.

"It's a beautiful apartment," he answers. "Very beautiful. Mine is not so nice these days. Too many cockroaches. I've been away too long—have they made more?"

In his eyes, a body convulses with chemical fluid. Those maniacal teeth gnash. I have my own memories tied to those images, imbuing them with visceral realism. My skin feels too tight and I can sense myself aging, the seconds counting to death. I am still young, but for how long? And I am no longer the kind of young I once was.

Red, maybe fifteen years older, propped up by an interior scaffolding of fillers, is barely hanging on. He is way past his prime. He might have some advice.

He has that twitchy, dying animal gait that Dom gets when she's on uppers. I made it my mission, after Mona, to learn how to spot any pill on a person. Ambien was a goblin lethargy. I suspect Adderall for Red, possibly Dexedrine.

I wish I had some to take the edge off. My head hurts. "What was it like?" I ask Red.

"Oh, honey," he says sadly. "If you're asking, you already know."

He leaves me, breathing shallow, electrified spots flooding

my eyes. My hands tingle and I scrape at the ripe skin around my nails, lightly at first, gradually adding pressure. I sat in the salon chair for close to three hours while the technician scrubbed and oiled my hands and wrists like she was preparing to descale a fish. I especially love the part when they push down the cuticles, cut them with the small scissors. Sometimes I bleed.

I can't stop touching my hands, baby-bottom smooth. I curl my fingers into my palms and squeeze. The skin over the knuckles turns sheet-white. I imagine unwinding the skin, starting at the corner of a nail and moving down each finger in swirls. Revealing the pink underneath.

Marigold enters in her mask, and then there is Tree. Bare-faced, regal Tree. Powerful, yet appealingly frail, a rescued kidnapping victim about to give her first press conference. Her weakness is her strength. Hair sharply parted down the center, clavicles showing, her arms slim and malleable. No hard muscles.

"Welcome." Tree clasps her hands by her stomach. Gasps ripple throughout the crowd, catching each guest in the chest. They are surprised, but maybe also not. Maybe this is the only logical conclusion.

"If you haven't figured it out by now, this is my apartment." Tree brings her arms out in opposite directions. Jesus on the cross. "I've brought you here for a singular experience, an introduction to the future of aging. Or shall I say"—her eyes sweep the room—"never aging.

"In the future, age will be a myth; we will speak of wrinkles and turkey necks the way veterans on the winning side speak of war. Tonight, you are invited to join the ranks of the immortal. If you come this way, we can begin."

Marigold pushes at a floor-to-ceiling bookshelf built into the wall. It rotates, revealing a hidden hallway. Those nearest to Tree follow her into the cavern. I fall in line.

Down the hallway the apartment unfolds. It is so dark that I can't see anything. I move by feel. Sounds are amplified, and the air smells like an old tooth. A glow emerges at the end of the corridor, accompanied by wet rustling like a fountain refilling itself. The light and sound grow and swallow us, and then I am in a new room, the last to enter. I make sense of what I'm seeing: several large claw-foot bathtubs like the one in Tree's private bathroom are placed at intervals. Plastic drop cloths strewn about. It calls to mind the aftermath of an orgy. But it's just the beginning.

What registers first is the white racing over my vision, blinding me to color. But the red is everywhere. White holds the red the way the midnight sky does the full moon, cradling and amplifying it. Blood fills the tubs, stopping mere inches from the rounded rims. So much blood. Too much blood. An impossible amount to have come from one person.

Jamie. It could not all have come from Jamie.

I move to the nearest tub. In some spots the blood is thick and chunky, like poorly blended tomato soup, watery in others. I sink a pinky to the root and the blood clots around it.

The guests don't wait for a signal; they climb into the tubs fully dressed. Blood races up their bodies, fusing the white fabric of their clothing to their torsos and upper thighs, making them so vividly naked it's hard not to stare.

I pause at the tub's snarled lip and grip the porcelain and I wait for the hidden morality inside me to take me over. I picture myself running from the room. Riding the elevator down until it hits the floor. Barging into the nearest precinct. The preposterous story spilling from my mouth like bile.

That isn't me. It has never been me. I climb into the tub. Sinking down, the blood covers me, a vital blanket. Around me, splashes and warped shadows cast by hundreds of pillar candles. I make butterfly motions with my arms. I close my eyes. Odors and sounds amplify. The room smells like the inside of a cleaned mouth, a whiff of periodontics. Spitting mint and blood into the little paper cup, the wax dissolving with moisture.

Orange glows behind my lids. I am Ophelia floating in the water, becoming a memory. I am Mona and Dom.

When I open my eyes, two dark-haired women are stripped down to scaled nipple covers. Their bodies are streaked with green and gold glitter, sticky red trails like they doused themselves in Bloody Marys. They flirt with another woman. A river of blood trickles from one corner of her Merlot-colored mouth. Her lipstick is still impeccable.

My hair is heavy, plastered over my forehead and neck. I feel mummified, covered in papier-mâché. Susannah from the elevator is in the next tub. Her ribbon has come undone, the ends stained with rust. White dress soaked, sheer with blood, forms a second skin. Her mouth opens and blood spills out; she is laughing and gargling and then she jumps and liquid surges over the tub and onto the floor. The tile runs slick. I think of cracked skulls. I could light the room on fire. I could tell someone, anyone. Go into Witness Protection and start over. Change my name.

But it's too late for all that, isn't it? I'm implicated. As teenagers Mona and I would mark others for death. Teachers, classmates, even random people we passed at the mall. Their crimes were varied. The world is one giant injury to a teenage girl.

That feeling never really went away for me. I thought, back then, that it originated from Mona; she egged me on. Now I see that the hate was in me all along.

Red is sitting alone, his white mesh shirt brutally stained, looking troubled. His face is dotted with splatters from a rowdy group in the adjacent tub. He touches one of the spots and licks his finger. I catch his eye and his lips break into an unpleasant smile.

I realize I have been waiting for Tree to give a speech, to gather the evening under one stated purpose. But she is content to watch her creation take its monstrous shape. The room maintains the frenzy of a massacre, blood everywhere, and a cauterized death odor. My mind wanders to the most famous school shooting of my childhood. When I got to high school myself I would often imagine my bland, quotidian world turned sideways. Here, the blood on the faux wood grain table. There, the stacks of musty books in plastic covers sprayed with brain matter.

The mood in this room is more like a garish playground. I can't imagine anything truly bad happening here, among the innocent splashing. I begin to massage the blood into my neck and shoulders. Drawing the collar of my dress down, I rub some across my chest. Holding my breath, I go under. I stay down for as long as I can. I break the surface sputtering and Tree is there, bone dry.

"Having fun?"

"Why didn't you tell me about this?"

"The fewer people who knew ahead of time, the better."

"But I'm a Storyteller, aren't I? You could have used me. You told Marigold."

"She is my executive assistant. And she suggested Jamie as our victim. We wouldn't be here without her."

The implication that Marigold means more to this operation than I do hurts, but I'm distracted by the sheer amount of liquid in the tubs. "Too much," I mutter.

"Hm?" Tree says.

"It's too much blood for one person."

Tree laughs. "Oh, silly. It's not just one person."

"But Jamie . . ."

"She's in there, don't worry. But we had to round it out somehow for the display. Less potent than the mixture in the cream, but good enough for this. If we imply that it's a magic elixir, they'll love it whether or not they see results."

I'm watching her, and I'm not understanding, and then, somehow, I am. The young, raw addicts in Tompkins Square Park. Girls with knotted hair, beautiful beneath the dirt. Tree, vanishing into the bushes with that boy. In my mind they wear Dom's face, which morphs into Mona's, which morphs into mine.

I SHOWER FOR so long that my skin becomes soft and dimpled like deboned chicken made ugly and pale. The blood, syrupy and turbid, clings to the hairs on my arms and I wonder if, after all, it's only paint. Gore drips into the basin of the shower and swirls down the drain. The nasty death scent intensifies. I scrub with HEBE's neroli bathing oil. Combined with the shower steam, the odor turns to one of flowers doused in gasoline.

My head aches, an angry pressure like a small hammer drilling my temple, and I rest my forehead against the condensation-slicked glass. I get dressed in cashmere sweatpants and a waffle knit. The dress from the party is hopeless. I shove it into a garbage bag, put the bag into the closet behind a row of designer purses I moved from Dom's room to mine.

Speaking of Dom, she's slumped on the bed where I left her. I turn up the air-conditioning and her smell circulates, a chemical-and-mold odor. Musk and pepper incense helps a little, but not enough; I'll have to move her soon. I prop her up with beaded Jonathan Adler pillows. Oval Le Specs hide the bludgeoned caverns within the orbital bone. I apply concealer around her mouth and the sides of her nose to hide the drawn cavities, blush on the high points of her cheeks. Her rubbery, fake skin shifts unnaturally. I snap a few photos, experimenting with the angles. I find that if I put the phone into her hand and fold my own hand over both I can fake a selfie convincingly enough.

Caption: *Life update! Taking a much-needed digital detox. See you on the other side.*

I post the photo to Dom's Instagram. Then I drag the body to Dom's room, shut her inside, and go to the kitchen. In a drawer by the refrigerator, Dom's cell phone slides among loose knives and a can opener. I place the phone on the counter. The screen is blank, a dead brick. I shouldn't turn it on, I know about surveillance, but I can't help it. I plug it in to charge and type in her password. Two-seven-four-three.

The apple swims from the abyss, then breaks away to deliver the home screen littered with apps. Her wallpaper photo has been the same for as long as I've known her—Joan Didion's Céline ad. Large sunglasses dwarf a face collapsed in age. I contemplate the yielding swell of her jowl and touch mine, mercifully hugging the jawbone.

Texts and voicemails flood the screen. Dozens of Signal messages from someone called Skittle advertising specials on pills and coke. Ten voicemails—snippets of chaos. Voices cymbal-crash with ambient EDM and grunge music: friends calling from various parties, wondering where she's been. Former one-night-stands sending up flares.

I open her email. Bank statements, promotional emails from SSENSE and Net-a-Porter and Lisa Says Gah. Missives from Lyft, GrubHub, and Uber saying how much they miss her, offering discount codes. Alerts about new comments on *MAKEUPSEX*.

Navigating to the site, I see her last post was three weeks ago. Published the day she died, it's about the best fashion and beauty looks from her favorite movies. Isabelle Adjani's soiled blue dress in Andrzej Żuławski's *Possession* is at the top of the page.

I remember the night we watched the 4K restoration at Metrograph. I longed to appreciate strange and difficult things, but Dom actually did appreciate them. I had been bored for most of the movie which, on its simplest surface, was about a couple going through a divorce, but really seemed to be about madness in one form or another. While I'm reading the post, Dom's phone dings with a new email. My blood runs cold as I read the subject line. It's from her mother. I expect a worried missive but it's more of a screed, a five-paragraph rant about how irresponsible Dom is, how hurtful it was that she didn't call her mother on her birthday. I quickly mark the message as unread, exit the email app, and throw the phone on the counter. Heart hammering, I deep-breathe until I can bring myself to turn the phone off, wipe it for fingerprints, and put it back in the drawer.

MISSING POSTERS FORM a fungus on the telephone pole. Overlapping, multiplying. New ones crop up seemingly by the day. They flutter in the exhaust breeze of an oncoming truck.

I examine the row of white girls. DayGlo blond leaps off the page like a bonfire. Face nondescript, but the hair. Oh, that hair. I know it immediately. A blond intern who left in the middle of June. *A family emergency*, Tree said. My fingers prickle, the nerve endings coming alive. I move closer to the poster, which is the newest one added to the pile, on top of all the others. Another Ashley. Ashley Summers.

Cops came to the office again yesterday, different uniformed officers. They spoke to Tree for nearly an hour. I nervously shifted my gaze from her office to the clock on my desktop. Twice I walked slowly by the office door ostensibly heading to the bathroom. All I made out were dull vague shapes, the walls impressively soundproof. They left and I barged into Tree's office against Marigold's protests. Tree rocked a pen against the desk, wearing a groove in the lucite. Turns out the cops had heard about the event at Tree's apartment. "I said it was corn syrup," she said, and scratched a dry circle on her chin. Cracks formed on the surface of her face, flakes settled like dandruff. She stopped scratching and met my eyes. The cords of her neck stood out. "Whoever narc'd is off our PR list!" She laughed, but I could tell she was furious.

Ashley Summers covers a Samantha and an Alyson. I take down Ashley's poster, crumple it into Dom's Staud bag. My wardrobe has improved drastically.

The missing posters I've brought home clutter the kitchen island. I haven't made a meal in days, surviving off soy yogurt, wedges of cashew cheese, and handfuls of almonds. I don't hide the girls. Who comes here? The apartment is mine to do with as I please. I've been sleeping in Dom's room, making myself comfortable among her things. She would want me to have them, I think. It would make her happy to see me get what I deserve.

Dom is relegated back to her bathroom; she smells worse all the time. Her skin shrinks, giving her a taut, dehydrated appearance. Nostrils huge and receding like a cave entrance, mouth puckered and dry. It's true what they say, that nails continue to grow after death. I cut hers in the bath, the irony of our role-reversal almost funny. *Take care of it however you want*, Tree had said when I asked how to dispose of the body and the evidence.

I light Cotton Candy Peppermint incense and lay the new Ashley among her sisters, the pendant light above the island illuminating my hand. I can't remember the last time I really looked at it. I've begun to take my hands for granted.

But something is off about them in this light. They are gray-toned. Flesh whorls at the knuckles. I slide the skin around. There is too much. And the texture is dry. It hurts to flex and contract my fists.

I run over to the window. The setting sun highlights the cracks in the cuticles, the yellowed nails. Ancient hands. Lifelong smoker's hands. My real hands. I scream, and then a knock at the door stops me. A pause. Then another knock.

Then: "Dominique? Are you in there? Dominique, let me in, please!"

I stay very quiet and still, hardly daring to breathe, until I'm sure the woman has left.

A HORRIBLE DEATH mask greets me when I step on HEBE's floor. Two purple planets where eyes should be. Lips split down the middle and bleeding. A volcanic pustule on one cheek. Curls brittle and limp. Starla gives me a weak wave. Hebe's goblet has vanished, leaving the pink marble plinth to display air.

She is not the only one. Gemma has a baseball cap tipped over her forehead, two long scratches flowing from the waterline of her right eye all the way down to the ruffled collar of her PVC Batsheva mini prairie dress with puffy shoulders. The office feels empty without interns. None are remaining. We've used them up. Every last one.

Marigold's post is abandoned. I charge into Tree's office. The lights are off. She's draped on the couch in a blue nap dress with a silk eye mask on her face. When she hears the door slam she rises like the undead and pushes the mask down around her neck.

I can't help it; I gasp. Tree is ghastly. No color in her cheeks. A pink triangle beneath one eye. White flakes around her mouth. The moisture has been sucked out and her flesh droops. Her neck is peeling off in strips of dead skin that flop over the neckline of her dress.

It's not that she looks old. She's coming apart at the seams. Blood trickles from the corner of her lip. She licks it. "What do you want?"

I was going to show her my hands, which looked even worse this morning. Chunks of nail split off while I slept and littered the sheets, leaving cuts on my arms and legs. I'd even put an old pair of gloves on before coming to work. But now, faced with this living corpse, this rotted shell where my boss used to be—my problems seem petty.

"Are you okay?"

"Just a little migraine," Tree says. "I'm sure I'll feel better in no time. If you don't mind, I'd like to continue my nap." She lifts the mask over her eyes and lies back.

"But—"

"Get out, Sophia."

THAT WEEKEND, I bleach my hair. Then I use my HEBE company card to buy industrial garbage bags and cardboard boxes at a hardware store near Tree's apartment. I hide my face behind a pair of Dior sunglasses and a cashmere hoodie. Then I go home and carve Dom's reeking body into pieces, storing the legs in separate garbage bags, the torso and head inside cardboard boxes. Wearing the same disguise, I take the parts on a tour of the city. I ride in several unmarked cabs, figuring they're harder to track than Ubers, and once again pay for everything with my HEBE card. The torso goes into the Hudson by way of Chelsea Piers. The legs are deposited into the East River. And the box with the head, stuffed full of ice packs, comes to Coney Island.

Dom and I ride the B train. Stopped on the Brooklyn Bridge, I imagine normal lives playing out in the apartments that dot the horizon. Young couples having late morning sex, feeding their pets, showing each other memes on their phones while still in bed. A lonely old man shaving in a fogged bathroom mirror, pausing a beat too long with the razor's edge pressed to the mound of his Adam's apple. I picture a beauty influencer talking to the camera while applying foundation. She pretends there's a woman standing beyond the lens, someone who wants her story. *Tell me more about the staying power? Is it good for oily skin?* I give her Dom's beehive and winged liner.

She stamps her face over and over with the butt of a pink egg-shaped sponge. It's permanently stained, no matter how often she washes it with soap, and the water runs beige, then clear, and the sponge sits out all night and dries. Come morning, it's tan on the bottom, an inescapable reminder of the changes she makes before she dares to enter the world. I clutch the box tighter. It's wrapped in three plastic bags. Dom's voice hisses through the layers, urging me onward. Taunting. I smell her still, that putrid old perfume.

The car lurches, the buildings vanish, and then we crawl through the tunnel to the DeKalb station. I lived in Brooklyn when I first moved to the city, a rat-infested building on Bedford Avenue with four City College seniors, but I haven't been back since I moved in with Dom. There are so many neighborhoods I haven't visited. The city remains a mystery to me no matter how long I've lived here.

A woman climbs into the car, laden with overstuffed garbage bags, wearing a Christmas sweater that used to light up. Bulbs that no longer work frame a snowman's maniacal grin. My version of New York is not the real one. My New York is the set dressing that blocks out the guts of the theater, wires and boxes and props the detritus of neglected life. Stagehands just out of sight make it run. I lift the box in greeting and the woman scowls, faces away. She settles a few seats down, and I'm hating myself for the way her scent wrinkles my nose. I really, really want to move farther away, but I don't. I sit up. I look at the woman and smile, but she doesn't see me. She sings into her lap. *It's beginning to look a lot like Christmas.* I wonder if she knows it's summer. I keep looking and smiling. The woman angles her knees and hugs one of her garbage bags to her chest. I'm making her uncomfortable, but I just want her to notice me noticing her, notice me acknowledging her humanity.

But she doesn't, and eventually my cheeks start to hurt and I sit back and stare at the blurred tunnels through the window and cradle Dom's head to my chest.

At Newkirk Plaza a group of rowdy teens climb on. Handsome boys with backward baseball caps and low-slung pants, huge grins, girls wearing hoop earrings large enough to put a hand through and small shirts. One of the boys plays music from a tinny speaker. A girl in a plaid skirt and dirty Converse, a tiny crop top with a Care Bear on the front, appears to be in love with him. He speaks and she laughs. It could be anything. At one point he remarks "Almost there," and she dissolves into giggles as if he's doing a set at the Laugh Factory. She pushes out her curls, which cascade prettily over a dainty shoulder, and the boy doesn't even see it. He's got his eyes closed and he's bobbing to Ludacris, a song that was probably, no, definitely released before he was born. Mona and I once knew every word. Now, only the shape of it is familiar.

The car is nearly empty, and the kids are spread out like seaweed on the orange plastic chairs. Their skin glows translucent and metallic in the flat subway light. The lights blink out for a second and maybe this is it, maybe it's my time. That would be its own freedom. I could forget the past few months, wipe the slate clean. No corn husk Emily in Tree's hall closet, no bloody bathtub, no dead interns, no gruesome Dom scavenger hunt spread across two boroughs. It's a Sunday, I'm still in bed, a shift at Think Coffee ahead of me, an alarm that hasn't gone off yet, Dom in the doorway with a story about last night.

Then the train stops, the lights blink on. Everything the way

that it is: Gum on the floor. Teens yelling and swinging from
the poles, leaving slick handprints. A white woman in pearls
and a blazer even though it's the weekend glaring at them. The
woman in the Christmas sweater with the snowman missing
an eye. Me. A head in a box.

Lights flicker and turn holographic, the shadows pool on
the grubby tile, then they widen, swirl and draw together, a
dark blob with a bright ring that resembles Tree's bleached
hair. Breaks in the gloom create eyes, a grinning mouth. Too
many teeth. I dig the heels of my hands into my eyes and rock
back and forth.

Stillness. A warm hand on my shoulder. I look up. The boy
who the girl loves is there, a concerned furrow tunneling the
perfect skin between his brows. "You okay, miss?"

No matter how kind the slant to his mouth, he can't help
me. I can only help myself now. I say nothing, and the girl
in the plaid skirt tugs on his psychedelic tie-dyed sleeve. He's
reluctant to leave, but he does. Not before raising his hand
in a sad little wave as he steps onto the platform at Kings
Highway.

I miss him, I miss them all when the doors close and I'm
left with silence. Even the Christmas sweater woman is quiet
now, having fallen asleep using her garbage bag as a pillow. She
snores softly. I consider getting off at the next stop, dumping
Dom's head in the first trash can, but I am close to the end of
the line. Coney Island. I'm not much of a beach person. The
sand, the sun blazing overhead like a warning, the screeching
children's laughter. Growing up, the beach felt like punish-
ment. My parents brought me about twice a summer, when
my mom's sister who'd moved to California was in town for
a visit. It wasn't until college, when I went to Jones Beach

over spring break with a friend, that I realized there were ways to mitigate the discomfort. Umbrellas and fold-out chairs. Card games to pass the time. The beach with my parents was a dour affair. My mother would slather us both in sunscreen that left a gluey sheen and never fully dried, our limbs gritty with sand. We arrived early, before ten, and the best part of the day was when my father unpacked the bagels that we'd bought on the car ride out. I'd eat mine, everything with scallion cream cheese, before the sun could turn it mealy and warm. Poppy seeds stuck in my teeth for hours. Full, I'd lie out on the towel and try to read a fashion magazine, *Vogue* or *Harper's Bazaar* or *InStyle*, whichever cover starred the model or actress I liked most that month. The models taunted me with their slim, gluten-free hips while the bagel roiled in the spirals of my digestive system. Eventually my mother and aunt would cajole me into a brief dip in the ocean, and for the rest of the afternoon we watched other beachgoers play volleyball, get tan, and swim out farther than we would ever go. Fun was for other people. Around one o'clock, my father pulled out plastic containers of fruit and pasta salad, passing us forks and paper plates. I'd eat it all, whether I was hungry or not, and then spend the afternoon nauseated and sunburnt.

But Dom, she loved the beach. The sun took to her like a lover. She'd come home tan and smiling, adorable freckles sprinkling her nose and shoulders. I owe her the consideration of a pleasant resting place. So I stay on until the B chugs into Brighton Beach, then I leave the train. The woman in the Christmas sweater stays on.

The houses near the station look like clay left too long in the oven. I'm glad I have the sunglasses and the hood on, even though it's way too hot for cashmere and I immediately start to sweat. The box is heavy and I have to pause every block to readjust my grip.

It takes twice as long as it should but eventually I'm at the boardwalk. It's bustling, a carefree summer afternoon. All the way out and it doesn't feel like New York City anymore. We're somewhere else, a carnival at the edge of the world.

A woman with a shopping cart almost runs me over. Her eyes are rimmed with navy liner, the whites are rheumy and red. I hurry down the boardwalk. Booths line either side, hocking classic snacks and games where patrons can win stuffed animals as prizes. The candy-colored roofs evaporate in the July haze. Tourists trawl the beach like toxic ants, eating popcorn from striped bags and walking slowly, gawking at the spectacle. I'm sweating into the cashmere, but I can't take it off, can't even chance lowering the hood. There's a girl who sings showtunes, an open guitar case with a few loose bills tossed inside, and a bunch of coins glinting in the sunlight. Her voice sounds perfect from a distance, but as I get closer, I hear the strain of her vocal cords at the high notes. She's wearing a brown leather vest as a top, and her chest and shoulders are spackled with copper freckles. Not cute like Dom's were. These are the type of freckles that morph into melanoma.

No one pays much attention to her performance. Some passersby idly toss money into the maw of the guitar case as they pass.

There's nowhere really to be. The water isn't hospitable, and the sand is lined with trash. Yet the steady drumbeat push and pull of the city, the torque, remains. Close your eyes and you could be in Times Square.

I walk down to the beach, struggling with Dom's box, and

almost walk into one of those guys with a huge snake wrapped around his neck. I rear back, bracing for the strike. Then the man and his snake are swarmed with tourists, blocked from my sight, and my heartbeat slows.

Close to the water, women lie on the sand. Alone or with friends, the occasional couple. Not a single man by himself, and it strikes me as the only time I've seen that in the city, women dominating the landscape with all the authority of their bare skin, their muscled calves. Tree would love it. A feminist oasis, she'd say. Drawing nearer, I see cracks in their tans, brown gathered in the creases at their ankles and the wrists indicating at-home application. Fine wrinkles winged between heavy, sideways sloping breasts.

My mom once told me not to worry about getting old until I'm fifty. "That's when you lose your estrogen," she said. But I'm twenty years to fifty already, and then what?

Paranoid itching starts at my fingertips. I'm too scared to use youthjuice now that I see what it's doing to the other women. It's like the more you use, the worse it gets. I move down the beach to a spot where there are fewer people. Near my feet, an empty Doritos bag shifts in the salty wind. I approach the water's edge and kick off my sandals. Then I sit in the sand, put the box next to me. Cool water kisses my mint green toenails. Beads form on the polish as the tide recedes.

A seagull swoops and plucks at something in the waves. If I focus my eyes, cutting my peripheral vision, I could be anywhere. Montauk, or California, or Greece. A little to the left, and there's the snake man again. The reptile shimmers like scattered sequins as the man lifts it onto a woman's shoulders. She snuggles the animal around her like it's a shawl while her friend snaps a burst of photos. The women confer over the images, while the snake pokes its nose curiously into the first woman's hair.

The gesture sends a shudder through me, one that deepens when, in tandem, the two creatures, woman and snake, turn their heads toward me.

Then I'm up and dragging the box with Dom's head inside, my feet sinking deeper into the sand with every step, a comical lurch. I wade farther into the surf. How far out do I need to go for the box to submerge? I walk until the waves hit the bottom of my shorts, then go out until I'm soaked and then I release the box. She's really gone now. I can't get her back. As long as I had the head that housed her brain, I still possessed her. I could tell her my secrets. There's a physical ache in my gut, a festering. But when I imagine a school of fish nibbling the cartilage off her nose, I can't help but laugh out loud.

The nearest sunbather giggles as if we're in on it together. It makes me turn in horrified panic, before I remember I look nothing like myself. I step out of the water, momentarily cold, my ocean-darkened clothing turning me into a true spectacle.

More laughter, amplified, appearing piecemeal, in snippets over my head like birds with snatching beaks pecking at my hair.

Inhaling deeply, I sit down on the sand. I breathe in through the nose and out through the mouth, to try and still the beating of my heart. The exercise opens up a primal urge, and suddenly I'm crawling in the sand, stretching my legs into a downward dog. Brighton Beach recedes, and it's my hands gripping the Earth, the burn in my muscles reminding me that I'm alive. The itch relaxes. Blood rushes to my head. Then it comes back. I'm a criminal. I scramble to my feet, lose my balance, and collapse onto one hip. A man stands above me with a crumpled cardboard sign. He stares down the length of my body like he knows it intimately because he has been watching me bend and shift my limbs out of line, and his creased face implores me to give him something, but what? He thinks I'm just a woman but I'm so much more. I'm a killer.

I get my weight under me, and then I'm running again.

Back on the boardwalk, heart thrumming in my throat. Four girls wearing Friday night clothes on a Sunday morning are lined up like candy hearts on a bench. The prettiest one is wearing sheer black tights with small bows up the sides and a dress slashed down the middle to show her upper ribs, small breasts tucked politely to the sides. She lights a joint, puffs, and passes it to the next girl, curls frizzed around her shoulders, a Madonna's veil, a sweet lemon-colored dress with a Peter Pan collar and a hemline that shows the very edge of a pair of bike shorts. She looks, with her unnaturally pale hair, a bit like Tree. Her mouth is slightly too wide for her face. There's a smudge of blood on the inner corner of one eye, but when she turns her head to relight the joint, I see that it is maroon eyeliner.

And then, through this lens, I see myself the way they must see me. Pushing thirty in a ratty sweatshirt, moth holes in the neck, damp shorts crusted with salt. Cracks around the eyes. Gloves in ninety-degree weather. Thumbnail scraping middle finger, digging.

I AM YOU! I want to scream at the ethereal blonde as she slides her eyes over me, mouth tucked in a toothless smile. Amused, like she has unlocked the secret to everything. The searching nail presses harder. The girls snicker. The pretty one pulls from the joint.

The girls' laughter multiplies, a hundred church bells. The

sound concentrates inside my ears. The laughing girls are of my recent past. Versions of me who believed the future would remain ever beyond my reach. Now I am running as hard and fast as I can away from these girls with their flashing teeth and last night's sleep caught in their tear ducts and their yeasty morning breath, back toward the boardwalk. The crowd has doubled. Tourists meander behind me and on either side. I'm caught in the wrong flow of the pedestrian traffic, an onrush of strangers blanched nearly invisible, foreheads patent with sweat. It drips into their eyes and off their chins like the off-melt from an old icicle. Bodies push together. A buffet of limbs and crumpled summer clothes comes at me. Men with hairy knees and women with beige bra straps breaking the lines of their garish dresses. Damp spots bloom like mold under breasts and arms, between legs. Toes curl around sand-flecked orthopedic sandals. Parents tug and jostle their children. A middle-aged woman's sickly cool upper arm flesh grazes mine and I keel to the side, onto all fours, knees and palms pressed to the splintered slats of the boardwalk.

The ground trembles with the force of so many feet. Sand embeds in the outcropped bony fissures on my legs. It's a satisfying pain, and I lean into it, grating against the grist. I hear Dom and Mona whispering, *you bitch, you thought you could outrun us?*

I sit back on my heels. The onslaught has intensified, a dense pack surges and surges like an unrelenting river, obliterating my senses. Pushing them to the maximum, a saturated sponge overrun with color, taste, sound. I am almost knocked over again but regain my sense of balance in time. I wash up at the edge of the boardwalk, gripping a fence post.

Blue eternity spills in front of me. Calming waves hit the

shore in flat bursts, like CBD oil on the tongue. I inhale, exhale.

Inhale, exhale.

Inhale, exhale.

Inhale, exhale.

My heartbeat slows. The ocean in my ears drowns the human din. I focus on the wash of cerulean where the horizon meets the sea. My thumb finds a hangnail through the gloves and presses down. A bright spot of pain spreads and spreads.

2008

I pressed against the window. I wanted to crawl inside, to take her in my arms and be with her. By that point, it was impossible to tell how many pills she'd taken. She'd swallowed them idly here and there however long I'd watched her. Periodically she sipped from a bottle of Yellow Tail Moscato.

Even when, draining that, she moved on to a caramel liquor, I did not know to worry. Mona was, to my mind, indestructible. Human qualities of mortality eluded her; she could be counted on to plumb the depths and resurface with the treasures of the underworld.

And so, I was not expecting her to lurch forward as though she'd been administered a shock treatment and slump against the soft arm of the couch. Slowly, she began to shake. Her hands flapped in and out of sight, batting the dull brown couch. In the night, however late it was, minutes and hours became one and tangled on into a riot of aching seconds.

I started toward the front of the house. Brambles and weeds scratched my ankles, and one flip-flop tangled in a dead rosebush. I left it behind and hobbled the rest of the way on a single sheathed foot, treading lightly on the bare one. I tried the front door, which was locked, and stood for a dumb moment on the stoop before I remembered the spare key under a stone toad. It was heavier than I thought. I got my hand under, grasped the key, and jerked it free before the toad thudded down into the dent it had worn within the dirt. Forgetting the mask, and with shaking fingers, I jammed the key into the lock and twisted until the bolt retracted and the handle depressed like a welcoming tongue.

The long front hallway reached the recesses of the house, grasping for me as I slowly pushed toward the dim light pulsing from the den. Turning the corner, I found the couch empty. The cushions molded to her shape, leaving me with the distinct impression that she remained there, invisible. The hair on the back of my neck prickled with the sensation of being watched. On the television, which I had not been able to see from the window, the muted spell of teen actors performing a song and dance routine in a high school gymnasium. This musical and its two follow-ups could be found any time of day on their own special channel, as reliable as the Long Island Rail Road. Silent cheerleaders waved their hips, metronomed their pom-poms overhead. They kept time, marching the slow line of history all the way to eternity. I felt I could follow them into hell. Those dancers would greet me on my deathbed, ticking out a solemn beat to usher me into the next life with flowers in their hands.

A wet sound pulled me out of my trance, and I followed another long, low whimper into the kitchen and around the corner to the basement entrance.

She seemed dead already, or that was my excuse. Lying in the stairwell, head cresting the top step, Mona was like a lost corpse drifting on a river. Arms bent at the elbows; her hands were loose in prayer over her heart. She had thrown on a blue smock dress, and, as I stepped closer, I saw that it was layered over the old Six Flags T-shirt she'd been wearing. She burbled again, and I detected a sharp, fermented smell. Vomit. Her hair spilled onto the cracked linoleum like a dark fountain.

I stood above, our faces yin and yang. I imagined us as twin flourishes, one girl pale and small, half in this world and half in hell; the other solid and tan, of this earth.

Mona's eyes grew wide as marbles and she rolled to the side and puked some more, and then I remembered the Ghostface mask. I must have seemed, to her, like a messenger of death. Did she know that it was me? I like to think she did, and that she found some comfort in that at the end.

Mona writhed, tried to stand, but only dislodged her perch on the stairs and rolled down with a series of horrible, heart-dropping thuds. Once again the mask slipped my mind, and I flailed through the house, screaming as I bumped furniture.

Mona's front door spit me out; I tripped down the stoop and fell, scraping my knee on the concrete. Blood gushed from the wound as I struggled to my feet and dug around in the brush for my phone, which I found tucked in the arms of a dead rosebush. I ran all the way home and locked my bedroom door, then finally tore off the mask and buried it in my underwear drawer.

Footsteps hesitated outside the closed door, and a series of awful possibilities flitted through my mind. Police. Mona. Chase. The feet resumed a hesitant slippered shuffle. Not a disaster after all, but a parent. I could hear the question on their breath humidifying the paint on the other side. I answered to the best of my ability, by grazing a knuckle on the wood.

Shortly after, the footsteps shuffled away and I heard a door at the end of the hall swing open, then closed.

Truly alone, I sat at the foot of the bed and looked out at the street. Our Subaru Forester stood guard outside the house. There was a slim line of trees, through which cars endlessly raced the parkway. And me, a teenager, seated on this bed, knowing the world went on but unable to see beyond this street. There were only these cars and these houses, only the slatted roofs. Only the people I had known since birth, even the ones I'd never seen before marked with a stale familiarity.

Without a doubt, Mona was dead. I knew from the pain in my core. It felt like an ax breaking through a log. The agony of unspeakable loss, and my own complicity. The cataclysmic thud as the basement's concrete broke her fall echoed in my ears.

I felt a crawling sensation start on my skin. It intensified in the tiny ridges where nails met flesh. I lifted my right hand and examined it for an entry. I had never looked that closely at my hand before; it was unremarkable, but that made it special. Finally, I found a hairline crack in the index nail. I shoved it between my teeth and clamped down. *Pop!* The corner of the nail came free, and I spat it onto the purple shag carpet.

My mouth descended, an animal all its own, and separate from me. Saliva and teeth. I was an ever-moving tongue. I ripped myself apart at the seams. I unraveled, a monster of a girl. Nails fell in shards and embedded in the carpet. Later they would splinter my feet.

Skin tore, blood beading the crevices, the delicate wrinkles gathered at the knuckles and the whorls of my fingerprints. The essential elements of Sophia.

I chewed until I collapsed, exhausted, among the pillows on my bed. I had started to cry without noticing, and tears and snot mingled, flooding my chin and mouth. It tasted salty and fatty, like raw scallops fresh from the sea.

Pale pink curtains swayed in the window. I watched the moon, full and weighted, a lake pinned to the starless sky. The moon rose and rose. It took my consciousness along, and I felt peace. Craters stood out on the silvery white surface. The shapes had never been a man to me. I'd always believed I could see a girl in the moon, dark haired and wild, trying to tell me something I was sorry I could not hear.

14

I did think, for a little while, that the crisis had passed. I call in sick to work and spend Monday cleaning the guest bathroom. I light a cluster of candles to fight the scent of decay. In the following days I stop applying youthjuice, and soon my hands are crossed with the old scars like I'd suffered an attack.

And in a way, hadn't I? The harm we do to others is nothing compared to the harm we do to ourselves.

The strangest thing: I don't feel like biting or picking. It's like I was baptized in the salty waters of the Atlantic Ocean, the snake-ribboned man and the sunbathers and the next-morning party girls as my witnesses before God, and now I'm cured. Cured for good, and not dependent on anything to heal me. I put the half-empty jars of youthjuice in the bag with my blood-soaked clothes from the launch party, stock up on luxury cuticle oils at Sephora, and buy a new wardrobe of gloves in sumptuous textures. All of it paid for with a fistful of cash from a hole in Dom's mattress. Every few days the same woman comes by the apartment and pounds on the door for fifteen or thirty minutes until she gets tired or a neighbor screams at her to stop. This must be Dom's mother, whom I never met in ten years of friendship. Each time I shut myself in the far reaches of the apartment and sit in complete silence until she quiets.

Back at work, the office displays a level of degradation I did not think possible. For a company beloved by It-girls on track to become a startup unicorn, HEBE has faded remarkably fast. Communal desks are mostly empty, which could be chalked up to the fact that July is a popular month to take PTO, and the fact that we have no interns left to speak of, but it strikes me as suspicious nonetheless. Phalaenopsis orchids and pink clouds of baby's breath in the designer floral arrangements lose their blooms and start to reek. Fresh ones used to be delivered on Fridays for the following week.

Marigold is rarely seated outside Tree's office. Instead I catch her slinking around odd corners, whispering into her phone. I haven't seen Tree or Gemma for three days. When they return to the office they are draped in mesh veils like widows with good taste, prairie-style dresses with full skirts and long sleeves, tights.

I derive wicked pleasure from the knowledge that their greed has destroyed them completely. At least the rest of me is unscathed—for now. Each morning when I head to the mirror I expect to find new damage, but so far I'm the same—just the normal wear and tear of twenty-nine years, eleven months of living.

HEBE's daily operations are suspended and there's nothing much for me to do, but I return to my desk from ten to six without exception, breaking periodically to prepare a mediocre coffee with oat milk or use the bathroom. Mostly I stare at the giant monitor I requested at the end of June in order to cultivate an air of professionalism and refresh the various social media sites on which I have profiles. People on these websites start to look the same shockingly quickly, and then I cycle through a folder of high-brow websites I bookmarked in an effort to improve my attention span with longform journalism. Skimming headlines from *The New Yorker*, *The New York Times*, Vulture, Vox, *Harper's*, *The Baffler*, etc., I end up on The Cut, from whose homepage Tree's headshot beams at me through the glow of the screen. *What's Happening at HEBE?* I don't recognize the writer's name.

The post details the missing interns, Emily's disappearance, and what avid commenters on our social media and Reddit pages consider to be a precipitous drop in product quality and customer service in recent weeks. A HEBE representative (Marigold? A lawyer?) contributed a comment: the company appreciates employees of all levels and treats them like family, most of these girls have not been employed by the company for months, we are working closely with law enforcement to help ensure they are safely found, etc.

I bounce my cursor on the X to close the tab. I feel sick and exposed, though the article didn't mention me or any of my coworkers by name, and focused on Tree and the interns. In the bathroom I remove my gloves, splash water on my face, dab a few drops on the pulse points of my neck where you're supposed to apply perfume.

Still, I don't feel the need to bite my nails. It almost bothers me. All these years and it's gone, just like that. I'm cured. Money and time wasted, and what did it take—a murder and a dip in the sea. Like a day at the spa.

Commotion spreads among the few of us remaining. I examine the women of HEBE who I paid little attention to while in thrall to Tree. Could they not have known? I think about Mona. You can know without knowing, I reason. That doesn't absolve you.

I HAVE NO friends. Eventually I'll have to do something about that, but for now I keep to myself. The empty apartment still feels like a novelty. Dom adopted a "what's mine is yours" mentality in our friendship, but now the apartment really does feel like mine. If HEBE goes under, I'll need a backup plan. I'll have to move. But for now I luxuriate in playing the kind of sad-girl indie rock that Dom hated. I cook elaborate meals with obscure ingredients from the specialty market in the neighborhood and leave the dishes for too long. I lie in Dom's bed, foul her linen sheets with my herbaceous sweat, and play around with an app that promises to tell you if your face is symmetrical, a filter that analyzes how old you look, an app that produces a series of AI-developed portraits in the style of famous artists. I set the Pop Art–inspired image as my profile photo on Twitter and use the surrealist one (mouth and eyes in a straight line) in the carousel on the dating app I've signed up for, now that I might be ready for a relationship, or at least a date, again soon.

Symmetry of the face, I've been told, is the degree between *attractive* and *breathtaking*. According to the app, mine is several millimeters shy. The left eye is higher than the right one, and my nose is crooked. I click through an online gallery of supposedly symmetrical faces and find them unnerving and lacking in substance, which makes me feel better. It's the difference between a technically perfect art student who produces photorealistic work and a true *artiste*. The real artist, while likely proficient in the essentials—illustration, figure-drawing, painted landscapes—displays their mastery vis-à-vis a point of view. That was what made Dom's writing special, her ability to put the reader in her shoes, even if said reader was broke without a bachelor's degree and living in a railroad apartment with three other girls and a closet full of Shein tissue-paper "going-out tops" that disintegrate at the whisper of sweat and business-casual pieces several degrees too slutty to pass muster anywhere more professional than a trendy media startup.

I plug in Dom's dead MacBook, navigate to *MAKE-UPSEX*, and click through the archive. The comments section going back two or three years includes a trail of missives from the most loyal followers wondering where Dom has been. I'll admit, I hadn't thought about what would become of the blog after Dom's curtain call. I guess I assumed it would be forgotten like thousands of dormant websites before it.

Under the influence of chaga mushroom coffee, I craft a "Where Have I Been" in my best approximation of Dom's voice. Inhabiting Dom's mind leads to longing, and I cry matter-of-factly as I type. Tears blur the content platform so that it becomes akin to automatic writing practiced by the spiritualists. I've summoned Dom by accessing the backend of her blog using her computer, a latter-day séance. Typing faster, I enter a flow state and begin to sense Dom's spirit guiding me through this exercise. She tells me what to say and lets me become her, thus giving me her blessing. I dry my eyes with an old Kleenex on Dom's windowsill and read over the post, changing words and phrases here and there until I'm confident no one will be the wiser. I hit publish and shut the laptop.

Then, out loud, I ask Dom's spirit if I'm doing the right thing. A picture of the two of us at Coachella—arms tossed around each other's shoulders, flower crowns gently grazing—wobbles and then topples off the dresser, landing face-first on the floor. I take the sound of smashing glass to mean: *yes*.

THINKING BACK TO early May when I started at HEBE, I recall an article published on *The Dew* that was a departure. Instead of interviewing a collagen-fluffed DJ or Young Hollywood ingénue, Emily brought in a professor-type in literal bow tie and tweed, a scientist whose research in skin-renewal technology had shown remarkable promise in the cell turnover of burn victims. Google tells me that he has published a study. Normally the websites of old men in STEM fields aren't noted for their comprehensiveness, but Dr. Dorian's is easy to navigate and provides a convenient contact form.

I send the study to the printer. The pages are warm to the touch.

I march into Tree's office holding the wedge of pages. She's at her desk, veils running down her face to her knees, elbows on the table, hands interlocked. Old food molds in piles on the desk, the coffee table, the couch. Takeout cartons transparent with grease, wax paper dotted by ketchup and clotted clumps of cheese, an open clamshell box with a layer of nachos at the bottom covered with a scrim of blue mold. The smell of cold French fries hangs in the air.

Tree doesn't react when I sit and place the printed-out study between us. The veils glisten with the subtle glitter of snow-dusted branches. Underneath she is a frozen eyeless mannequin. I push the papers closer and ask her to read them. Tree doesn't move from her beseeching position. She's Mary, virginal in pearl Chantilly lace and a wide-shouldered prairie dress. Desperately I come around to kneel in front of her, jamming the papers onto her lap. She's too smart to watch the empire she's created spin out of her control. "Tree, if you would look at what I found, I really think it could help—"

She emits a moan like that of a mournful boat's siren. Her head throbs, carrying the veils in a wave. The veil is attached to a satin headband. She's a doomed bride in an old photograph, like Sharon Tate on her wedding day. Only Tree is no casualty.

"Tree." I take a gentler approach. "What's wrong? Why is this happening?" A croak comes from deep inside the frothy veils. "I can't hear you," I say.

Tree coughs. Her throat-clearing is the dusty rattle of death. "youthjuice." That's what she's saying. "youthjuice did this."

"But I don't get it, it was working . . ." I'm shaking the pages of study, really getting in her face. She starts to rock in her chair, whining, and pushes my arm to the side. I let go and the pages flutter to the floor.

Then Tree screams and tears the headband and the fabric petals away, revealing her face. And then I am screaming too, our screams mingling in a hideous chorus. Virulent pink worms of flesh writhe in her lap. Chunks are missing from her cheeks. The skin she does have is crisp and cracked like oven-fried chicken. When she tries to cover her face with both hands, more pieces fall off. They come to life on the fabric of her skirt, staining the twee fabric with brilliant bloody spots. Dried blood and pus erupt in the craters on her forehead, in the cavern where her buccal fat should be. She is ruined satin on a ballerina's shoe.

Tree starts to cry, and the salt from her tears stings her wounded face, so she cries harder. I ask her what's wrong, what's wrong, what is happening. I want any answer but the right one.

The dead skin on her lap is alive. It's coming together in the dip between her thighs, forming a wriggling mass like a beating heart. That's exactly what it is, a new heart forming independent of a body. I hear the slap of pumping life.

More clumps of skin drip from Tree's face, feeding the swelling organ. From far enough away they might resemble tears. I take a heavy book from a stack on the floor, use the spine to sweep the heart onto the floor. It clings to the fabric of her dress through the initial swats, a toddler holding its mother on the first day of school. But each impact dislodges the orb of tissue a bit more until it falls to the floor. Three solid wallops with the side of the book and the monster is pulp, a smashed grapefruit.

I glance at Tree. She's rocking back and forth, back and forth. Her mouth is a black hole, the skin of her lips sucked of Restylane, it's telling me to get out get out get out get out get out get out ge—

MARIGOLD IS RESPLENDENT, not a pore out of place. We're in one of the Ovaries, squared off on either side of the conference table. A dead bouquet behind her severe bob, an outer ring of fruit flies lending a primordial goddess effect.

"You never used it?"

Marigold flips through the study, avoiding the spatter from Tree's face. "Interesting stuff here," she says. "We could use this."

"What's happening to Tree?"

"These results are astounding."

I slam my hand on the tabletop. "Answer me!"

Marigold doesn't flinch. She gingerly lowers the page she's holding to one side of the stack. "No, I've never used youthjuice. I think Tree's obsession with aging is juvenile. People get older, it happens all the time. It's not a tragedy."

She sounds so wise that it's tempting to believe her. But all of life is one great tragedy for a woman. You're born, you have a brief, shining moment when you're in control, you matter, you age, you die. Each passing day is a small death that prepares you for the end.

Marigold traces the edge of the papers, flinches when they nick her, and sucks on her finger. Then she says, "Why do you look normal?"

I peel off one glove and lay my bare hand flat in front of Marigold. The scars are worse than before, puffy tunnels like creatures under the surface. Marigold's nostrils flare. She grinds her teeth, the tendons in her neck tight and distended.

"I only used it on my hands. When I noticed them deteriorating, I stopped before it got worse. And I only did the full bath twice, maybe that has something to do with it."

Marigold considers. "I think it's the level of exposure. The moisturizer is a highly concentrated formula. Tree's taken baths for close to a decade, but she dilutes them." She gives a wry chuckle. "I suspected it would catch up with her somehow. I thought it would be the police, but her own body beat them to it."

"You went to school with them. Tree and Gemma. I saw you in the background of the snapshot in her apartment."

Marigold adjusts her jacket's ironed-flat lapels. "I lived on their floor our sophomore year. Had a couple of classes with Tree."

"They weren't your friends, though, were they?"

Marigold frowns. "It took them a while to realize they needed me. Tree is brilliant, but she's erratic. I'd hear her in the common room talking about the untapped potential of plasma's healing properties, how one drop of someone's blood could tell you everything about them. She sounded crazy to me, but her talks always drew a crowd. I thought, this must be what it's like to watch a great leader at work.

"She found this girl in one of our lectures with a bloodletting fetish or something. The girl had insane skin, no pores. She used to give Tree these tupperwares with her blood and Tree would make a soak—a few drops mixed with lavender oil. I think she just wanted to see if there was anything to it. Back then it was about eczema, not aging. Tree used to suffer from the worst eczema on her chest and back. Every time she had a breakout, she'd use this girl's blood in her tub, and it cleared things up like that." Marigold snapped her fingers. "Seeing those results made me a believer. I thought she could do amazing things, if I were to guide her toward realistic goals. The idea we came up with was, we start with a beauty brand, earn enough money to fund the experimental research on the side. But she got distracted from the original mission."

"Which was what, exactly?"

"We were going to cure extreme skin conditions, like Tree's eczema."

"By killing people."

"We'd only take a syringe or two at first, from volunteers. It wasn't until Tree and Gemma fixated on the anti-aging effects, what it did for fine lines and wrinkles, that they realized we'd never have enough that way. We had to start taking it by force."

"And the younger the better."

"Of course. But I don't think that's it: I think she loves killing those girls. I think that's why she can't stop. If her face wasn't falling off, I think she'd still be doing it right now."

Marigold seems almost human in the washed light of the Ovary. In the corner, the dead bouquet, the largest flower, a single tear-shaped petal with a plastic sheen is covered with black dots. The dots are moving. Fruit flies feeding off the petal's dead flesh.

LATER I'M WATCHING TV. Sheet masks on my hands, a coat of Vaseline sealing in the serums on my face. The limitation on movement gives me the opportunity to lie stock-still and let the mind wander. When the timer goes off, I drop the masks in the trash, rub the serum in, and then apply a lip-shaped gel over my mouth, sealing it shut for the night. With my mouth closed and the television's nonstop light and sound, I rest on the couch and think through the day. The blue light from the screen subdues me and I enter a dream-wake state. Something white on the floor catches the corner of my eye. It's the card with a contact number the officers investigating Emily's disappearance gave me.

I read the number over and over until it's a song in my head, then I dial.

THEY COME IN the morning. Boxes carried from the depths of the office. Employment records, research materials, cartons of youthjuice. My heart does ache to see it go, but it's for the best. Our computers are confiscated. Tree, Gemma, Starla, and the director of R&D are cuffed and read their rights. Marigold is gone—the kidney-shaped desk is wiped bare, and her work accounts have been terminated.

The remaining HEBE employees look on, bewildered, but maybe not shocked. This place was built on decay, its stench seeping through the quartz-pink walls. I recognize Officer Rodgers gruffly guiding Tree by the shoulder. She brings us face-to-face. A Rorschach of blood and sebum seeps through Tree's Chantilly veil. She gets as close as the cop's grip will allow, six or seven inches from my nose, and growls, *You fucking bitch.* Spittle flecks my lips and chin. I keep my cool; I smile. It isn't until she's ushered off to rot in a jail cell that I wipe my face, her saliva melting into my ivory satin glove.

Epilogue

It's a beautiful day. Sun shines through the windows on the left side of my office. I've settled in nicely. Gemma left a couch behind, and a few abstract paintings. Eventually I will take them down, add decor that's more *me*. I'm eyeing an original Anna Weyant oil painting. There are two photos on the desk—the one of Dom and me at Coachella, reframed in pink lucite, and the picture of Mona and me on the swings.

I have my own Marigold now, a sharp-ponytailed Yale graduate whose freckles disarm the most skeptical venture capitalists. Her name is Barley, and she flosses after every meal. I found her in a boutique; she was telling her friend which dresses and shirts to try on, which ones to buy. I hired her on the spot after consulting her opinion on a sage green dress for my court appearance testifying at Tree's trial. They got her on twelve counts of first-degree murder. Gemma, Starla, and the R&D woman whose name I never learned provided information in exchange for leniency. I never saw Marigold again. After our conversation in the Ovary, she took off like a whisper in the night. Maybe she's in Prague. The police won't look for her—they have their scapegoat.

From the window I can see the billboard for the latest HEBE launch. Artistically directed by me, it brings the viewer into the world of the revamped youthjuice formulated with Dr. Dorian's proprietary technology. *Live forever.* Behind the tagline, a row of collarbones. The backward L-shape of several women's necks swelling elegantly to the slope of their shoulders. Naked and contrite, marching out of the frame and into the distance. Their skin sheened and their hair scraped into low, youthful ponytails. Robbie in the center, the only one making eye contact with the viewer. One eye open, the other flattened into a wink. Millions will see it. And it's all because of me. HEBE is mine. The board voted unanimously to install me as CEO. They said I demonstrated great loyalty to the company when I turned Tree in to the police, when I got justice for those poor girls, our sacrificial lambs. Our valuation exploded following my press tour, a spate of interviews on morning shows and social-justice-themed YouTube series, with features in the major media outlets and the more popular niche feminist publications. When they inevitably asked why HEBE should continue in light of its brutal history, I let the tears surface. We owed it to the victims, I said, that their deaths should go on to mean something, not just for the dead girls, but for womankind as a whole. They would want us to continue, I insisted. HEBE would become an ethical company in their wake.

It's a nice idea. I don't know what's in Dr. Dorian's youthjuice, but it's nearly as potent as the original.

At the helm of my desk, a wide acrylic ocean, I gaze at the photo of Dom and me squinting against the sun. I flinch and turn away from the lens, but she stares straight into it. From the desk drawer I unearth lipstick in a matte purple tube. *Dom* is spelled in sans serif type on the side. The color is lavender gray with a hint of gloss.

Turns out that Tree was right; a lipstick is the perfect tribute. I smooth the blunt tube across my lips in the dull reflection of the picture frame's glass. Smile a purple smile, remembering all she did for me in our brief but eternal friendship.

I rest my pristine hands on the keyboard. Opalescent nails flash, the cuticles well-oiled and pushed neatly into the cushion of my nail beds.

I smile, and I am beautiful.

Acknowledgments

Thank you first to my agent, Maria Whelan, for your unfailing belief in this book, and in me, and the tireless work on my behalf. And to my amazing editor, Taz Urnov—your vision and enthusiasm gave me the push I needed to take *youthjuice* to the next level. I am eternally grateful that we met and had the chance to work together. Beauty IS possible!

My eternal gratitude also to the team at Soho Press— Bronwen Hruska, Rachel Kowal, Lily DeTaeye, Rudy Martinez, Emma Levy, and Janine Agro—for publishing my work with so much care, attention, and passion.

Writing is a solitary pursuit and I'm very lucky to be surrounded by a community that makes it feel less lonely. Thank you especially to my parents for letting me read basically whatever I wanted, whenever I wanted and only occasionally telling me to "look up." To Gabrielle Moss, my blonde Hitchcock doppelgänger—I do not want to know what life would be without you to engage in Deep Talks about art, publishing, and everything else in the middle of the day/night. Much love and gratitude also to my beloved group chat, "the

Daves"—Bee, Egg, Hope, Jojo, Kelsy, Liri, and Sha'Nicka—
for ferrying me through apocalypses large and small with
humor and endless support, and to Logan, Erik, Emma,
Katie, Katherine, Sarah, Zac, and Zach for being the friends
that are more like family.

Speaking of family, thank you to the Donnellys, Sathues,
Soccorsos, Perrys, and Moores for always being there. And,
finally, Benjamin Perry, John to my Joan—I look forward to so
many (many, many, many) more decades of reading, writing,
and laughing with you. Thank you for being my first reader.

Bringing a book from manuscript to what you are reading is a team effort.

Renegade Books would like to thank everyone who helped to publish *youthjuice* in the UK.

Editorial
Alexa Allen-Batifoulier

Contracts
Megan Phillips
Amy Patrick
Anne Goddard
Bryony Hall
Anniina Vuori

Sales
Caitriona Row
Dominic Smith
Frances Doyle
Hannah Methuen
Lucy Hine
Toluwalope Ayo-Ajala

Design
Nick Evans
Jo Taylor

Production
Narges Nojoumi

Publicity
Millie Seaward

Marketing
Emily Moran

Operations
Kellie Barnfield
Millie Gibson
Sanjeev Braich